DANGEROUS TO KNOW

THE CHRONICLES OF BREED: BOOK ONE

K.T. DAVIES

SCIMITAR MEDIA

This is a work of fiction. Names, characters, organizations, places, events, and incidents are either products of the author's imagination or are used fictitiously.

Published by Scimitar Media

www.scimitar-media.co.uk

ISBN-13: 978-1999747404

Cover design by Scimitar Media

Original cover art by Michael Gauss

To Raven and Gabe,

the best rum crew a cove could wish for

Dangerous to Know

The Great Ocean
Pharria Province
Appleton
Valen
The Empire
The Grundvelt Protectorate
Grundvelt City
Tomarzsk
Lescarr Province
N
S
W
E

Valen
Little Lea
Ruins
Appleton
The Empire

Chapter One

There's nothing quite as exhilarating as heedless, headlong flight, when fear of the unknown is banished by the sure and certain knowledge that whatever is ahead cannot be as dreadful as that which is behind. It's liberating, like being a child again, free of all constraints born of thought or reason. Although, truth be told, as wild as my childhood had been this was the first time I'd ever been chased by a dragon.

Even though my situation was sliding rapidly from dire to fatal, every fiber of my being sang with the joy of being alive. I let out a loud whoop as I leaped a boulder and glissaded at speed down an ice-sheathed slope, scattering talus in my wake. My shout rang across the mountain, a challenge as much as an exultation.

Not to be outdone, the dragon answered with an ear-splitting roar. Thus warned, I dived into a stand of knotted pines as it spewed a mouthful of frosty bile in my direction. A wash of ice glazed the copse. Leaves shattered like glass, trunks and branches cracked like old bones. I escaped all but the merest lick of cold fire, but the slight splash was enough to peel the skin from my shoulder.

I stumbled, arms windmilling, feet scrabbling for purchase. The second I regained my balance, I dug my claws into the frozen ground and propelled myself down the mountain. My thoasan father had blessed me with his race's superior speed and agility, a gift that had kept me alive longer than I probably deserved. Alas, my human mother had cursed me with the stamina of her breed. The pace was hard and the dragon relentless. Though I sped downhill like an arrow, the beast was devouring my lead with every furious beat of its coriaceous wings.

It seemed that, in this rare instance, crime had not paid. It was a sad state of affairs, but not one that I'd live long enough to regret if my icy friend had anything to do with it. Thus disillusioned, although highly motivated, I sprinted from the snarling jaws of death. Provoked by necessity to exert itself, my mind began to race as fast as my feet. The thought occurred that if I discarded the sapphire I'd stolen, the dragon might let me be, but then the wise words of Mother leaped to mind. 'Hope is for fools, and only losers rely on luck. More wine!' I could almost see the old dear, slouched gracelessly across the Rat Bone Throne, majestically drunk, and sneering at my predicament.

Tossing the stone would be pointless, the last act of a desperate cull. Why on earth would the great, flying turd-sack let me go when it could retrieve its treasure after it had turned me into a frozen smear on the mountainside? It wouldn't. Like me, the big ugly bastard was greedy and vicious. Even if throwing the gem worked and I escaped from this particular pot of arsepickle, I'd be leaping from the jaws of one monster into the arms of another, deadlier fiend. To return to Mother and the Guild empty-handed would invite a far harder death than any the dragon could mete out. My dear mama had elevated brutality to an art form, nay, a philosophy, a meditation on suffering.

Another roar whipped snow and dirt into an icy shroud, a thunderous stomp sent jagged fractures racing down the mountain. I narrowed my eyes against the blistering glare and glanced over my shoulder. The dragon was tearing its way through the knot of pine less than thirty feet behind me. It paused a moment, fixed its pale, blue gaze upon me and bared its saber fangs. In that moment, the air was awed to stillness and the beating of my heart seemed to falter. There was death, sharp and cold. While my eyes drank in the full measure of my doom, my legs kept running, trying to save with speed what I had failed to protect with wit. They were doing well, up to the point that I stepped into nothing.

I pitched forwards and rebounded off the rough sides of a deep fissure. The breath was hammered from my lungs. I fell, clawed at rock and earth, tried to latch onto anything to slow my descent. Darkness yawned beneath me, but before I was swallowed by the baleful unknown I managed to grab an outcrop of stone and hang there, legs swinging in the inky void. A steady drizzle of grit and snow rained from above. I adjusted my grip so that I could pull myself back up into the fissure but the rock I was holding came away in my hand.

My thoasan instincts trumped my human ineptitude and I landed prone, arms and legs outstretched spreading the impact of the fall. Myriad stars exploded before my eyes, lighting the darkness. I squinted through the fireworks at the grey hole far above me. When the hole vanished I had wit enough to roll aside. A torrent of icy vomit gushed down the hole, turning the ground where I had been lying into a hissing mirror of brittle glass. I laughed before I passed out, lulled by the sound of the dragon venting its impotent fury on the mountainside.

* * *

I'm not sure how long I was unconscious, all I know is that when I came round, everything hurt. My hair spines had saved my skull from cracking like an egg against the hard floor but the brain within was feeling somewhat scrambled. I pawed my face and traced tears of dried blood to a sticky gash on my forehead. As I flexed each limb to see what still worked, a chorus of aches and pains sang a song of cuts and bruises. I sat up and brushed the grit out of the raw flesh of my frost-burned shoulder. Considering that I'd just been chased by a *very* angry dragon, I'd got off lightly.

When the world stopped spinning, I peered into the darkness. I was in a cave that a human might describe as ‘pitch black’, but I could see through the varying layers of darkness. Upon inspection, I adjusted my initial appraisal. It wasn’t a cave, it was a large, carved chamber with several exits. The ravages of time had taken its toll on the room. Once beautiful sculptures and carvings had collapsed into piles of rubble. I drew breath, tasted fetid air, the musty stink of decomposition, and something else. There was another scent in the mix, something I couldn’t quite place. I drew a deeper breath, let the smell roll over the buds of my partially bifurcated breed-muddled tongue. It was an acrid-smelling taste, a mix of fear-sweat, sulfur, and anger.

I wasn’t alone.

Shaking off the effects of the fall, I sprang up, drew my blades, and scribed an arc in the air before me. It was my way of showing anything that might be sizing me up that it wasn’t worth the pain of trying to find out what half human, half thoasa tasted like. Nothing moved, but the smell lingered, clawing at the edge of my senses. As much as I enjoy playing ‘stab in the dark’, time was against me. I had to get out and get home with my prize before Mother sent my fellow Guild Blades to hunt me down.

I summoned the words of a spell to mind and a fist-sized ball of light bloomed before me. I sent the pale sphere towards the recess where the smell of anger was strongest. Sure enough, hunched beneath an arch of fallen masonry was *a thing*.

No bigger than a malnourished, human child, its skin was mottled grey and its wrinkled head was far too big for its spidery body. It was wearing a ragged shirt and breeches of an ancient design. It blinked a pair of large, pure black eyes, and scratched nervously at the cobweb wisps of hair that garnished its head and pointed ears. It was a pathetic looking creature, a cross between a very old human and a very young one, but I did not lower my swords just yet. I'd come across some dangerous coves prowling the sewers and back alleys of Appleton that had looked just as harmless as this scrapling.

It raised its hands to shield its eyes from the light. "Don't hurt me. I mean you no harm, I did you no harm as you lay there insensible." Its voice was little more than a hoarse whisper, as though it was unused to talking.

"What the fuck are you?" I demanded, holding it at sword point.

"Isn't it obvious?" it asked.

"No, why should it be?" I didn't give a damn what genus of goblin it belonged to, I was more concerned with how I was going to get out of here and off the mountain without being eaten by an angry dragon. The thing took a wary step towards me, mindful of the steel between us. It scratched the tiny horn buds that sprouted from its forehead, marking it as a descendent of the infernal demonspawn that fought in the Schism War. It stared at me with its huge, dark eyes and folded its arms.

"You're an imp of some kind." I ventured unenthusiastically.

It straightened up, puffed out its bony chest. "I, am a demon."

I snorted. "Are you indeed? A demon of what, pray tell?"

It cleared its throat. "I am a tormentor of scribes."

"A who of what?" I wasn't sure that I'd heard it correctly.

It set its wizened face in what I suspected was supposed to be a righteous frown and planted its bony little hands on its hips. "I steal nibs, sometimes entire quills, and upon occasion, sealing wax and the odd scrap of vellum." I didn't hear what else it said as by this point because I was laughing too hard. Not only had I almost been frozen to death by a dragon, admittedly, one that I had provoked, but I was now stuck in a subterranean somewhere, with a mad goblin for company. You couldn't make this stuff up.

"That's very petty," I said when I finally stopped laughing.

It did its best to glower. "I'm a specialist."

"I thought demons were supposed to ravage and destroy and lay waste to civilizations, that kind of thing, not steal pens."

"Have you ever seen a scribe hunting for a favorite nib? Or been there when one has discovered the ink has dried up because someone, me, has left the lid off the pot, hmm?"

"I can't say that I have."

It wagged a finger at me. "Well, let me tell you, it can lead to a great deal of destruction when you steal the pen of a scholarly type. They are, by and large, a highly-strung breed, given to wild fits of temper."

"Angry scribes, eh? I'll be sure to watch out for them. D'you have a name, or shall I just call you Destroyer of Pens?"

"Stupid human. Do you think I would tell you my name and give you power over me?"

"Human?" I gave myself an exaggerated once-over. "Are you blind?"

My feet are covered in red and orange scales, and I have seven, taloned toes on each foot. He couldn't see the scales on my shoulders and back because of the tunic I was wearing, but the liver-red stripes on my arms and neck were plainly visible. I smiled just enough to show him the tips of my sharp canines. And even if it hadn't noticed my feet or hair or stripes, it had looked me in my bright, yellow eyes and must have seen the flicker of my third eyelid.

The demon shrugged dismissively. “Mortals all look the same to me. What’s your name, half-breed?”

“Mind your own business, imp.” I gave it my best, broken bottle glare before sending the globe of light up to the ceiling. It hovered beneath the stopple of rubble and ice that choked the hole about forty feet above us. It would take days to melt even with the aid of magic and longer to dig through. I needed another way out if I was to avoid a bounty being placed on my head.

“I came when I heard the dragon and saw you lying there. I thought you were dead,” it said while I surveyed my surroundings.

All thought of escape was momentarily banished when I was struck by a sudden, horrifying thought. I groped at my chest. After an agonizing few seconds of panic, I found the sapphire, still nestled in the folds of my tunic where I'd stuffed it. Relieved, I chuckled. Some demon. Not only hadn’t it cut my throat while I lay senseless, but it hadn’t even bothered to search me. The youngest kinchin cove in Appleton would have had the wit to do that.

My stomach growled. I wasn’t a natural when it came to sorcery. If I maintained the spell for much longer the hungry weakness would really start to bite. I searched through the debris and found some wood dry enough to fashion into a torch.

The imp sneered at my efforts. "Real warspawn can see in the dark."

"They also rip little shits like you in half. Do you want us to go down that route?" It didn't answer. "I didn't think so."

I sparked the torch to life with my flint and tinder and wafted it towards the imp. It leaped away from the wash of amber. "That's better." I gave it a knowing look. "You never know when you might need to burn something and as I'm neither a real sorcerer or a real warspawn this'll have to do me."

The imp snorted. "The Mage Lords were too afraid to give the warspawn the ability to use magic. They were scared that their creatures might use it against them. Cowards, the lot of them."

"That's fascinating, really, it is. You should write a memoir, get some use out of all those pens that you've nicked." I didn't give two shits what had happened hundreds of years ago, but I had the distinct impression that there was more to the little scutbucket than merely tormenting scribes. Another time I might have delved deeper into its history but the pressing need to find my way out of here pushed all further thought on the matter to the farthest corner of my mind.

The chamber had four exits. One was blocked, and none of them looked any more promising than the next. I tasted the air. A full-blood thoasa would have been able to discern the finest thread of freshness in the turgid atmosphere, but my human-blunted senses couldn't pick anything out above the musty funk of ages. If indeed there was another way out.

As I pondered which way to go, my gaze roamed over the heavily embellished walls. The sputtering torchlight sheened the drab stone with gold and lent a semblance of flickering life to the vicious demons marching towards an unseen foe. This was no ordinary dwelling or common tomb buried under a rock fall. A knot of gloom tightened my gut.

"What is this place?" I asked the imp while not really wanting to know the answer.

It sat down on the severed, stone head of a demon and drew its knees up to its chin. Its blank stare echoed the enigmatic vacuity of the statue's gaze.

"Shallunsard's Keep." The imp's breath curdled the frigid air.

"What?"

"Shallunsard's Keep? The Bright Star of the Morning?"

I shook my head.

"The jewel that glitters in the crown of Helel? The Keep of the Bright Star?" It arched a feathery eyebrow, gave me the all-knowing wide eye, as though I should know what it was talking about and be impressed.

I didn't, and I wasn't. "I think you mean *was* the bright star of wherever. In case you hadn't noticed, a mountain fell on it."

"Ah. Yes. The fall, I remember."

"That's wonderful. Pray, sirrah, d'you also remember the way out? Only I have to be somewhere yesterday."

"I do. And I will show you."

"Splendid."

"For a price."

I waved my sword at it, all casual like. "Let me stop you there, shorty. My body and soul are owned by my mother, and she's one demon I will not cross."

It made a sound akin to that of a cat throwing up a hairball. I think it was trying to laugh. "I want nothing so prosaic. I just want you to take me out with you."

"You can't come with me. My mother, who is also my employer, wouldn't be at all happy if I brought an imp home. She has a strict 'no pets' policy."

"I have no wish to travel with you, breed. Just take me across the seal." It wrapped its arms around its legs. "Agree, and you'll be out of here in a matter of hours. Don't, and you can spend the rest of your life, short though it may be, lost in these ancient and labyrinthine halls."

"Breed?" I laughed. "Am I supposed to be offended? If I am you'll have to do better than that because I've been insulted every day I've drawn breath. As for surviving down here, I'll wager that I'll last a few days longer if I spit-roast your carcass, arseling."

"You think so, eh? the restless dead might have other ideas."

I was about to reply with a stinging riposte, but my attention was diverted by the sound of something shuffling behind me. I tilted my head and caught a whiff of deathly decay. Without further prattle, I dropped the torch, pivoted to my right, and rammed my blades into my unfortunate stalker before I'd given much thought as to what or who it might be. I'd apologize later if it was some lost cull looking for directions, but where I come from sneaking up on a person is a declaration of murderous intent. Nobody plays 'guess who?' in Appleton, not twice anyway.

I knew something was wrong the moment I felt my swords bite into something more akin to rawhide than flesh. I have a good working knowledge of human anatomy and knew that if it was a human of average height, both of my blades should have been sticking in a gut, or the transverse colon as quacksalvers name it. There's a satisfying pressure one encounters when stabbing guts, a comforting suck on the steel. It's like a warm handshake, one that tells a bloody-handed cove that they've hit their mark. I'd hit nothing. My blades hung loose within an empty husk. The knot in my gut tightened another notch.

"Oh, this isn't good."

While I stood there, goggling at the walking corpse it grabbed me by the throat. I was somewhat perturbed by this and screamed like my arse was on fire until it tightened its grip and choked off my air pipe.

Shocked into action, I twisted my blades and ripped them through its desiccated body. The death-hardened flesh was tough, but fear lent me an extra measure of strength, and I cut the thing in half. The legs fell away, but the divorce of top from bottom didn't encourage it to loosen its bony fingers. Choking, I sheathed my blades in its chest, took a firm grip on its hawser taut arms and wrenched the skeletal hands from my throat. Free from its deathless grip, I threw the damned thing to the floor, retrieved my blades, and stomped on its bits until it was nothing more than an inlay of old flesh and bone.

"Neatly done." The imp clapped. "As you can see, this place is dangerous, infested with the restless dead and worse. I know how to avoid them, most of them, at least."

"I've a mind to make you one of the permanent dead for not warning me that thing was behind me."

"What do you expect? I'm a demon, I don't do nice, helpful things, it's not in my nature." The smug little snotstain picked a fleck of dry skin from its ragged shirt.

"You would also be wasting your time, nothing stays permanently dead down here. This place is cursed."

"Of course, it is." I kicked a sliver of skull across the floor. "Does it flood too? Is the air poisonous? Will blood drinking rabbits attack at midnight?" I sheathed my blades. "Just my luck to be trapped in a fucking dungeon with an irritating, half-sized demon and gods only knows how many walking corpses, and if I don't get back to Appleton in the next few days it's open season on my head."

The demon chuckled and steepled its fingers. "As they say in the common argot, you're fucked, unless you agree to my terms, which I have to say are rather generous, considering your predicament. Now, do we have a deal?"

I sighed. "Very well. Just show me the way out."

The demon grinned, displaying a neat row of tiny, needle-sharp fangs. It offered its hand. "Remember, Breed, a deal is a deal. You promise to take me over the seal, alive and well?"

I didn't know much about demons, other than what I'd heard in the Nest when some lag wanted to impress their cronies. I recalled something about it being a bad idea to make deals with them, but I didn't see that I had much choice. I clasped its hand. "Deal."

Chapter Two

We walked for hours along lavishly carved corridors piled with moldering furniture and heaped with bones. Lots and lots of bones. After trudging along what looked like the same corridor for the second time, I was starting to think that the mad little skunkpizzle was leading me in circles.

Demon or not, I swore that if it was playing me false, I'd gut the little bastard. My frost burned shoulder ached, and I was running out of time and patience. I was also heartily sick of looking at the endless procession of grim-faced heroes and heroines battling snarling demons.

Some of the rooms we crept past piqued my professional interest, especially when I spied a glimpse of a chest or the gleam of something shiny winking from the shadows, but my demonic guide insisted that we press on without exploring. Even though I had a sapphire the size of a chicken's egg tucked into my shirt, it pained me not to steal everything of value that wasn't nailed down.

"So, what are you in for?" I asked, bored of listening to my breathing and the wet slap of the imp's feet against the flagstones.

It tilted its head to one side and narrowed its eyes. "What are you talking about, Breed?"

I cleared my throat. "WHY. ARE. YOU. STUCK. IN. HERE? WHY. CAN'T. YOU. LEAVE?"

It wiped its face and scowled. "A sorcerer imprisoned me, something of an overreaction in my opinion, all because I stole her favorite pen which as I recall was albino peacock, silver nib, very classy."

"That's it? How long have you been here?"

"I was bound here in the year that Halda the Red Witch and the Hammer of the North united in battle against the Lord of Dawn."

"Really? You do know how long ago that was, don't you?"

"Seven hundred and sixty-seven years, six months, one week, three days, and nine hours." It stomped off along the corridor.

"You've aged well, considering."

When I got around to bragging about this adventure in the Nest, I'd paint over the image of the 'small, insane demon'. I would instead claim that my dread companion was seven feet tall, with flaming eyes, wicked horns, and great, leathery wings. I'd also tell my awestruck and fawning audience that I'd cut a far more advantageous deal than just 'get me out of here'.

We passed more rubble-strewn chambers and the occasional pile of ancient corpses. Clad in rotting armor, the dead lay where they had fallen, names and deeds forgotten, their passing marked by none. And all those purses still hanging from their belts. Sweet salvation, but it was hard overcoming the habit of a lifetime and not filching their chink.

After a couple more hours of walking in silence, the lightest kiss of fresh air brushed my cheek. I sniffed, caught a hint of ice, pine, and moss. It seemed that my little goblin friend was steering us right after all. I turned to my companion. "So, what'll you do when you get out? whores and ale, or is it straight back to business for you?" I was feeling much happier now that I knew we were going in the right direction.

It sighed. "'Tis not a business. A demon's wyrd, its nature, is written in its blood. I do what I was made to do. 'Tis as strong an imperative as the suns' need to shine, the rain to fall, the seas to—"

"All right, I get it. You're a committed pen thief."

Silence fell again, and we continued until we reached a junction. The imp raised its hand, bringing us to a halt. The passageway snaked off to the left. Before us was a pair of impressive double doors. "Which way now?" I asked.

The imp pointed at the doors. "Through the hall. We're close now."

I believed it, the scent of trees and taste of cold, fresh air oozed under the doors. It was like nectar, and I made to enter the hall, eager to be away. The imp grabbed my arm and pulled me back. It had quite the grip for something so small. "What?" I wrenched my arm from its miser's grasp. "What is it?"

"You remember I said I could avoid *most* of the restless dead?"

"Urgh." I handed it the torch and cast a light spell.

The shimmering globe banished the shadows from the hall, revealing more than a dozen, shriveled corpses lying on a black-and-white tiled floor. The ancient dead were wrapped in dusty, silken shrouds that had been woven by countless generations of spiders. Some of the corpses were human but there were also warspawn like me, as well as demonspawn. All of them were locked in combat when they died. I wondered what calamity had befallen this place to slay them all so suddenly. Skeletal hands tore at bony throats, mouths were open, frozen mid-shout, swords were buried in skulls and chests, fists were raised in short-lived triumph. I didn't care what had killed them, I just hoped that the demonspawn with four arms and tusks like longswords was permanently dead.

Despite the silvery radiance of the magical light, the furthest corners of the chamber remained cloaked in shadows. To my right, an obsidian throne stood brooding atop a raised dais. I half turned to speak to the imp when something on the throne caught my eye. Curious, I directed the light over to it. There was a sword lying across the armrests, not of itself particularly interesting, a sword was a sword, this one was interesting because it glittered.

The imp tugged my sleeve. "The surest way to traverse the hall without waking these poor souls is…"

I stopped listening. The sword, the lovely glittering sword had captured my full attention. The hilt sparkled like frost in the moonlight. As vulgar as it was valuable, the whole of the hilt was encrusted with diamonds, an irresistible lure for a rogue like me. Before I could stop myself, I was halfway across the room, my eyes locked on the twinkling prize. It was at this point that the restless dead distinguished themselves from the permanently departed.

* * *

When I'd finished the last of them and the clamor of battle had stopped ringing in my ears, I sheathed my blades and drew a deep breath. The imp was rolling around on the floor, laughing its skinny little arse off.

"What are you laughing at, you little bubo?" I was tired but had sustained nothing more painful than a scratch on my leg during the scrap. The dead might have been restless, but they were a slow lot.

The imp's raucous laughter dwindled to a giggle. "I have never seen something that wasn't under the influence of a powerful geas act so recklessly." It shook its head. "Thy wyrd is greed, halfling."

I snatched a verdigrised coin from the floor and threw it at the demon. "Here you go. When we get out, find yourself a nice inn and buy a big, frothy pint of fuck off, on me." Chuckling, it plucked the coin from the air and then idly toed a skull into the shadows. A moment later, the braincase skittered back towards us, this time accompanied by the dry clatter of bones.

"You missed one," the imp sang.

"Why did you do that?" I sighed and drew my blades, again.

"Demon." It shrugged and settled its arse on the dais.

The restless dead lurched from the shadows. Creaking muscles worked its rotting jaw as though it was trying to speak or shout a battle cry, but all I could hear was the sound of its teeth grinding.

The bag of bones was wearing the remains of ancient plate armor and wielding a longsword. It wove its blade in a loop before launching an overhead blow at me. It was fast for a corpse but nowhere near fast enough to catch me. When it was committed to the swing, I pivoted on my left foot and scythed my blades through its neck and torso. The head flew backwards and rolled into the shadows while the torso folded beneath the sternum. I sheathed my weapons with emphasis and swept onto the dais without so much as glancing at the goblin.

The throne was carved from cloudy obsidian and decorated with a writhing mass of dragons. The stone alone was incredibly valuable but the whole thing was far too big and heavy to move. The sword, however, was an entirely portable proposition. The blade was double-edged, deeply fullered and tapered to a fine, diamond-cut point. The pommel and crossguards were covered with glittering, white-blue stones. Time had been kind to the gaudy weapon and the steel was unblemished. I picked it up, gave it a swing. It was perfectly balanced and sang through the air.

"Do you see how it's been forged?" the imp asked. "The metal is rare, Stellaris Metallium only sorcerers can work it. The Shen call it star steel because of the way the crystals shine like stars in the night sky."

While the imp prattled on, I took a firm, two-handed grip of the hilt and smashed the blade against the arm of the throne. There was a loud crack and the steel snapped neatly just below the rain guard. I let the now useless blade lie where it fell and stuffed the hilt into my tunic. As I turned to leave, I saw that the imp was staring at me, wide-eyed and open-mouthed.

"What?" I asked.

"That was Dawnslight, the greatest sword of the age. It, it was priceless." The little rat-dropping scuttled over to the broken blade, picked it up and cradled it like it was a sleeping babe, before gently placing what was left of it back on the throne.

"I know it's priceless, that's why I broke it up. I mean, where in the Empire d'you think a breed like me could fence such a relic?" I laughed. "If I turned up waving a great, shiny pig-sticker like that and tried to sell it, I'd either end up doing the gallows jig or be vented by one of the Guild before I'd seen a penny of its value. Now, loose stones I can fence. Sell a few at a time so as not to draw attention to myself and I could keep the wolf from the door for many a month on the proceeds. Anyway, what's it matter to you? It's a sword, not a pen."

The imp didn't answer. It wandered out of the hall with its head bowed.

* * *

After a few hundred feet, the passage widened. Decapitated statues stood either side of a gaping wound where I assumed the outer doors must have once been. A cold wind greeted us, carrying with it a hundred mundane smells and tastes that I never thought I'd miss so much. Beyond the ragged arch, the rose-infused glow of the setting suns melted into the dark line of the horizon. I ran outside, opened my arms, and drank in a lungful of the racing air.

I was standing on the ravaged lip of a cobblestone promontory that ended abruptly some fifteen feet from the entrance. Below, a bare slope stretched about fifty feet before giving way to a broad sweep of pines that flowed into the vast, green sea that was the Arrak Basin. On the far side of the forest was Appleton, my hometown. A thick pall of smoke from the calthracite burners marbled a patch of sky, marking its location. I turned to my companion who was lurking nervously in the shadows of the entrance.

"I need you to take me over the seal," it whispered. It didn't look me in the eye, instead its gaze flitted nervously from one foot to the other as it shuffled from side to side.

"Oh, right, the deal." I went over.

It held out its hand. I saw it was shaking, could smell the acid tang of fear and apprehension rising off its diminutive body. I picked it up and carried it into the sunslight.

"Put me down, stupid breed," it squeaked, kicking feebly against me.

Laughing, I put it down on the other side of the large steel ring that was set in the cobbles by the doorway. I guessed this was ‘the seal’ because of the arcane scribbles incised in the metal rim.

“Oh,” it said surprised.

“The words you’re looking for are ‘thank you’,” I said and went back over to the edge of the plateau to plot my route down. It was steep but not a difficult climb. The imp was silent. I guessed it was embarrassed for having misjudged me.

This wasn’t the first time I’d been wrong about something important.

As ever when something went awry, my body was quicker to react than my brain, so when I heard the soft implosion of air followed by a wave of heat and sulfur, I didn’t spring into action and draw my blades. I turned around but before I had chance to raise my hands in the universal sign for ‘I surrender, don’t hit me’, I was grabbed by the throat and hoisted off my feet.

The demon was over seven feet tall and naked but for a few shreds of cloth clinging to the bony scales that jutted from his dead white shoulders. He had long, curving horns like those of a massive ram, and fine, sharp features. He flexed his shoulders and a pair of black, leathery wings unfurled. The only thing that hadn’t changed were his eyes. They were the same smooth pools of obsidian and they were staring at me.

"You broke my sword, Breed," he said in a voice that I felt as much as heard.

"Sorry?"

His laughter sounded like a rock slide. "Oh, Breed, there are some trivial imps and some petty demons, I'll grant you that, but a demon dedicated to stealing pen nibs? You really believed that?" He laughed again and squeezed a little harder. "You are without doubt the most stupid creature I have ever encountered. Some might say, too stupid to live."

"I helped you." The growing pressure lessened, but I was still dangling by my neck over a precipice.

"Helped? We made a deal. I showed you the way out, and you took me over the seal."

He took a step back and released me. I fell in a heap and sucked in a huge gulp of air. The demon rolled his heavily muscled shoulders and cracked all fourteen fingers that terminated in gleaming black talons. Preferring one death to another, I got ready to leap over the edge.

"What are you the demon of?" I asked, trying to buy myself time to come up with a better plan than jumping off a cliff.

"Oh, you know, vengeance, destruction, laying waste to civilization, crushing empires under my heel that kind of thing. The more pressing question is, what am I going to do with you?"

“Let me go?” I asked, somewhat hopefully it must be said. The demon reached a taloned hand towards the seal. A lance of white-hot fire leaped from its fingers and engulfed the ring. The air burned black and bitter as the metal melted and ran between the cobbles.

“That’s better,” he said. A curtain of steam rose between us. “Let you go? That would be fair, I suppose, only I don’t want everyone to know I’m back just yet. I’d like to surprise them.” He winked.

“I won’t tell anyone anything, I promise.” Even as I said it I knew it was a lie, and so did he.

Before I could leap backwards and take my chance with rocks and gravity, he grabbed me again. Once again, his iron-hard fingers closed around my throat. This time he swung me so hard into the rock face that it felt like I’d dented the mountain with my head. Now I fought like a cornered thoasa. I kicked, I punched, and I bit and made no impression whatsoever. With my eyes bugging out of my skull, I used the last of my breath and hissed, “Shallunsard.” The pressure lessened.

“That is the name the world knew me by.” He released me.

I slid down the wall, I was saved. I had power over a demon lord. I was,

“Of course, that isn’t my true name.”

Fucked. I was fucked.

The demon threw his head back and laughed like thunder. "What? You didn't really? Ah, Breed, if only the rest of the world was as stupid as you." It held out its hand.

I fished the hilt of Dawnslight from my tunic and handed it over. Caught by the dying rays of the suns' light the gems flashed a crimson farewell. The demon raised his free hand above his head, the air grew heavy and crackled with energy.

"Let's make a deal," I begged, cringing away from the blast of fire that I knew was coming.

His hand hung over me like a hawk's claw poised to crush a rabbit's skull. The suns haloed him in scarlet. I held my breath. After an eternity, the demon lowered his hand.

"Very well, Breed. I have a task for you, perform it and I won't kill you, fail and, well you know the rest."

"Anything. Thank you." I could have kissed him.

"Bring me the Hammer of the North."

Euphoric at being alive, it sounded like a fine idea. "Certainly, right away," I said, and then the magnitude of what he asked sank in. "You mean the Hammer of the North's hammer, don't you?"

He nodded. "Yes, I do."

"He's been dead for a very long time."

"You owe me a debt, Breed."

"Funny, that's how I ended up being chased by a dragon."

"Why doesn't that surprise me? Now, do we have a deal, or do I turn you into a pile of ash?"

"Since you put it that way."

The demon held out his hand. I gripped it.

"How long do I have?"

He grinned. "A year and a day."

"Deal."

As soon as the words left my mouth, my hand began to burn. I tried to pull away, but the demon held me fast. When he let go I saw that a black sigil had been burnt into my palm, marking me out as the demon's own. I looked up, a salty oath on my lips, but Shallunsard had vanished

.

Chapter Three

Appleton does not smell of apples. Appleton smells of shit and misery, which perfectly summed up my situation.

My father was a Thoasa, the toughest breed of warspawn. They can survive for weeks on nothing more than a few mouthfuls of brackish water, run for twenty miles without tiring, and still fight like ten bastards in a sack at the end of it. So, it's a shame that my mother is human. That less hardy side of my lineage was currently desperate to add the contents of my stomach to the corrosive salmagundi of viscera sloshing around in the bottom of the honey pot in which I was hiding.

As I slipped and skidded in the greasy waste, I tried to follow the thread of events back to where everything had started to unravel. Stealing the sapphire from the dragon hadn't gone exactly to plan, I'll grant, and then I'd inadvertently loosed a vengeful demon on the world.

What irked me more was this latest indignity. I had been forced to hide in a gong pot just because I was a couple of days late getting back to Appleton. Two poxy days and my own mother had put a bounty on my head.

The honey wagon slowed. A yelled greeting-come-warning was followed by the creak of gates telling me we'd arrived at the city. I hunkered down out of habit rather than fear of discovery. Not even the most zealous greenshanks would think to search a honey wagon for fugitives. Why would they? Only a lunatic or a desperate fool would hide in a shit pot.

The team of urux pulling the wagon bellowed lugubriously when the driver encouraged them on with a few licks of the lash. My fragrant carriage jounced against its neighbors, and I slid around the pot like an oily rag. After a halting, five-mile journey from the dump to the city, I was covered in filth, and despite the best efforts of tear ducts and nictitating membranes, the stinging fumes were blinding. My finely tuned sense of smell had also been bludgeoned to uselessness by the olfactory assault of putrid effluvia.

After the last outbreak of plague, all tannery waste and night soil was required by law to be dumped at least five miles from the city. The Imperial Factors who ran Appleton didn't give a crusty scab about public health, but they did need a workforce to dig and refine enough calthracite to supply the Empirifex's Royal Cannoneers. It was almost funny that a rogue like me had benefitted from an Imperial law. I would have laughed if I wasn't trying not to breathe.

The pots clattered hollowly against each other as we rolled along, much like the heads of the two Blades who'd waylaid me on my way back to the city. After a brief and pointy exchange with the pair of foolhardy opportunists, I left them in the shallow grave they'd prepared for me. It was a bit of a squeeze fitting them both in there, but where there's a sword there's a way. Their clumsy attempt had at least warned me that Mother had made good on her threat to put a bounty on my head should I be late. I wasn't surprised, she had a vicious reputation to maintain.

The wagon slowed almost to a halt. I lifted the pot lid a finger's width and saw that we'd reached the crossroad of Pater Lane and Main Street. Seven-foot mounds of grey-dusted urux shit banked the busy thoroughfare. Everything in Appleton is gray, even the shit. Height of summer, depth of winter, the soot that falls from the calth burners paints all seasons the same uniform shade of hopeless.

After we crossed the Silverlight River the urux gathered pace and channeled their breath through the hollow bones of their crests. The beasts' ululating cries rolled through the timber and daub canyons of Old Town's shanties and dilapidated mills. Minutes later, the mournful cries of their stablemates flowed back towards us.

I didn't leap out as soon as the cart pulled into the gong farmers' yard. I lifted the lid a crack and waited for the dead-eyed driver to unhitch the urux. Unsurprisingly, the yard was empty save for her and the animals. As she led them to their stalls I saw the locked bronze cuff on her wrist that marked her out as a self-indentured servant. It made sense, given the job. Pawning yourself to the state was common practice amongst the poor of Appleton and this was the fate of many a poor cull who had fallen on hard times. With the animals bedded down, she grabbed her coat and left the yard. I waited a few minutes before tipping the lid and vaulting to the ground.

I landed with a squelch; rancid fat oozed between my toes. It was times like this that having seven, clawed toes on each foot was a massive pain in the arse. I wished, albeit briefly, that I'd inherited Mother's fleshy little human feet that could be shoved into a neat pair of shoes and not get covered in filth every damn day.

Cursing under my breath, I squeezed a handful of stinking, gong juice from my hair spines. It did nothing to improve my grimy appearance, but I felt a yard less wretched without rotting viscera dripping down my back. My left hand itched. I scratched it, remembered the black sigil of the demon Shallunsard that was embedded in my palm.

I had a year and a day to find the hammer of the Hammer of the North, the weapon of the greatest hero the world had ever known, if Mother didn't do for me first. I laughed at the absurdity of the situation and tore a strip of cloth from the lining of my jerkin to bind around my hand. There was no point adding 'demon-marked' to the list of reasons to kill me.

Despite my appearance and exotic aroma, nobody gave me a second look as I made my way along Tannery Lane. In this part of Old Town, I'd have drawn more attention if I wasn't covered in filth. I took a few random turns to make sure that I wasn't being followed before heading down Grinder's Snicket. Wedged between clapboard warehouses, at the end of the narrow passageway, a flight of steps led to the cellar under Blookmann's Grindery.

In a dark corner of the cellar, behind a row of storage racks that were never moved, used, or inspected, there was a cunningly hidden sewer entrance. The Blookmann family and their employees were well paid to ignore it, along with the shady types who used it.

I was about to congratulate myself on evading my brothers and sisters of the blade when I saw something move under a piece of sacking that was crumpled by the cellar door. The suns hadn't quite set, but thuggish shadows mobbed the alley and fell heavily across the doorway. I tried to arrow my gaze through the murky depth only to find that it was a little too dark down there. I sniffed the air. Someone was using hedge magic. The spell to deepen shadows was a favorite among the stealthily inclined members of the Midnight Court. Scribed on bloodclay tablets, they could be used once.

They were a nice little earner for sorcerers of modest skill or for those who wanted to stay on the right side of the Paradox of Power.

Whoever had cast this one had used it in the right place, but they hadn't taken their smell into account. Free of the gong pot, my senses were my own again. I tasted the air and let the ambient funk of the alley wash over my tongue. The lurker was human and either a male or someone who had recently been pissed on by a male. Whoever they were, they hadn't washed in a while and had recently dined on pickled garlic. Nevermind a thoasa, a rotnosed poxmonger would have been able to smell the tang of cheap wine vinegar that cut through the alley's background perfume of cat piss, pigeon shit, and grindstone dust.

It was an amateur mistake, very sloppy.

Outwardly, I affected an air of feckless nonchalance as I strolled towards the cellar. Inside I was drawn as taut as a bowstring, ready to spring into action. I waited until I was half a stride from the steps before I snatched my blades from their scabbards and leaped.

As planned, I landed inches from my would-be ambusher, leaving him scant room to maneuver. He spat a curse and threw the sack aside. Like me, he was using two long knives, the weapons of choice for discerning, back-alley brawlers. Unlike me, he wasn't very good. He swung his steels, but I parried both blades, inside to out, and kneed him in the jewels. As he folded I butted him in the face. Gargling snot and blood, he took a seat in the corner. I rocked him off to sleep with a smack in the teeth and then had a quick rummage through his personals. The ghost of a familiar odor clung to the tumble of silvers that I found in his purse. I gave the coins a lick and a sniff. They smelled of failure and self-abuse. They smelled of my old mate, Sketh.

* * *

There are those who say that Appleton's sewers are nothing more than a shit-smeared, fat-calked labyrinth. A treacherous maggot burrow where only the desperate or the deadly venture willingly. Here be monsters, they say, which I know to be true, for I am one, and this is my home. The passage under the grindery isn't the safest way to get to the Nest and therefore seldom used, which was why I chose it. From here I could either take a long and time-consuming detour, or a shorter but more perilous route. I paused briefly to weigh up the relative dangers of keeping Mother waiting longer, against the risk of taking the potentially fatal shortcut. An image of her scowling visage floated before my mind's eye, tipping the scale decidedly in favor of the shortcut.

* * *

Nobody knew if Ludo had ever been a single person. Some speculated that it had been a sorcerer who'd pushed the Paradox of Power too far. Other's said that they, he, she, or it, had always been the way it was, just another freak birthed too near some old Schism-tainted battleground. The only fact about Ludo that was beyond speculation was that it was a deadly cove of the highest order.

I was hoping that the guardian of Mother's backdoor would be out fishing the sewer flow for 'treasures' when I passed through its lair. I am often disappointed and today was no exception. I paused before the bloodstained door to Ludo's lair which was swinging gently on well-oiled hinges. Long before Mother had moved the Guild into the sewers, someone, perhaps Ludo itself, had blocked all but two of the entrances to the collection chamber that lay between me and my destination. It had been Ludo's home for as long as I could remember and as all knew, if the doors were locked, it meant that Ludo had a visitor, as it liked to call the poor culls it lured to their deaths.

"Come iiiin," Ludo sang in an unsettling twine of baritone and falsetto. I sheathed my blades and entered. Previously, when I'd gone to see Ludo to beg a favor for Mother or take the shortcut through its home, I'd felt a thrill of fear as invigorating as it was disturbing. I was therefore disappointed to find that after almost being killed by a dragon and a demon in the space of a week, the thrilling terror of a visit to Ludo was somewhat muted. Thoasa hadn't been bred to be emotional, they'd been bred to kill demons for the Mage Lords. Even now, seven hundred years after the Schism War, the descendants of those mage-bred warriors were known to be a coldly practical breed of warspawn. It was the human in me that enjoyed the spikes and troughs of stirred emotions.

I took in the room with a casual glance. A rusting walkway spiraled up the wall before tapering off beside a blocked-up doorway. As usual, it was piled with a wide variety of objects that Ludo had either fished from the sewer or stolen from its many victims. Today I hardly thought about the coins and jewels that lay scattered amid odd shoes, broken buckets, and yellowing bones. I just wanted to get in and out in one piece, although at a push, I'd settle for alive.

As usual, Ludo was dressed in a motley outfit sewn from mismatched swatches of fabric that the more ghoulishly inclined gossips swore had been cut from the clothes of its many victims. It had artlessly posed itself for my benefit and was leaning against a broken alabaster column with a mildewed book held daintily — and upside down— in its giant, red claw. Belying Ludo's imitation of gentility and refinement was the collection of severed heads that had been nailed to the wall. In various states of decay, from skull to still dripping, the gaps in their ranks were a grim reminder to be extremely wary around this cove.

Over the years there had been several doomed attempts by heroes and rogues alike to kill Ludo and plunder its hoard. Mother had never officially sanctioned any of those attempts, although I know she would have happily taken her cut of the loot had any of them succeeded. Officially, Ludo and Mother had an understanding. She didn't move against it or kick up a fuss when one of the Nest's less cautious patrons vanished, and Ludo kept an eye on the back door to her territory. It was a pact between monsters which, thus far, had extended some protection to me as Mother's only offspring, but hereabouts I never took my safety for granted. Ludo flipped the book it wasn't reading closed and beamed a wet-lipped smile with both of its lopsided mouths. Imagine taking two humans, sticking their eyes on stalks, replacing the right arm of one with a massive lobster claw and the left arm of the other with a flaccid tentacle. Then imagine the two unfortunates had been squashed together in some infernal vice. That's what Ludo looked like. Its smell was equally unique, akin to a bowl of overripe fruit and maggoty bread, with a subtle hint of licorice. Its gender was another mystery, as not even the lowest slubberdegullion in the sewer had dared a sniff of that hem and lived to tell the tale.

It watched me intently, both pairs of gray eyes dancing merrily on the end of weaving stalks. Like a fleshy jigsaw, its vaguely human skulls were distended, flattened, and bulging where nature had deemed necessary in order to accommodate its warped design. Greasy fronds of hair the color of curdled milk clung to its sallow pate. Two extra legs unfolded from somewhere beneath its gaudy raiment and the two halves glided apart. But not the voice. When Ludo spoke, its voices remained in disturbingly perfect unison.

"Dear friend has come to visit. Dear friend smells very tasty, like a ripe skin fruit plucked straight from the flow. Mmm… luscious," Ludo both rumbled and squealed. "What pretty thing have you brought Ludo, what treasure?" Its eyestalks contracted and extended excitedly, both halves licked their rouged, too-full lips.

I took out the ambusher's purse and tossed it to the half of Ludo with the pincer. The claw snapped shut on the bag like a bear trap. It weighed the pouch appreciatively before tipping the coins into its human hand.

"Only coins for Ludo?" It sighed and deposited them somewhere within its motley. "Ludo likes pretty things, likes eyeballs, and pigeon tongues, and sapphires as big as hens' eggs."

"Alas, dear friend, I only have one of those and it belongs to Mother."

The halves continued to slowly drift apart, casually flanking me like a pair of wolves. I tried to watch both without looking like I was watching either.

Ludo pouted and teased a lick of hair behind its ear. "Mother." It groaned, swung away from me like a petulant child. "Mother has a bony soul, a heart of flint, a mind of knives and wasps. Stay with me, dear friend. I'll kill you for much better reasons than jealousy." It licked its lips.

"It's tempting, friend Ludo, it really is, but I've already kept the old dear waiting and… What do you mean 'jealousy'?"

Ludo tittered. "You're a sharp cove, dear friend. You know the grip is slippery on the greasy pole of power. Old hands grow feeble, lose their strength." It fondled its nethers suggestively.

"Come again?" I said whilst trying neither to stare or avert my gaze.

"Mother fears you."

I didn't get a chance to answer, to say, with respect that I thought it had dropped a maundering whid and should stopper up its bunghole sharpish. I didn't get a chance to say anything because one minute both halves of Ludo were casually gliding around the room and the next it apported.

"Here I is," it breathed in my ear.

I didn't flinch. I didn't so much as twitch when the warty, red claw clacked an inch from my neck. Ludo giggled. The other half wandered over to the exit and clapped its hand and tentacle.

"Dear friend is very clever," it said from over there, and next to me.

"I do try, friend Ludo, I do try."

Its clammy, human arm slithered around my shoulders. It sniffed my neck. I flinched, not because I found Ludo repulsive, who was I to talk? But because the skin and scales on my shoulder were still tender to the touch.

Ludo noticed. “Ice burn, hmm? Has dear friend been playing kiss-chase with a dragon?” It giggled like a child.

“Something like that,” I said through gritted teeth.

It sniffed me like a boarhound on the hunt for truffle pigs before it grabbed my hand and tugged the strip of cloth aside. It sucked its teeth. “Dear friend is demon-marked. Dear friend is fucked.” The part that had been beside me vanished and appeared by the exit where it cozied up to its other half. It opened the door and with a flick of its claw invited me to leave.

I obliged without hesitation. As soon as I was out, the light behind me thinned to a narrow wedge. I glanced over my shoulder. The old villain had half closed the door but was still loitering in the doorway, eyestalks bobbing in thoughtful contemplation.

“Be well, dear friend,” it sang in tenor and bass. “But don’t come back too soon.” The door slammed, bathing me in echoes and shrouding me in shadows.

The booming noise of the door slamming ran ahead of me, rippling ever weaker as it spread through the tunnels. It was good to be back in the sludgy veins of the city. I knew this darkness, knew the way the shadows wrapped around flesh and stone, knew every nuance of every native stench and sound. I feared no evil down here. This burrowed corpse was the only home I’d ever known and as far as I was concerned there was no better place to dwell. But then, worms like me; coves who were hooked into the arsepipe of Appleton, had a habit of elevating the feculent passages far above their inglorious purpose. I suppose I was a bit of a romantic at heart.

* * *

Not long after leaving Ludo's, a burst of tavern babble breached the silence, welcoming me home with raucous laughter and slurred curses. I had almost reached the Mouse's Nest. The Inn was the epitome of dump and proudly catered to the vilest scum and most dangerous flotsam that dwelt within or passed through Appleton. The queen who ruled this benighted kingdom was the most evil, ice-hearted monster I'd ever met, and I'd parleyed with a demon, so I knew what I was talking about.

She was known as Mother Blake or just Mother to her gang which she had imaginatively named 'the Guild'. I was one of her Blades. That she also happened to be my birth mother was purely accidental according to the woman herself. I never met my father, a thoasa who apparently went out one day to buy a goat and never came back. I can't say as I blamed him, Mother was a difficult person to live with.

We did not get on, but for the most part bore the burden of our relationship with stoical and mutual disdain. After the demon, she was the very last person I wanted to see right now, but I had no choice if I was going to save my neck. By way of encouragement, I promised myself that as soon as I handed her the sapphire and she canceled the bounty, I was going to dive into a vat of cheap wine and stay there until I was entirely pickled, something which could take a while on account of my iron constitution.

My high-spirits lasted for about another four paces which was when I caught the unmistakable whiff of failure and self-abuse. I flattened myself against the wall just before a spiral of air riffled past my face. The crossbow bolt whined like a mosquito as it sped into the gloom. I cut sparks from the wall as I swept my blades from their scabbards and peered in the direction from which it had been fired.

About fifteen feet away, the skein of smells that were tickling my nostrils knotted themselves into a familiar lump of crap that was pressed tight against the corner of the wall. I'd wanted a legitimate reason to make Sketh bones for a long time so, in a way, I was grateful that he'd opened the account with this sorry attempt, although I could have kicked myself for not spotting the little turdling sooner.

I growled so he could hear me. "When I catch you, Sketh, I'm going to peel your balls like a couple of grapes." That was an exaggeration. I didn't have the patience to peel his poxy fruits, I was just going to stab him a lot. Hero that he was, my fellow Blade ducked around the corner and ran. The wet slap of his feet receded at a pace. I followed at a walk because I knew where he was going. He kept running until he reached his destination. Soon after, a blast of conversation and the smell of stale beer billowed through the tunnels. Sketh had reached the Nest.

Chapter Four

There wasn't a sign above the door of the tavern, but a literal representation of the inn's name. Set in a rusting cage was a broken human skull that had been carefully packed with rags and straw by the now long dead and desiccated rodent still curled within the braincase. Nobody had ever dared to ask Mother who the skull had belonged to on the off chance she was in the mood to redecorate.

As well as being the only inn in the sewers, the Mouse's Nest had the dubious honor of being the headquarters of the Guild. Mother had built both from nothing with only her wit, powerful sorcerous skills, and efficient stock management skills to aid her. I sheathed my blades. There weren't many rules in the Guild, but few sane people entered the Nest looking like they wanted a fight. Before going in, I straightened up, loosened my neck with a quick head toss, and composed my expression to read 'cross me and I will stab you in the face'. I'd been away a while and the heady stench of piss, pel, and beer tickled my nostrils as soon as I opened the door. I wanted to sneeze, but stone-cold killers don't sneeze. Instead, I swaggered through the crowded bar. For the briefest of moments, I thought that news of my adventures had somehow preceded me as lags and bravos all but fell over each other to get out of my way.

Then I remembered.

I could tolerate the stink of the gong pots, but non-thoasa weren't as resilient. Even down here, in a tavern in the sewers, I must have stunk. Deflated, I gathered the tattered shreds of my ego and hurried through the main bar.

Members of the Guild tended to congregate in the dimly-lit back room of the inn. Casual drinkers were allowed but were often discouraged from staying with a polite smack in the teeth. This shady den was where deals were made, fates sealed, and the well-heeled with their faces hidden behind masks came to have awkward problems permanently solved. It was like a temple, silence ruled, except when someone came in smelling of rotted brains and fermented pigeon dung. A couple of the patrons gagged, several threatened violence. One shrank back into a curtained booth, quiet as a murderous little mouse.

"Evening, Sketh," I said as I strode past.

"Er, aye. Evenin'," he mumbled.

I had no intention of starting anything in here, not when I was already in Mother's bad books and besides, it was dreadfully rude to fight while people were trying to have a quiet pint, but it didn't hurt to make Sketh sweat before I closed his account. It served the bastard right for attempting to vent me, but before I could have a short, sharp word with my brother-in-arms, I had to square things with Mother.

The stairs down to her den were hidden at the back of the room behind a faded tapestry of an Imperial knight. The image of the armor-clad bastard was a warning to the Guild Blades of who'd come calling should they screw up. I took a deep breath. The thrill of fear I'd thought lost was now dancing light fingers up and down my spine. I pushed through the tapestry.

* * *

Lediss was slouching at the bottom of the stairs. The door guard's once muscular bulk hung like sacks of sodden wheat on his tired bones. The ogren glared at me, his solitary eye gleaming angrily from beneath his heavy brow. He snorted, rubbed his stomach with a grizzled paw. He'd been with Mother for as long as I could remember. The big oaf was slavishly devoted to her but hated everyone else, including me. Over the years I'd watched him slip from being Mother's red right hand to her doorman. The next step down was working behind the bar. After that, it was sweeping the floors and emptying spittoons, and then he'd be out on his arse and prey for those with long memories and axes to grind, something which couldn't come soon enough for my liking.

"You stink," he said, spittle flying from his broken tusks.

"I can wash, you, however, are always going to be an ugly, one-eyed bastard."

He growled. So did I. It was good to be home. The ogren shoved the door open and tossed his head impatiently. I spared him a sneer before sauntering inside. All conversation died, all heads turned in my direction.

"Where have you been, you miserable, half-breed bastard?" said Mother.

"Hello, Mother," I said cheerily, even as the leaden surety of doom settled over me.

"Don't you fucking 'Mother' me."

* * *

Imagine a room that has been decorated by someone with a lot of money but no taste whatsoever and that would give you a fair picture of Mother's audience chamber. It was an eclectic goulash of the most expensive and gaudy fixtures and fittings money could buy, in Appleton. Now imagine it upside down.

Upon my arrival, Mother and I engaged in an unfortunately spiky bout of bear garden badinage. Soon after which I found myself disarmed and hanging by my ankles over the pit, suspended from a rope held by that grinning, rut-stuck bucket-fucker, Lediss.

The pit was a sheer-sided hole that Mother had dug down into the uncharted tunnels where the dog rats lived. It had taken her months of patiently feeding the feral creatures juicy morsels of miscreant to train them to come when she called. The pit was now the centerpiece of her audience chamber, much like an exquisite crystal chandelier might be in the house of a less bloodthirsty noblewoman. Unfortunately for me, there was nothing more than the whim of a madwoman and an arthritic, one-eyed ogren between me and an unpleasantly bitey-chewy end.

Mother sprawled across the Rat Bone Throne in her usual pose. A bird-thin leg was hooked over the arm of the glazed mountain of skulls and bones and a silver goblet hung from her bony fingers. She nailed me with a pin-sharp stare as I slowly spun to face her and her bodyguards.

The Dumbrovski twins flanked her throne like a pair of malformed bookends. The identical goblin brothers liked to think of themselves as the killer elite of the Midnight Court. Killer elite my arse. I didn't fear them, but I had a healthy respect for the handcannons they were carrying.

One of the pair, Klaus I think, going by the stink of fermented fish drifting off him, tightened a sparkling zanthe crystal in the priming screw of his gun. That the weapon could blast a lead ball through Imperial plate armor at fifty paces was why I was hanging upside down over a pit of massive rats, instead of stabbing the smug grins off their faces.

“Two days late,” Mother intoned. Candlelight etched a deep v between her eyes. Neatly coiffured waves of dyed black hair shone darkly and framed her vulpine face. Like a lot of humans, she valued her appearance as much as, if not more than, her abilities. Beside the throne, an incense clock smoldered on a cracked alabaster table. Another string burnt through and a tiny brass weight dropped into the boat-shaped metal tray, signaling the death of another hour and the approach of my demise. The next string began to smolder.

“I lifted the fucking sapphire *from a dragon*, what more do you want?” I said with as much indignance as I could muster, although I admit, it’s hard to be taken seriously when you’re upside down. When I swung round to face Mother again, I saw that she was examining the stone in question.

She slammed the rock against the arm of her throne, sending chips of rat bone flying. “You also lost my fucking shipment of pel.”

“The fucking guards weren’t supposed to be there,” I snapped back.

A foot of rope slipped through Lediss’s hands. Mother laughed. Some of the more sycophantic Blades joined in. Sensing a meal was in the offing, a few of the bolder rats leaped at the tail-ends of my hair spines. Mercifully I was still out of reach. Blood flows almost to the tip of each leathery strand and it damn well hurts when they get bitten or cut.

"Guards or not, you shouldn't have dumped my pel." She wrinkled her nose at the huge rock like it was a turd. "This bauble will barely cover my costs, let alone compensate my clients for the inconvenience."

"Most of your clients don't notice when they've shit themselves." I rejoined. What was really biting her arse was that they had gone and bought their drugs off Pork Chop Jing instead of her. Angry as I was, I didn't point this out or mention her rival's name, not with the furry masses staring up at me, eyes bright with hunger.

Mother tucked the sapphire into her sleeve and took an angry slurp of wine. A dribble of scarlet ran down her chin and joined the widening stain blooming on the delicate brocade of her blue satin gown. She stabbed me again with another accusing glare as hard and sharp as coffin nails. It was a solid fact that the dragon had a friendlier visage, even when it was trying to kill me.

"If I'd have known what an utter and complete fucking lackwit I was growing in my womb, I'd have gutted myself with a rusty spoon rather than give birth." She spat as though even the memory of my birth was distasteful. "Useless. Just like that flyblown, bastard father of yours. Two cocks and you are all he could produce!"

Nobody in the chamber had the guts to address Mother's willful ignorance of thoasan biology, least of all me. To emphasize her displeasure, she lobbed her goblet at my head. I was well used to such shows of affection and easily dodged the improvised missile. Lediss didn't. The cup struck him on his blind side. He yelped, which would have been funny had he not fumbled the rope as he pawed at his injured face. I dropped another couple of feet before the fat-fingered idiot caught it. The rats screeched. I curled my body up to my knees to avoid the more athletic rodents who were scaling their companions to reach me. Backed against the walls by the force of Mother's anger, the Guild Blades all watched in silence, except one.

Wulfrun pushed through the ranks and approached the opposite side of the pit to Mother's throne. The warrior from Grundvelt's stance spoke of confidence just shy of confrontational. He was bold, but not arrogant, strong but not overbearing. He walked a fine, dangerous line with Mother, one I'd never seen any cove walk for long. As I swung between them like a pendulum, or a worm on a hook, depending on your point of view, I could almost feel my skin burn from the intensity of their staring contest. I tried to look inconspicuous, which isn't easy when you're six feet tall, upside down, and swinging from a rope.

"There's no need for this, Mo," Wulf said. "The stone's worth twenty times what you lost." He had one of those voices that made you want to listen. A born leader, he was liked and hated in equal measure in the Guild, but nobody regarded him with indifference.

He'd only been a full member for a few months but in that short time he'd made his mark and proved he was as clever as he was big, something that had fatally surprised the Blade he'd replaced. The double-headed ax strapped to his back belied his talent as a cracksman but advertised well enough that he was a more than competent enforcer, something Mother hadn't missed. She liked him and let him get away with more than many who'd been with her for years.

It was obvious that there was a strong, physical attraction between them from the moment they met over a pile of blood-drenched corpses and a consignment of stolen rum. He was just her type; big, muscular, and intelligent. Although, being human, I assume he only had one cock.

"What do you suggest, Wulf?" All trace of fury left her voice and the snarl was replaced by a purr.

"Timekeeping aside, Tails got you the stone." He gave me a sly wink when I drifted between them on my slow, elliptical rotation. "Didn't you tell me you had an awkward job that needed doing? Maybe it's something Tails could do, t' make up for being late?"

So, they not only shared a bed, but she'd confided in him too. I felt no slight, she'd never told me anything, but there were others in the room who I could sense were recalculating Wulfrun's worth and their relative positions in the Guild.

Mother's lips curled into something like a smile. She clicked her fingers and Melpinin flip-flapped from behind the throne. The amphibane's moist skin shone like verdigrised copper in the tallow gold light that was dripping from the candelabra. A powdered wig that was made for an entirely different shaped head was perched awkwardly on his warty pate. He filled another goblet and offered it to Mother on the platter of his wide webbed hand. She snagged it without acknowledgment and took a thoughtful slurp.

My fate was dependent on so many unfathomable and irrational factors that I'd already started planning how I'd get past the slavering pack of dog rats and out of the pit tunnel before they could tear me to pieces. As for Mother, I didn't have time to waste hating her, although it did cross my mind that perhaps I should at some point in the future when I wasn't in imminent danger.

The amphibane's gaze flicked in my direction before he hopped back behind the throne. He might have given me an encouraging double blink of his saucer eyes, but it was hard to tell from my inverted position. I couldn't remember how long I'd been upside down, all I knew was that my head felt as swollen as a blood-soaked sponge. My hair spines were near rigid from the amount of claret that had pumped into them and I was still covered in shit. Much longer like this and I'd have to cut the rope with my claws and rescue myself.

"You might be right, Wulf." Mother turned the stem of the goblet between her bejeweled fingers. "Ah, but what about my furry friends?" She gestured to the dog rats with a languorous wave. "They will be ever so confused if they don't get their treat and it took an age to train them. You see my problem?"

The very next instant the goblet clanged against the empty throne. A sharp burst of summer fruit soared from the spilled wine, momentarily distracting me from what had just happened. As usual, my body was much quicker on the uptake and was already twisting to face Wulf.

To his credit, the barbarian was reaching for his ax before Mother appeared behind him and shoved him in the pit. He didn't cry out as he fell, he wasn't the type. As soon as he landed on the writhing mass of hungry rodents he was on his feet and laying into them with a fury that matched their ferocious hunger.

It was a mistake.

He must have realized that the tunnel leading from the pit was big enough to accommodate even his bulky frame, so why hadn't he run for it? I suppose Mother's surprise attack had thrown him. Whatever the reason, his choice to stand and fight was the wrong one. If I'd been in any position to make a wager my money would have been on the rats. The other Blades in the chamber were of a similar mind and didn't pass on the opportunity for a quick bet. As soon as coins were exchanged they began cheering and cursing depending on where they'd put their money.

After a tense handful of minutes, Wulf let out an anguished cry as a rat tore the sausage of his guts through a bloody gash in his stomach. It was over quickly after that. The last I saw of the warrior was the butterfly blades of his ax drowning in a spray of scarlet. Mother watched every bone-snapping, flesh-rending second, and I watched her, watched the play of light and shadow scratch frowns and chase smiles across the livid canvas of her blood-splattered face.

I almost didn't blame her. As a sorcerer she was subject to the Paradox of Power, the more magic a sorcerer channeled, the less stable, physically, and mentally, they became. The clever ones got round this by developing strategies to cope with and contain their abilities. Meditation, drugs, regular bleeding, and quite commonly, limiting what they did and how often they did it. Mother handled the Paradox by embracing murderous insanity, I would say 'like a lover', but it meant more to her than that.

Twenty minutes later, the feeding frenzy of the alpha rats gave way to the scrap-hunting of the pack. The spell of slaughter broken, Mother looked up and fixed me with her viper stare. If I was lucky, the bigger critters would be sated after eating their way through a mountain of Grundvelt bred prime beef, and I'd be able to make good my escape through the tunnels. Ready for the drop,

I waited for her to give Lediss the order to let go of the rope.

"In half an hour your fucking hero will be nothing more than a pile of rat shit," she said to me. Her voice was husky, thick with the iron blood scent that perfumed the room. "There's a lesson for you in that. Fail me again, and you'll learn it the hard way."

The echo of her words died away until the only noises were squeals and the sharp crack of bones being splintered. She turned her algid gaze on the Blades who were all trying to look less worthy of note than the next cove along. Satisfied they were all suitably cowed, Mother spat into the pit and then vanished. I spun round to see her sitting on her throne like she'd never moved. You had to respect skill like that. Only a master of her art could apport with such precision. It was why she was still queen of the Midnight Court after eighteen years, probably why she and Ludo held to their little arrangement. The Dumbrovski twins cracked matching, toothy grins, vicariously smug and no doubt relieved that someone they'd seen as a rival was now passing through the digestive tracts of fifty or so dog rats.

Melp flip-flapped from behind the throne again. His tongue flicked out and snared the dropped goblet which he duly filled and handed back to Mother. She drained it in one. Suffused with the heady mix of wine and murder her cheeks flushed. Nobody said a word. The silence dragged on. Below me, I heard metal scraping against stone. I looked down to see a pair of smaller rats had the leather wrist strap of the ax clamped in their teeth and were dragging the weapon across the blood-soaked clinker towards the tunnel.

Other than a few wisps of sun-bright hair and scraps of leather harness, there was nothing left. Wulf the leader, the hero, was gone. It wasn't supposed to be like this. My would-be savior was rat food and here I was, still alive, dangling arse over head, surrounded by leering Blades. Still, I'd had worse days.

"Let the lackwit down," said Mother.

Dutifully, Lediss let go of the rope. I rolled when I hit the blood-soaked ground. Bright green eyes glowed in the shadows of the tunnel.

"Not like that, you fucking moron!" Mother bellowed at Lediss.

I was about to slash the rope when it was pulled taut and I was yanked off my feet and hauled from the pit before the sluggish rats could reach me.

* * *

The audience chamber was cleared of everyone except the Dumbrovskis, Melp, Mother, and me. The grille over the pit was replaced and covered with an orange and purple floral carpet.

"I suppose you think you're off the hook now?" Mother held out her goblet for another refill.

"Er, yes. I rather thought I was." I tried to sound contrite even though I was anything but. She smelled of wine, raw meat, expensive perfume, and the tiniest hint of sweat, just a grade sharper than mere heat perspiration. It couldn't be fear because nothing scared her but there was a subtle hint of apprehension. If I didn't know better I'd have said she was wary of me, which was worrying as she'd been wary of Wulf. I suppose it could have been worse, she might have liked me.

"Well, you're not, and you stink. Why were you late? Never mind," she spoke too quickly for me to do anything except open and close my mouth a few times which was all the response she required.

"I need you to kill that louse farmer, Pork Chop. Don't bother trying to work out why, just get your arse over there and do it. I don't care how, just do it tonight, now. I was going to send Sketh, but the vapid little turd-sack has vanished."

"It wasn't me," I blurted too quickly.

"What wasn't you?"

"Nothing."

* * *

I was in desperate need of a wash but I daren't risk visiting a bathhouse. Even one that catered to warspawn would probably balk at letting me in like this. Not to mention, if Mother found out that I'd stopped off for a scrub, she'd have fed me to the dog rats, again. 'Misunderstanding', my arse. That cock-stain Lediss was going to pay for dropping me.

I did stop off at the room I rented in the Nest to pick up my bow. Not even Mother would object to me arming myself for a job that I had no idea how I was going to accomplish. I knew it was the Paradox that kept her dancing on the edge of madness. She threw a lot of power around and there was a price to be paid for that. The trouble was, I seemed to be the one paying it.

Now that I had a moment to breathe, I saw that my faithful jerkin, my only jerkin, was beyond repair this time. The back had been ice-burned by the dragon and it had half a dozen ragged tears from when I'd fought the restless dead in Shallunsard's Keep. That it had soaked up a goodly amount of *liquor* from the gong pot was the final nail in its sartorial coffin. I'd never be able to sneak up on anything smelling like a rancid shit pot, not even in Appleton. I tossed it in the corner, regretting that I'd never thought to keep a spare.

Other than the mattress, the only piece of furniture in the room was an iron-bound chest and only then because it was bolted down. Despite what they say, there really isn't any honor among thieves. After disarming the needle trap I'd rigged on the lock, I dug out a spare shirt. Unlike the jerkin, it offered no protection but the mud-brown homespun would at least hide my stripes and paler human skin. I also found a pair of fingerless gloves. They were old and speckled with mold, but they'd do a better job of hiding the mark in my palm than the strip of cloth.

My heart did a drunken waltz that might have been akin to human dread when I thought about what Mother would do if she found out about the deal I'd made with the demon. I told her that I'd been late back because I'd run into a gang of ogren after escaping the dragon. It wasn't the most convincing story but as I was dangling from a rope at the time of telling, I forgave myself for the lack of bardic flair. She was so drunk and angry that she barely heard a word I said anyway. I'd decide what to do about the deal I'd made with him later. Right now, I had to kill a gang boss for her. Dragons, demons, Ludo, and Mother. "There are just too many monsters in my life."

I wrapped my bow and quiver in an oilskin and took a last look around my little corner of heaven. It was strewn with month-old rushes and was as damp as a drowned rat. I wasn't sure, as I knew no different, but I had a nagging suspicion that there must be more to life than this.

Chapter Five

The Silverlight River crawled through Appleton and separated Old Town on the east bank from New Town on the west. Two gangs controlled the midnight economy that kept both halves of the city moving. Mother's Guild, the headquarters of which were under Old Town, and Pork Chop Jing's outfit, the Pearl. Jing and his crew fancied themselves as more upmarket thugs and had their den just west of the river, on the Street of a Thousand Lanterns. It was what you might call the entertainment district if your idea of entertainment was being robbed blind and catching the pox.

The street was named for the lanterns carried by the whores of every stripe who worked the long meander. They lured customers with bright paper lanterns that dangled enticingly on the end of gilded fishing poles. Poorer culls, miners and calth smelters and their ilk, would head for the river end of the street to squander their meager wages. The more fastidious amongst them might even visit a bathhouse before picking up a whore or falling into an inn that best suited their purse.

The more affluent denizens of Appleton, those out for a good time would visit the theaters and expensive brothels furthest from the stink of the Silverlight. Young rakehells would dare the bawdier backstreet establishments, hunting for cheap thrills and pel. The whole, wild jig was a lucrative business, ably orchestrated by Pork Chop Jing and the Pearl.

To avoid Jing's lookouts on the bridge I swam the Silverlight. I climbed out downriver of the main street, near an inn called the Grinning Dolly. It was a ramshackle flop-house which was slowly falling into the Silverlight. Canted towards the river at a jaunty angle, the Dolly catered to those hard-up culls whose next stop would be a dip in the drink with their pockets full of stones. After my swim, I emerged much cleaner than when I dived in, which goes to show how filthy I'd been because there are days when the Silverlight is so stiff with garbage you can walk across it.

Jing's compound was at the midpoint of the street. Impossible to miss, the brazen scarlet and gold pagoda stood three storeys higher than any of its neighbors. Cleaned daily by nimble amphibane servants it was a spike of brightness in an otherwise drab and dreary city.

Unlike Mother, Pork Chop wasn't a sorcerer. He was warspawn and therefore lacked the ability to use magic.

It didn't stop him hiring sellspells when he needed a few fireworks, but he tended to rely on a sizeable retinue of well-armed guards to enforce his will. Being as I was half human, Mother had managed to beat a couple of simple spells into me. Unfortunately, apporting wasn't one of them.

I strung my bow before threading my way through the maze of back streets, dodging pel-smoking sentries and bored city guards, until I reached the high walls of Jing's compound. The mournful peal of distant temple bells rang out the tenth hour. The suns had long since surrendered Appleton to night's charitable embrace. Unfortunately for me, Jing's pagoda was lit up like a bonfire.

Climbing the wall of the compound wouldn't be difficult. Not being seen while doing it just about impossible. A burst of laughter rippled on the breeze as though mocking my predicament. It was followed by the opening strains of a dolorous tune. The smell of succulent roast brachuri and the sickly-sweet aroma of grilled pigroach wafted towards me and made my stomach growl. I sniffed, caught the undercurrent of tea, beer, and Grundvelt Blast Whiskey. Curious as to the reason for the celebration, I made my way to the back gate of the compound.

Unlike the front entrance, which was richly decorated with giant insects and gilded arrachid warriors, the rear gate was unadorned, iron bound and to my delight and surprise, wide open. 'Now, tonight' hadn't just been

Mother raving. She must have known that Jing was holding a banquet. Security would be tight, it always was, people like Jing and Mother only survived by maintaining a ridiculously high level of paranoia, but guards would be less focused on the dark and silent places, whether they chose to or not, their eyes and ears would be drawn to light and movement. The influx of guests, the loud music, and abundance of pel and drink would wear down the senses of even the keenest sentry. Born for dark work, I would slip into the shadowed corners like a hand into a glove.

Feeling a little more enthusiastic about the job than I had been before I set off, I jogged down the street behind Jing's place. Just before the corner of the block, I squeezed behind a stack of broken barrels from where I could watch the road unseen.

Like my old friend the ambusher, I cast a spell from a bloodclay tablet to deepen the shadows around me and then settled down to wait, snug in the magical fold of darkness. A fistful of minutes later a pair of amphibane link boys hopped into view ahead of a couple of wheezing humans carrying a sedan chair. They staggered towards Jing's, followed closely by a nice big coach which was what I'd been waiting for. Although the rattler was unliveried, it must have belonged to a wealthy cove because it was being drawn by no less than four horses. Only one of the valuable beasts acknowledged my presence. The grey mare bestowed upon me an imperious snort as it high-hoofed past my hiding place. Despite their pampered existence city horses were as inured to the stink of Appleton and its inhabitants as any plodding urux.

The driver pulled on the reins and applied the brake as the coach wheeled round the corner. When it was three-quarters through the turn, I sprinted from my hiding place to the rear of the carriage, dragging shreds of shadow with me. Holding my bow tight against my chest with one hand, I gripped the rear axle with the other and slid under the vehicle. Supporting my weight on one arm, I wrapped my legs around the brake beam and gripped the leather through-bracing with my feet. It wasn't the most comfortable way to travel, but it was unquestionably better than riding in a gong pot.

When I'd scouted the gate earlier I'd taken note of the two, beady-eyed ogren guards. All I could see of them now were their big, hairy feet and the butts of the firelances they both wielded. Substantially bigger than handcannons, the firelances worked on the same principle. Calthracite powder and lead shot were loaded into the barrel, and a zanthe crystal was locked into the firing claw beside a pan filled with more calth powder. Firelances not only made really big holes in whatever was in front of them but as their name implied, they often set fire to it. The bloody things were as dangerous as a drunken sorcerer but thankfully still uncommon due to the cost of zanthe crystals and calthracite powder. The situation was changing. The Empirifex had a taste for conquest and had recently decreed that more mines should be found. There was still work for handy coves like me, but I sensed that the days of the blade were numbered.

The horses' hooves clattered against smooth stone as the carriage entered the compound and pulled up outside the pagoda. I clung on, hardly daring to breathe. On one side, I could see a neatly trimmed hedge in front of several long low buildings. On the other, the footplate dropped. A pair of silk hakama approached the step. A moment later, a dainty, slippered foot descended before being engulfed in layers of brocade-edged satin. Whoever they were, they smelled of emerald water and tincture of pomegranate. The carriage rocked and a pair of long, brachuri hide boots followed the gown. Why some of Jing's guests chose the rear entrance perked my professional interest, but I pushed the thought aside in favor of concentrating on the task ahead, which was to slot the host.

A door opened, and light spilled across the courtyard. I tried to think small and inconspicuous thoughts whilst being very conscious of the spatter of gold that clipped the frame of the carriage and fell across my back and hip. All it would take was for someone to look and connect the abstract shape with that of a living being and then, just for a change, I'd be in a right pot of arsepickle.

I pressed myself as close to the underside of the carriage as I could and willed the driver to move off. A long minute passed before the reins snapped and the horses pranced away, drawing murmurs of delight and admiration from those present. The haughty beasts were unimpressed and shat a trail of steaming, partially digested grass across the impeccably clean courtyard.

What little I knew about the layout of the compound told me there wasn't enough room for all the carriages to wait inside, this one in particular as horses and urux do not enjoy each other's company. When we were about fifty paces from the pagoda I dared a quick look round. This end of the compound was framed by a collection of single-storey buildings that crouched against the outer wall. The driver turned the rattler to face the gate, which I took to be the best time to alight. When the rear axle was facing into the darkest corner of the compound, I dropped, flipped, and scrambled from under the swaying belly of the carriage. Supporting myself on my claws, I scuttled over the hedge and wedged myself in the shadow-clad corner of the buildings like a six-foot-long cockroach. I lay still and held my breath and waited for sounds of alarm. None came.

My bow was made for thoasa and was long and flexible, which allowed me to bend it beyond the tolerance of lesser weapons. The quiver of arrows wasn't as forgiving, and I'd heard a couple of loud cracks as I crawled from under the carriage, luckily nobody else did. I felt inside the quiver. Two shafts had snapped leaving me twelve, which was plenty. Given the task, I'd be lucky if I had the time and opportunity to use one.

The music drifting from the first floor of the pagoda changed tempo. The reedy agony of an arrachid ballad scratched the skin off the air like the dying cries of a cat being slowly eviscerated. Jing would be in that room as the gang boss fancied himself a cultured cove when he wasn't extorting coin, selling drugs, and peddling flesh. He'd be sitting there, smoking pel and enjoying the scathing vibrations of the arrachid 'music' the very same as was making my ears bleed.

The windows on that level were set high on the wall and partially overhung by the flaring skirt of the roof above. I quickly and quietly crossed the compound, climbed the wall, and vaulted over the balcony of the first floor of the pagoda seconds after two of the four sentries disappeared around the left-hand corner. Without waiting, I reached up, grabbed the lip of the sweeping roof, and swung myself up and under the eaves. I was safely tucked upside down in the darkness before the next pair of guards rounded the right-hand corner.

Gripping the cedar lintel above the window with my feet, I braced my back against the underside of the roof. Wedged as I was in the angle of the roof, I could see into the room and remain hidden in the shadows of the eaves. If the guards patrolling the balcony looked up they'd see me, but why would they do that? There were far more interesting things happening in the hall, the courtyard, and the street beyond the compound.

Even so, I was momentarily tempted to enhance the darkness with a spell, but I changed my mind, just in case the rumors were true and the place was warded against magic. I carefully drew an arrow. The last thing I wanted, other than to miss was to spill the contents of the quiver all over the balcony. I licked the flight smooth and threaded the shaft between the string and stave before searching for Jing among the gentry gathered within.

There's something deeply unpleasant about the smell of arrachids. It's like old shoes that have been left to marinate in lemon juice and earthworms. It's not a strong smell, nothing that a human would notice, but I did. Not all the jasmine-scented fountain water and eaglewood incense in the world could mask the stink of a nest of them. As well as being the national dress of their adopted culture, the Shen silk kimonos that Jing and his offspring favored also concealed their six, double-jointed legs, which apparently made some humans feel uncomfortable. I watched Pork Chop's dutiful sons and daughters as they mingled with their father's guests, making polite conversation, and laughing at unamusing jokes.

Old Pork Chop was content to rest his bloated abdomen on a pile of plump silk cushions and smoke his double bowled pel pipe surrounded by his favorite concubines. The gang lord's long black hair hung to his waist and his violet silk haori perfectly matched the color of his two pairs of eyes. It was said that the best arrachid silk was produced by virgins. If that were true, the amount of the good stuff floating around in this room would have made a brothel keeper weep. Jing nodded politely at his guests as they passed before him and paid their respects. He favored some lucky few with a word or two, but for the most part, he sat and watched, as impassive as an arrachid gang boss in the heart of his web.

I didn't go straight for the kill. I first made a note of the security that would blaze into action the moment I vented Jing. The ogren standing guard by the sliding doors was of interest, partly because she must have been seven feet tall, but mainly because she was carrying a very large, bronze handcannon, the barrel of which was cast in the form of a roaring dragon. Although the imagery was laboring the point, the beast slumbering in the ogren's arms was due serious respect. Like the creature it represented, the weapon breathed ruin. I counted another four sentries positioned around the room, but as they were only armed with halberds and spears, they were not as much of a concern as the ogren with the cannon.

The main door to the banqueting hall was directly opposite me, but Jing's dais was against the wall on my right, so I had to lean left to get a better angle on the King of the Midnight Court. I re-nocked the shaft and drew the bow until the stave was tight against the window frame and my elbow was touching the rafters. I could have got a few more fingers' width of draw, but this would be enough to put a shaft through Jing. I took a deep, slow breath and was about to loose when, for some reason, someone else in the room snared my attention. Irritated, I relaxed the draw and took a proper shufty at them.

I couldn't smell much above the blooming reek of arrachid, pel, and incense so I had to rely on my eyes but there was no mistaking the grizzle-chinned, pig-nosed, tiny-eyed lackwit strutting into the room, arm-in-arm with one of the Pearl. It was Sketh. The miserable little snot-gobbet had turned traitor. That it was probably my fault was not the point. The little toad-gobbler looked right at home and was grinning wide as a cheese rind. They'd even dressed him in a fancy pair of hakama and coiffed his greasy hair into a top knot. The tomb-toothed puke must have spilled his guts to the roots to earn such pampering. No wonder Jing looked happy. My aim tracked from Jing to Sketh.

As much as I wanted to vent the traitor, I knew I shouldn't. I had my orders. Mother really would kill me if I messed up this time. I re-aimed at Jing. Sketh snagged a drink from a passing servant. He was laughing at something his new best friend had said. I drew the string to my lobeless ear. Jing. *The target is Jing.*

I've often found that it's one thing knowing what you should do, but quite another doing it.

The arrow entered Sketh between the pectoralis major, or at least between where chest muscles would have been if the little turd-biscuit had any. A rose of deepest red stamped my fatal brand on his nice new haori. I knew Mother was not going to be happy but, by all the gods, it was a good shot.

It takes a lot to really rile me, but Sketh had succeeded where a demon, a dragon, and Mother had failed. It wasn't just that he'd tried to ambush me, or that he'd come close to putting a bolt through my head, that was just embarrassing. It was the gong pot. When I should have been strutting along Main Road, I'd had to hide in a shit wagon to avoid my greedy comrades and that was why Sketh was dying on his feet.

The ex-Blade, ex-Pearl member stared at the ever-widening scarlet bloom, confusion written across his rabbity features. The game was only truly up when his companion tugged the yard shaft out of the tatami behind him. She frowned at first and looked questioningly at Sketh, who answered by slowly pitching forward and crumpling into the folds of his silks.

"Guards!" she yelled.

One shot. That's what I'd promised myself, even if I'd missed Jing. So by the time the ogren had blasted the window frame and a fair chunk of wall and roof into flaming matchwood, I was already halfway to the ground. Almost on the beat of my feet touching the cobbles, a gong hammered alarm into the languid night. You can always trust some bastard to ruin a party and tonight that bastard was me.

I sprinted across the open ground and leaped up to the roof of the single storey building before anyone outside the pagoda knew what was happening. Given that they were in the same business they caught on quickly and by the time I'd dashed across the roof and had my foot on the compound wall, I heard the heavy *thwunks* of crossbows being discharged in my direction. A velvety ripple of air preceded a searing whip of fire that lashed my left bicep. It was nothing, a sting that served to spur me on to greater effort when I leaped.

Darkness flowed beneath me as I launched myself over the gilt-edged void. Landing softly, I wound the energy from the drop into a roll that spun me across the slates, thrust me up, and set me off running. I knew that if I could reach the river I'd get away. A jarring impact on the roof behind me underscored the *if.*

The sagging joists creaked and groaned. I didn't slow or turn around, I didn't need to. The smell of old shoes soaked in lemon juice and earthworms rushed at me on a following wind hot, hard, and angry. Arrachids didn't swim well but they were experts at tearing people into tiny pieces. With that in mind, I summoned an extra measure of speed and ran for my life.

I don't like to brag, but I've outrun dragons, which was a good thing to bear in mind with one of Pork Chop's broodlings inches from taking a chunk out of my scaly arse. Their species of arrachid had a pair of vicious sword-like foreclaws, tucked just below the abdomen. I know it might not sound like it but being chased by this kind was preferable to being pursued by those that spat gobs of sticky, poisonous web-snot from their nethers.

Of course, given a choice, I'd rather not be chased by any kind of arrachid.

Ahead of me, the river gleamed invitingly like a shining rod of rippled obsidian, framed by crooked chimneys. I vaulted the pots. My many-legged pursuer smashed straight through them. Who would have guessed that Sketh was so well loved? Thus encouraged to greater effort, I surged forward and was just starting to pull away from my ardent pursuer when the roof collapsed beneath us.

When you're falling, you reach out for anything; it's an instinct common to every creature that has limbs. I watched, quite detached from the act, as my hands and feet groped at timbers and slates until they eventually found something substantial and grabbed hold of it. Alas, the 'it' turned out to be the arrachid. She'd had a similar idea and so, like boon companions, we fell together, briefly visiting a grimy, rat-infested loft before crashing through to the next floor, and the next.

By now I wasn't sure which were my limbs, and which were hers. There was a mass of flame-red hair in my face and her arms were locked around my waist, but as luck would have it I was sitting on her pincers, so she was unable to fulfill her screamed threat and stab me to death and beyond. In truth, we both did a fair bit of screaming and cursing as old plaster, dead pigeons, and roof rained down around us. Finally, we hit a floor that didn't break.

I landed on top of the arrachid, the air *whoomphed* from her bellows, leaving her gasping. Two pairs of angry, green eyes shone from amid the mass of hair, giving me a general target to aim for when I headbutted her in the face. She groaned, her grip on my waist loosened. I disentangled myself and sprinted for the nearest exit. Floral wallpaper, paintings, and bemused faces peering from doorways flashed past. The sound of three pairs of feet charging after me drove me on. I hurtled along the corridor and through the door at the end without stopping to open it, which quite surprised the occupants.

A red-robed human male with a black beard glared at me. He had another human pinned by the throat against the wall opposite the door. In his other hand, Blackbeard held a slender bladed knife. The other human was wearing rough brown robes and was struggling ineffectually against the bigger man. I leaped at the bearded cull and knocked his head against the wall. While he decided to have a little sit-down, I relieved him of his pig-sticker and threw it at the arrachid, just before throwing myself through the window, again without bothering to open it. The blade found its target, the arrachid yelled and crashed to the floor in a tangle of hairy limbs.

I was prepared for a hard landing and so was surprised when my fall was broken by a group of late night revelers who just happened to be passing. With nary a scratch, I untangled myself from the skirts of a pleasantly doughy cull and was about to leg it when one of her foppish friends had the suicidal urge to draw a blade on me. I say blade, it was more a hairpin with a hilt.

"How dare you. You, what the devil are you?" The fop stared down the barrel of his bony nose and quirked one of his plucked eyebrows. "You should have stayed under your rock, lizard,"

A rouged, 'punch me' smile gashed his powder-pale face in response to the laughter of his friends. Playing to the crowd, he whiff-waffed the hairpin and took some kind of stance that I assumed a dancing master must have taught him.

I'd never had the patience to bandy words with halfwits, so I snapped the blade and slapped him across the chops for fear that a punch might kill him. He sprawled. Alas, the distraction was enough to give the wounded arrachid time to join us and for a sizeable crowd to gather. I don't like crowds, especially when I'm the subject of their attention, and I certainly didn't like the arrachid who was aiming a murderous glare in my direction.

I drew my blades. She advanced, kicking a couple of the fop's friends out of the way with casual disdain. She'd come off worse in our little roof dive and her arm was bleeding where I'd caught her with Blackbeard's dagger.

"What the hell?" exclaimed another of the youths. "Is it raining demonspawn?" He and his companions drew an assortment of glorified toothpicks.

"Who are you calling demonspawn, you little shitstain?" the arrachid snarled, pincers twitching.

Emboldened by his friends, the aforesaid shitstain puffed out his fashionably thin chest. "You, you four-eyed grotesque."

The arrachid reared up on her hindmost pair of legs. I'm not sure exactly what happened next as something akin to an anvil hit me on the back of the head. I saw white light and dropped to my knees, stunned but only distantly alarmed as pretty purple flowers burst into bloom before my eyes. My blades slipped from nerveless fingers, I fell. The last thing I saw before the press of fighting bodies closed around me was the brown-robed human. He was leaning out of the ragged hole I'd put in the wall of the inn, the one which the arrachid had enlarged. He was staring at me, his brow knotted in concentration.

What happened next is hazy, but I got the impression that the entire Street of a Thousand Lanterns decided that right then was the perfect time to have a riotous brawl. The night erupted in shouts and screams, accompanied by the sound of breaking glass and splintering wood.

Chapter Six

I woke up, face down on a hard floor. Pockmarked flagstones burnished by constant abuse swam into focus. There was something vaguely familiar about them and the wet metal stink of the place. Before I had a chance to ponder my location further, I was grabbed under the arms and hauled to my shackled feet. Now I knew where I was. I tested the manacles around my wrists and got a slap across the head for my troubles.

"Stop that," said the greenshanks. Coves like me called the local, Imperial Guard 'greenshanks' on account of their green uniform breeches. This one was short and had beady eyes set deep in a flat, expressionless face. She had the heavy build of a mountain goblin but must have been human because warspawn weren't allowed in the Imperial Guard.

I'd lodged in the cells under the law courts once or twice when I was a kinchin cove, but this was my first stay since I'd become a fully-fledged Blade. Other than the inmates, nothing much had changed since my earlier visits. The rows of cells looked and smelled the same. The cells on the right were for humans and were warded against sorcery. Those on the left were more heavily reinforced for warspawn but bore no sigils. Warspawn, true warspawn, not half-breeds like me, couldn't use magic.

"What are ya?" the greenshanks demanded. Her breath smelled sickly sweet like something was rotting inside her. She coughed. If she didn't already know she was sick, she soon would. "Well, what is it? Thoasa? Do you understand?"

Before I had the chance to earn another slap by telling her that I didn't speak dolt, the door behind me opened and another guard came in. He looked tired and was sporting a week's growth of facial hair. I don't know how humans can stand all those bristles. They must itch something terrible, and then there's the lice. An old scar running across his cheek and nose spoke of past battles. Like a lot of the greenshanks in Appleton, he'd probably served on the front, fighting to gain the Empirifex another acre of nothing much at all.

He gave me a cursory once-over. "S'just another breed, Tori. Put it in four."

Tori grunted and prodded me towards cell number four on the warspawn side. Such a pity that the most dangerous spell I knew was how to boil water. Mother had taught me the cantrip when she was going through a phase of drinking hot chai. There was a chalkboard nailed to the outside of the door. The guard looked at me expectantly.

"What? You're not going to give me a test, are you?" I asked.

Neither smile nor smirk marred the unleavened perfection of her pasty face. She took up the stylus that was chained to the board. "Name?"

"Breed," I said straight-faced. If she got the joke she didn't let on. She invited me to enter the cell with a toss of her head and patted the butt of a cudgel that was hanging from her belt, implying punishment would follow should I refuse to comply. If there hadn't been an entire garrison of greenshanks hanging around, I'd have taken the tickle-tail off her and shoved it where the suns don't shine. As it was, I acceded to her invitation without argument. In truth, I wasn't in any particular hurry to get back to the Nest. I needed some time to come up with a plausible lie to tell Mother as to why I'd killed Sketh instead of Jing. 'Because I was annoyed' would lead straight back to the dog rats, if I was lucky.

The cell smelled no worse than anywhere consistently used as a toilet. I slumped against the door, grateful for a chance to sit down. Now that the excitement had passed, I was starting to feel the various cuts and bruises I'd earned during my recent adventures. The cells sounded busy, which told me it was still night. They'd empty in the morning when all the scallywags were sent before the beaks. While I sat in the shadows, listening to rats crunching through cockroaches, I briefly regretted killing Sketh instead of Jing. But then I remembered sitting in the gong pot and the feeling went away. One thing I could be sure of was that nobody would finger me for killing the little bunghole. The Guild and the Pearl had few agreements, but it would be a dull day in hell when either went to the authorities seeking what passed for justice in Appleton. I closed my eyes, tried to get a little sleep for the first time since I'd got back to town.

I shouldn't have been surprised that the sleep I snatched was far from restful. The thunder of a dragon chasing me down a mountainside accompanied by the laughter of a demon resolved into the sound of someone banging on the door and shouting at me to get up. It didn't feel like more than a few minutes had passed since I closed my eyes, but it had been long enough for the guard to change. A skinny cull with a cauliflower nose and weeping acne unlocked the door.

He squinted at the slate and snorted. "Right, Breed. It's your turn in front of the magistrates. C'mon, look lively, they're in a hanging mood this mornin'." He laughed, no doubt like he did every time he made the joke, which was probably every time he unlocked a cell.

I was stiff and thirsty and in no mood for light-hearted banter and I didn't have any coin to pay a fine, but that was the least of my concerns. By now Mother would know where I was. I'd delivered enough bribes for her to know how the wheels of justice were greased and just how much sway she had with the official government in town. Whichever of the magistrates she owned would pocket a nice sum of gold, set a low fine, and make sure that I was sent off with a stern warning not to transgress again. I didn't for one moment consider that Mother might leave me to rot. Even if she was angry, she'd pay to get me out so that she could kill me herself.

Me and a dozen other coves were chained together and taken up through the barracks to the City Hall, where the official if only slightly less nefarious business of running the city was conducted. Burghers and merchants, sycophants and toadies congregated in the lobby to exchange bribes, gossip, and backhanders. As our not-so-jolly band of resigned ruffians, penitent drunks, and tired whores shuffled past, the honest gentry squinted at us through spectacles, monocles, and lorgnettes in order to properly turn up their noses.

We were shoved into the holding pens outside the courtroom just off the main lobby. I claimed my place in the cramped cage and watched the great and the good of Appleton go about their very important business. Ugly little pet dogs, smaller than your average sewer rat, pissed on the grubby marble floor and barked incessantly at everything. Bedraggled jadewings squawked mournfully from tenuous perches on the limp wrists and sloping shoulders of the more fashionable pillocks of society. The birds were the current 'must have' amongst what passed for the social elite of Appleton. Mother preferred to deal in pel, murder, and larceny rather than smuggling exotic pets. She didn't have the patience to peddle anything that needed gentle handling. She had tried it once, but when twenty birds suffocated, she gave up and spit roast the rest of the consignment.

"Oi, Breed. You're up," The greenshanks crossed my name off the slate. I eyed the handcannon in the crook of her arm and obediently shuffled out.

The court's sickly yellow walls were bare save for the Empirifex's gaudy crest painted above the magistrates' bench. The leaded windows looked out onto Four Gallows Square where the five city gallows were situated, indicating to all and sundry how brisk business was in Appleton. It was a point of pride for the good citizens of the town, not so much for me and my fellow rogues.

Three periwigged magistrates sat on the bench above the court, shuffling papers, taking snuff, and muttering amongst themselves about proceedings and other tiresome preoccupations of their day-to-day existence. A bored-looking scribe sat beneath the bench idly sharpening his quills. My palm itched. An image of the demon Shallunsard sprang unbidden into my mind. I thrust it aside. I had to try to think innocent thoughts and see if I could push them through the naturally sardonic set of my face bones.

I was shoved into the dock and the cage door was locked. A sorcerer's sigil etched on the heavy bolt ensured no magic could be cast from inside. A couple of guards stood either side of the door, fingers resting on the triggers of well-used handcannons. It did my professional pride no harm to know that they weren't giving me the benefit of the doubt.

Unusually for morning court, there was quite a crowd in the public gallery. Several of them had cuts and bruises some also had torn and blood-speckled clothing. Almost all were staring daggers at me. I guessed that they must have been the rakes that I'd landed on the night before. What with deals with demons and inadvertent assassinations I'd hardly given this crew a second thought. For their part, they seemed delighted to see me, in an angry mob sort of way. Sitting behind them, knitting furiously was an old human I knew well. Martha Ferney, or Mattie the Drop as she was known in the Guild, looked like your average grandmother, but you turned your back on her at your peril. She didn't so much as glance when I came in, but I knew she'd clocked me.

Her presence was reassuring. Despite Mother's constant admonishment never to hope, seeing Mattie meant that Mother probably wasn't too angry and that she'd sent the old mort with a bribe for the judge. I relaxed but tried to look contrite, which isn't easy with a face like mine.

The Chief Magistrate cleared her throat and cast a bulge-eyed glance in my direction. “Case the fifth on this the 10th day of Messidor, Year of the Pantheon, 766. By Empirifex, Dunstan the Seventh’s grace, the court will rise.”

The court obeyed. A lawyer in a black gown swept in and bowed before the bench. I was touched, I didn’t think Mother would go to the trouble of hiring an attorney.

As it turned out, I was correct.

“Council for the Prosecution begs leave to proceed, Magistrate Ornlably,” quoth the daughter of prattlement I had briefly mistaken for my defender.

“Yes, yes, go on.” The magistrate waved impatiently.

I very much wanted to object, struck as I was that I might be getting stitched for killing Sketh after all. My mind raced. Had Jing turned barley? Had he ripened into a yellow-backed coward, broken all the laws of hell, and gone to the authorities? Such a thing wasn’t entirely unheard of, lesser members of the Midnight Court had committed slow suicide by going to the catch-poles, but no one of Jing’s stature had ever stooped so low as to get the lurchers involved. It was downright dishonorable. I was shocked.

“Thank you, Magistrate. I’ll hurry to the quick, as the Court’s time should not be spent lingering over such overt miscreancy. I would be so bold as to say this is—”

"Just get on with it, Counselor Cheams," said the magistrate. As I was keen to know what I was being charged with I was inclined to agree.

"My client, Sir Mathorius Walmisus." The lawyer indicated a skinny cull in the public gallery with a black eye and swollen lip. "Was the victim of a vicious assault, and I, therefore, ask that the savage responsible." Cheams pointed at me. "Feel the full force of the law. Death... is too good. This gutter scum should serve the Empirifex in the calthracite mines for no less than twenty years," Cheams declared, shaking with bought and paid for indignation.

The magistrates exchanged weary glances. "How very thoughtful of you, Cheams," said the chief magistrate. "But we're more than capable of coming up with a sentence. All we ask is that you present the evidence."

"As you wish, Magistrate." The prosecutor straightened her wig. "Would the first witness, Sir Mathorius Walmisus, please take the stand."

It turned out that Mathorius Walmisus was the razor-nosed fop who'd pulled a blade on me.

He swaggered over to the witness stand and gave a curt bow to the magistrates. "Lord Harrin, Lord Reevis, Aunt Gwendolyn."

My heart didn't so much sink as dive majestically into the pit of my stomach, dragging my hopes down with it.

The chief magistrate, *Aunt Gwendolyn*, whiffled through a sheaf of papers and waved him to silence. "Yes, all right. Go on, Counselor."

Cheams strutted before the witness, hands clasped behind her back, no doubt contemplating the easiest conviction she'd ever won. "In your own words, Sir Mathorius, before the seal of the Empirifex, his duly appointed magistrates, and this court," she intoned. "Pray tell, what befell you and your companions last night on the Street of a Thousand Lanterns?"

"Thank you, Counselor." He inclined his head at her and cleared his throat. I rested my elbow on the bars, keen to hear what fantasy the simpering pisspeddler was about to spew. "My friends and I had just enjoyed a tolerable supper at Fausto's on Garrote Street and were on our way to Tremlaynes theater to watch a production of the Death of the Red Witch when that *thing*," he glared at me. "Leaped upon my companions and attempted to accost Lady Juliet." He waved his handkerchief at the gallery, indicating a pinch-faced froe I wouldn't tup with borrowed nethers. She sniffled, the gallery made a unified rumble of displeasure and threw facefuls of disgust in my direction, although not one of them had the cods to look me in the eye. The fop continued. "As a gentleman, I stepped in to defend my friend from the amorous advances of that creature, who, with its vile accomplices, proceeded to attack my comrades and I. I'm happy to say, we were more than a match for this gutterscum and had gained the upper hand by the time the city guards arrived." He puffed out his chest. "And lucky for this creature that they arrived when they did."

I noticed that the greenshanks guarding the dock exchanged wry smiles at that. I was interested to know why the arrachid had been left out of the account, and indeed why the rank virago wasn't in the holding pens waiting her turn in the dock, and then it occurred to me that Jing might have outbid Mother in the bribery stakes.

For the next hour, a long procession of ill-used ladies and gentlemen limped from the public gallery and took their turn on the witness stand. I was accused of all manner of grievous crimes, from beating the fop and his crew to attempted murder. Had I been conscious I probably would have done what I'd been accused of, far worse in fact, leaving a damn sight fewer of them to point their waggers at me today. Throughout it all no mention was made of the arrachid, not once. It was as though she'd never been there. Eventually, the Chief Magistrate turned her attention to me.

"Do you have anyone to speak for you, any defense counsel?" she asked.

I shook my head.

"Do you have anything to say in your defense?"

"Yes, as a matter of fact, I do." A startled murmur ran through the gallery. The magistrate regarded me suspiciously. "This is a travesty!" I tried to mimic the haughty manners of Counselor Cheams. "I wasn't even conscious for most of the fight. I am the victim here, Your Honor."

I would have continued, but she banged her gavel. "All right, that's enough. The defendant's evidence has been noted by the Bench."

As unfair as it was, I knew better than to argue. You never beat the law, especially if you looked like me. Once the beaks had you fast, you weren't going to encourage them to go easy by haranguing them. It was better to submit and get it over with as quick and as painless as possible. I'd been done up tighter than a miser's coin purse and no mistake, but there was no point bleating, who'd listen? I looked over to Mattie. She made a shrug face and cast another stitch off the formless mess she was knitting.

After a whole two minutes of thoughtful deliberation, Aunt Gwendolyn stamped her authority on proceedings with a sharp staccato rap of her gavel. "The court will rise," she said through a half-stifled yawn. "The defendant is hereby sentenced to seven years' hard labor in the Empirifex's calthracite mines. Case closed. Send in number six."

The magistrate set her seal to some documents, and the court sat. I stood there a moment, trying to work out how the hell I'd got into this mess, how the hell I was going to get out of it, and what the hell was going to try to kill me next.

While I pondered these questions, my gaze wandered to the public gallery. It wasn't the smug, fundament jugglers busily congratulating each other who drew my attention; it was a turnip-pated patri-cove who I recognized as the very same whey-faced cull I'd seen in the inn. He shuffled awkwardly past the spindle-shanked gentry but didn't leave the courtroom as I'd expected. Instead, he made his way over to the bench and beckoned the chief magistrate down from her perch. Much to my surprise, Aunt Gwendolyn didn't have him thrown from the court for his presumption or order him sent to the mines for contempt of her high office, she complied. Smelling deeds afoot, the lawyer followed, ears straining to catch the gist of the confabulation between Wheyface and the beak.

In the gallery, Mattie packed away her knitting and gave me a look that told me I was on my own. Meanwhile, Wheyface was heads down with the magistrate, locked in a heated argument over I knew not what, save that there was a lot of gesticulating and headshaking by both parties. It was then I noticed that the brown-robed cull's left hand was missing, the wrist being tidily sheathed in a leather cup.

After a hiss-whisper exchange between the lawyer and Wheyface, the magistrate shooed them away and returned to the bench where she knotted heads with her colleagues. Eventually, after a short debate, Aunt Gwendolyn hammered on the table. “Order. The court will come to order, or I’ll throw the lot of you in the bloody mines.” The chatter died. She fixed her dead-eyed gaze on me. I offered what I thought was a warm smile which didn’t appear to go down well. “Due to, *Mitigating circumstances*.” She glanced at Wheyface. “The court has decided to show leniency in this case and commute the sentence to five years’ indentured servitude to Brother Tobias of the Sacred Order of Scienticians of Saint Bartholomew.” The priest bowed his head. The magistrate grunted, unimpressed. “Case closed.”

Chapter Seven

Somewhat begrumpled by this miserable turn of events, I cursed all the way out of the court, laying all manner of vile imprecations upon the heads of my accusers, the magistrates, and the greenshanks who dragged me back to the cells.

Being condemned to the mines was an excessive punishment for falling on a bunch of over-privileged popinjays, but I could've escaped from the mines. I could have extorted some coin, used it to bribe guards, and grease the right palms. I'd have been out within a month with no one the wiser. Judicial indentured servitude reinforced by a sorcerous geas was an altogether different proposition.

Despite knowing there was no point fighting the catch-poles when they have you, I often rebel against my own wise counsel. It's like a disease. Very kindly, the greenshanks tried to cure my affliction by administering a dose of steel-shod boots as soon as I was out of sight of the ruffs and ribbons.

I woke in a cell, manacled to a ring set in the floor. My nose was crusted with blood and my jaw ached like I'd repeatedly been kicked in the face which, I blearily recollected, I had. As I lay there, contemplating the righteous vengeance I was going to wreak on the bastards who'd put me here, the peephole in the door slid open. From my position on the floor, I could just make out a worry-pinched face peering in at me. I forgot about the manacles and lunged at the priest. He recoiled despite the three inches of steel door between us.

"I mean you no harm," he mumbled. "I just want to talk to you."

"Well, there you go, you've talked to me. Now fuck off." I was in no mood to chat with someone who'd had me condemned to magical slavery.

"I saved you from the mines," he countered as though he'd done me a favor.

"I could get— Never mind. Just leave me alone." I couldn't be bothered arguing with the one-handed lackwit. I had to focus on how I was going to get out of this. I'd given up on Mother if she was going to help she would have done it by now.

"It was all I could think of at the time. I used what influence I have. I'm sorry," he said.

"Why? Why the hell did you try to 'help' me? What's in it for you, priest?" I think he looked confused, but it was hard to tell. He had one of those soft, book-bathed faces, pale and smooth from lack of sunslight or kiss of the wind. It was the kind of face that begged to be repeatedly slapped.

"Because you saved me." He shivered. "What happened after you went through the window was an accident. I was trying to help, but I was disorientated, and the spell went awry. I honestly didn't mean to knock you out, but with hindsight, it's probably for the best that I did."

Again, I forgot the manacles and lunged at him. The chain snapped me back to the cold stone flags. The moon-faced bastard loitered a while, staring at me with a look of pity and guilt painted on his milky features. Upon receiving nothing in return save a dead-eyed stare, he slunk away, head down, and shoulders hunched to his ears.

It was night when they came for me. I hadn't slept. I'd lain in the darkness, listening to doors slam and inmates proclaim their innocence while cursing, or weeping, sometimes all three. I was trying to decide if I was going to make the guards do this the hard way or if I was just going to submit, like a lag of the highest mark. What was churning my vitals was not knowing if the geas of servitude would dominate my survival instincts, something I guessed would come in handy given the many apple carts I'd upset of late. I didn't know how much of my free will would be curtailed and that worried me. I can't say I was scared, Thoasa were bred to be fearless and although I was only half thoasa, I don't think I'd ever experienced fear as powerfully as humans seemed to.

What I did know was that I'd been given a sentence of five years but had less than one to find the Hammer of the North before my life and possibly my soul was forfeit to Shallunsard the demon. And then there was Jing. He would most likely send the Pearl after me for slotting Sketh at his party, and of course, I couldn't forget dear old Mother. She would undoubtedly want to know why I'd disobeyed her. As nice as it was to be wanted, I couldn't afford to be bound in servitude to the milksop priest. I needed to go to ground, preferably in another country, until everyone forgot all about me.

Before I could formulate a brilliant plan to escape, the door was thrown open and a lantern lit up the cell half blinding me as I'm sure was the intention. The barrels of a pair of handcannons were thrust into the circle of light.

"So you're a Guild Blade, eh? You don't look much from where I'm standing," one of the cannon-wielders said from the darkness.

"Spoken like a true hero, from the brave end of a barking iron. Come out from behind the brass and we'll go tap for tap, see how ye fair then, eh, greenshanks?" I grinned. My offer was declined with the stony silence.

One of the guards unchained me, and I was dragged from the cell. The two gunners stayed behind us as I was taken down to the lower of the lockup. I didn't know anyone who'd been down here. All I knew was that it was where confessions were extracted and indenturing by sorcery was carried out. Any cove down on their luck could sign up for regular indentured servitude and sell their labor in exchange for work and food. Punishment indenture was another fish altogether. I should have been honored. Not just any lag got indentured by sorcery. Only those for whom chains were not enough of an impediment to making mischief suffered this fate, and then only rarely. It was an expensive spell from what I'd heard. Soul-binding, indeed anything to do with dominating the will of a person, extracted a high price from the sorcerer, whereas a hempen necktie was a less expensive cure for a fractious nature.

My stomach rolled as I was marched to my fate. I'd been stabbed, shot at, lashed, even burned by dragon breath, but this was something more worrisome. Pain only hurts. Losing my free will filled me with a greasy feeling of dread.

At the end of a blood-splattered, flame-scorched corridor was an iron door unlike any I'd seen in the jail. It was inlaid with alloys of a dozen different metals that had been hammered into overlapping sigils. It hummed with magical energy and the air grew stiff with power the closer I got to it. I stopped a few paces away. One of the greenshanks behind me stumbled to a halt. If I spun around now, I could take his cannon and torch and have a quick dance in the dark with his gun-wielding companion. I might even get the better of them with surprise on my side, but the chances of fighting my way out of the barracks were slim even with a pair of irons to back me up. With this in mind, I allowed myself to be shoved forward, although my guts were writhing like a sack of snakes.

On the other side of the door, a passage split right and left. A strong smell of dried blood and death emanated from the right. I was taken to the left. At the end of the dimly lit corridor, I was thrust into a room that was little more than a rough-hewn cave. There were no other exits. A half dozen rancid, tallow candles spilled a dim light across the floor and wreathed the low roof in oily ribbons of smoke. Unlike the building above, which had been designed to emulate the architectural style prevalent in Valen, this place was ancient and reeked of old magic and primitive rites.

The floor was obsidian, variously inlaid with groups of concentric and overlapping rings of copper, bronze, steel, and iron. Each ring was scribed with arcane sigils. I was invited at gunpoint to stand in one of a pair of overlapping steel rings, where I was duly shackled. The smell of strong incense blinded me to everything save the overpowering scent of attar of roses, camphor, and the sour undertone of knotweed.

After a few minutes, the door opened and my savior shuffled in. The one-handed cull swallowed hard when he saw me. He was followed by the sellspell or as they preferred to be called, Court Appointed Sorcerer. She cast a sharp glance in my direction and frowned before instructing the priest to stand in the ring beside mine, luckily for him, beyond my reach.

“Sweet Saint Bart, what happened to you?” the priest asked me.

“Juris impudence,” I said. The greenshanks stationed by the door chuckled.

The sellspell shushed everyone. Stooped and grey, she looked well past her prime but must have been good at her job given the gold trim on her robe. She obviously dealt with her Paradox through pain, as every sagging wrinkle on her face was pierced. Lips, nose, eyebrows, cheeks. Every inch of pliant skin was either scarred from previous insertions or hung with tiny silver rings.

She made no announcement, nobody gave a speech or read out the sentence. The sorcerer merely lit a censer and began to pace the perimeter of the circles, muttering the incantation that would bind me to the whey-faced fuck-knuckle. In her other hand, she held a thick silver wristband inscribed with sigils. My palm itched to the point of burning.

“I’m really sorry about this” the priest muttered, his eyes imploring like those of a beaten puppy. “I honestly never intended to hurt you.”

I growled. “You better hope this works, priest, because if it doesn’t, I’m gonna skin your pasty hide and wear it while I ravage your grandsire’s worm-infested corpse.” It wasn’t the most imaginative curse, but I was starting to feel lightheaded. It had the desired effect though. The priest flinched as though I'd slapped him. For a second, it looked like he might grow some stones and give me some stick in return. Alas for him, the fire that had briefly kindled in his eyes died and he shrank back into his robe. I felt no satisfaction as the room had begun to spin, and I was struggling to stay on my feet. The sellspell's voice bored into my skull, made my bones ache. The room spun faster, the inscriptions in the floor began to glow, and the world blurred as the ground rushed up and kissed me into oblivion.

* * *

I woke in yet another strange place only this time I found myself lying on an unpleasantly yielding mattress, somewhere that didn't smell of piss or mildew. I forced my eyes open. Hard sunslight streamed through a pair of gauzy curtains. I raised my hand to blot out the painful brightness and saw a silver cuff fastened seamlessly around my left wrist. I sat up and promptly puked. After emptying my stomach of everything but the lining, I lay back on the bed and shivered despite the warmth of the day.

"It will pass," said a familiar voice. I raised my aching head. A few feet beyond the end of the bed, the priest was sitting at a book-buried desk. His hood was down, revealing closely cropped yellow fuzz, set above watery grey eyes and a soft chinned face that was ill-defined by age or character. "The sickness is due to the magic. I felt awful for a few hours after, but I think it's worse for…"

"The victim?" I offered. It came out less angrily than I'd intended.

"Would you have preferred seven years in the mines?"

I sat up, swung my legs off the bed. "Yes, as a matter of fact, I would. Hard labor is preferable to slavery." The sharp note of defiance in my voice reassured me that I hadn't been turned into an entirely spineless drudge. I looked at my hands and was relieved to see that I was still wearing my gloves. At least the demon mark hadn't been discovered.

"You wouldn't have lasted seven years, nobody does," he said.

I grinned at him. "You're right there, priest."

"Brother Tobias of the Sacred Order of Scienticians of Saint Bartholomew, actually. You may call me Brother Tobias, or Father."

I snorted. "My scaly arse. I've never called anyone father and I'm not going to start with someone like you, no offense." I stood up, lights danced before my eyes. I was pleased to see him shrink back in his seat. Pleased to taste a faint whiff of fear sweat above his watery musk.

"Then Brother Tobias will suffice, or sir. You are my servant, my property for the next five years. You might as well get used to it."

Like fuck. Pain bloomed in my skull like a flower made of broken glass. It suddenly felt like I'd drunk a pail of the cheapest, sot-brewed, back-alley rum and had then proceeded to headbutt rocks.

"Yes, sir." The pain lessened. "You dumb-armed muff-fumbler," I whispered. The pain spiked again, I stumbled.

The priest came to my aid, his face knotted with concern. "What did you say?" He looped his arm around my waist and eased me back onto the bed.

"Nothing of import," I said when the pain gave me leave to speak. It hurt like hell, but the ache helped me feel my way around the geas and begin to get the measure of my bonds. I'd sprung a fair few master-crafted locks in my illustrious career, I'd find a way to unlock these chains, magical or not.

"So, what shall I call you?" he asked, all nicely, like we were newly acquainted friends.

"Breed."

He nodded, as though it was an entirely acceptable name for someone like me. I cracked a smile at his ignorance. "Have you ever been outside of Appleton, Breed?"

"No, sir," I answered humbly, ignoring the hammer tapping in my skull. I knew his type. Barely out of puberty but wanting to be thought venerable, to be called Father. As if reading a pile of books conferred wisdom as well as knowledge, as if the robe he wore was something more than clothing. The flash of contempt squeezed another pinch of pain from my noodle.

"Wait here," he said and left the room.

The only decoration in the chamber was an icon of a platter-faced human with a yardstick in one hand and a staff in the other. He glared down from a plinth on the wall, a smug look painted across its plaster face. The priest returned with a mop and a bucket of sweet smelling water. He handed it to me and chinned towards the yellowing puddle of vomit.

"Is that Saint Bartholomew?" I asked as I mopped up my puke.

"Aye, may his name be praised." He bowed to the icon. "Ours is a relatively new order, though by His grace it is gaining prominence and more followers with every passing year."

"How nice." I finished cleaning up the mess and offered the pail and mop to the priest. He pointed to the door. Outside an unadorned corridor stretched right and left. Long and low-ceilinged, the sandstone walls and floor had been scrubbed to the color of old bone. The air was tinted blue, and a strong smell of incense tickled my nose. It must have been one of the monasteries in New

Town's temple quarter, not a place I'd ever had much cause to visit, not during daylight anyway.

Of the hundreds of saints and gods in the Pantheon, a few dozen had opened shop in Appleton. They were mostly obscure or poor, run by scammers and sharpers hoping to find softheaded culls, lacking wit but not wealth, to swell their ranks. There were a few of the true believer kind who'd take the poor and exchange a hot meal and a bed for a sermon and a lifetime of unquestioning devotion.

The drab cloister and homespun garb of the pew-bashers creeping about the place told me that this wasn't one of the more affluent orders, which was a pity as I didn't have so much as a clipped penny to my name. A few of the brothers and sisters cast fearful glances in my direction as they passed. As I had a mop in my hand instead of a sword, they continued, offended but unalarmed by my presence. The brethren I saw all looked human, which was not unusual as humans and warspawn rarely shared anything, least of all religion. Thoasa had gods of their own, but I preferred to believe in that which I could see, smell, hear, and touch rather than otherworldly beings, except for the Annurashi. I believed in them because they made their presence known from time to time although I'd never seen one.

I handed the mop and bucket to one of a group of shave-pated priestlings shuffling by and went back inside. Tobias was at his desk, stuffing books into a backpack and stacking sheaves of paper which were covered in elaborate diagrams and elegant scrawl. Though I kept it quiet, I could read Imperial, Guldistani, Vrok, and a smattering of a half-dozen others. Mother believed that education was important and had book learning beaten into me from an early age. My tutors were mostly scholars who'd fallen on hard times and had a desperate desire to work off their drug or gambling debts by teaching me rather than lose their fingers. Given Mother's reputation, they needed little encouragement to make sure I remembered what they taught me, and I still had the scars to prove it.

"I must shortly return to our temple in Valen," the priest said. "I'll need you to carry my belongings and help with cooking, that kind of thing. Should we encounter any undesirables on the road, I give you leave to help me fend them off."

"With a mop?"

"What? No. Just your hands, er, claws." He flailed, searching for the right words. "Just, you know, do what you did the other night."

"I had my blades when I was saving your life the other night. Do I get them back?"

He laughed nervously. "You didn't use them as I recall, so no, they won't be necessary."

"Now, you say that, but there are some dangerous roads between here and the capital where all manner of scum prey on the unwary traveler and they will not be discouraged by fists and feet alone." I knew this to be true because from time to time, I'd been the scum doing the preying.

The priest seemed to think about it for a moment but then shook his head. "No, it wouldn't be right and besides, in his wisdom, Saint Bartholomew has seen fit to gift me with certain abilities that allow me to calculate both defensive and offensive angles of reality. Blades will not be necessary."

I shrugged. I had no idea what he was talking about and neither did he judging by the flush in his cheeks. "Remember you said that when you're being slow-roasted alive by some meat-starved ragabash."

He frowned. "Don't you mean when we're being slow roasted alive?"

"Nah, thoasa don't make good eating, it's the scales."

"Oh, I don't know." He grinned and made a show of sizing me up. "Other than a few patches here and there, you don't look to have too hard a shell to crack. I'm sure you'd make a perfectly excellent meal for some varlet, should the situation arise."

"If you let me use my blades, the situation won't arise. But if it does, they'll eat you first. Soft, white meat is a delicacy, after all."

"If I thought you were being insolent, I'd have you flogged."

I shrugged, looked him straight in the eye. “It wouldn’t be the first time.”

His pinked cheeks darkened to scarlet and he looked away, according me the victory. “I shall pack my books myself. Please don’t touch them.” He curled his left arm into his sleeve, a defensive habit if ever I saw one. If he hadn’t bound me to slavery, I might have felt sorry for him. Only might. I knew some dangerous coves who were missing the odd appendage. As an old acquaintance once told me, ‘It’s not what you have, it’s what you do with it that counts’.

***

The rest of the afternoon passed in near silence save for a few begrudging exchanges. The quiet suited me well enough as I had a lot to contemplate. Mattie would have told Mother what happened in the court. The question was, what would she do about it? The priest sent me on various errands within the monastery which gave me the chance to explore the limits of my bond while I recovered from the ill-effects of the indenturing.

Although not painful, the longer I was away from the little piss-streak, the more a nagging itch grew in the back of my skull. I wasn’t sure if it was a real feeling, like someone tapping me on the head or if it was just my imagination searching for some sign of the magic that bound me.

Out of sight of prying eyes, the cuff proved invulnerable to my attempts to smash, lever, and saw it off. I didn’t so much as scratch the metal, all I succeeded in doing was give myself a headache. It dawned on me sometime later that I hadn't really been trying as hard as I might to remove it. My heart, my will, wasn't in it and it didn't particularly bother me.

After a few hours' running errands, the dizziness wore off, and I stopped jumping at every noise that might be a Guild Blade or vengeful arrachid come to settle my account. The brothers and sisters of the Order of Saint Bartholomew were wary around me. Some delicate souls flinched when they came upon me unexpectedly, a few squeaked. That these timid culls survived in Appleton was the best and only proof I'd seen since I'd been here that they had any kind of divine patronage.

That night, drained from the indenturing, I fell asleep outside the priest's room within minutes of putting my head down. The corridor floor was pleasantly cool and dry, the swept flagstones smelled of lavender, shoe leather, and clean, garden soil.

A few hours later, I was woken by the sound of shuffling footsteps. I didn't leap to my feet because assassins don't shuffle. I opened one eye a crack but lay as still as a corpse. The smell of wool, sweat, and old human wafted past my face as someone swirled the hem of their robe away from me. Whoever it was knocked quietly on the priest's door and entered without invitation. I'd heard the bells chime midnight probably two hours before, so I was curious as to who was visiting the priest when all goodly, godly folk should have been long abed.

The priest and his visitor were too talkative for this to be a simple lovers' tryst. A wise Blade knows well enough that it's better to keep ears open and mouths shut, something neither of these prayer peddlers seemed to ken.

I put my shell against the door for a listen. They started their conversation at a whisper and I couldn't make much out above the odd word, but being the amateurs that they were, they quickly forgot the precaution. A couple of minutes in and they were chattering like a pair of excited children. Their naivety made me smile, I found it charming, in the same way that a hawk finds a pair of conies a delight to behold.

"I have no doubt the binding geas is powerful but more powerful than *that*, Toby?" As I'd guessed, the shuffler was old. His voice rattled and was occasionally lost to wheezing coughing fits.

"With all due respect, Benedict, I know what I'm doing." The priest spoke with more authority than I'd heard before. "I've prayed, and I've done the calculations. You have to trust me. The Order has to trust me."

"Marius has already tried to kill you. Sweet Saint Bart, just saying that makes me feel ill, that it has come to actual violence."

"He wasn't trying to kill me, just scare me. It's not the first time. But that's in the past now." The priest paused, something rattled. "No, try turning it the other way."

The old man grunted, straining against something. My mind jumped to all manner of prurient conclusions.

"I'm not convinced. Oh, right, I've got it," Benedict said. There was a pause and the rustle of what sounded like waxed paper. "Oh, these are rather nice. Thank you, Toby. Now, about Marius. I think you underestimate his ruthlessness and that of his order. This isn't about religion to them, this is about politics and power, albeit temporal."

"Glad you like them. My mother sends me a tin of them every month. No matter where I am, her care packages always find me." He laughed. "The blackbell cherries are particularly good, very sweet. And since when has there been a difference between politics and religion?"

"Oh yes, these are lovely," Benedict said as he munched a mouthful of candies. "Careful, Tobias, you're starting to sound like those jaded old sots in the Synod. But yes, it's a sad fact that the two things are oft entwined, or should I say entangled, to the detriment of all. But back to the matter. If you're right about that thing, and I'm not convinced you are, then malevolent forces could be rising as we speak, forces that are beyond the power of the Synod to contain. Please, for all our sakes, be wary of it. We do not want another Schism War."

Although I couldn't see, I was pretty sure that thing the old scrote was talking about was me. I can't deny that he was right. People should be wary of me, especially those who've landed me in a pot of arsepickle or talk about me behind my back, those folks should really watch out.

"I know what I'm doing, Benedict. No, please, take them. I don't have much of a sweet tooth."

"Very kind of you, my son. I'll do what I can to calm the situation, but I have little influence in Valen these days and Augustra is looking for any means to garner support for her challenge. If she can rally the orders behind a cause, any cause, even one as vile as this. Oh, Tobias. If only you hadn't given her the reason she needed."

"I couldn't lie. This is too important. I had to report what I'd found."

"But what you found is open to interpretation and abuse, as we're seeing now. You should have waited, or better yet, not told the Synod at all."

"No. I'm sorry, Benedict, but I cannot legislate for the evil in people's hearts. The truth had to be told, the world must prepare. It will happen. That thing is proof."

"If you fail, hundreds, nay, thousands might perish."

"I know. Enjoy the sweets."

"I shall. May Saint Bart guide you, my son." The old man sighed, defeated.

The latch rattled. I lay back down before the door swung open. A curl of warm air blew the same, pissy, sweaty smell of old human across my face, now sweetened, if not overly improved, by the syrupy tang of sugar and cherries. When the old man had shuffled off around the corner, I rolled on my back and stared at the whitewashed ceiling. A cold nugget of discontent lodged uncomfortably in my gut and refused to budge. They were scheming, and I was involved and worse of all, it didn't alarm me overmuch.

By the time I drifted back off to sleep, dawn had begun to wash night's shadows from the walls. I dreamed of the demon Shallunsard, saw him sitting on his obsidian throne, toying with the broken hilt of Dawnslight. He looked up, looked my dream self in the eye, and shook his head.

Chapter Eight

It wasn't the call to morning prayers that woke me. What roused me from my slumber was the frantic clamor of alarm bells ringing out across the city. Bereft of anything approaching a sense of emergency or purposefulness, priests and priestesses stumbled into the corridor and clumped themselves into babbling knots of confusion.

The air was tinged with smoke from bakery ovens lit hours earlier, but as dawn approached the smell thickened into something more sinister than baking bread. My first instinct when trouble called was to absent myself and yet, here I was, guarding the priest's chamber door like a faithful cur and wondering why. When he finally showed himself, I bundled him back inside, followed him in, and locked the door behind us. He flounder mouthed something incomprehensible, his words dictated by a sleep-fugged mind. I propped a chair behind the door, my hands twitching for blades I didn't have.

"What the hell is going on, Breed?" He rubbed his eyes. "What are you doing?"

"Looking after you, your priestness. Now, stay away from the door until I've had a look-see out the window, there's a good fellow."

I noted that I was concerned for his welfare. While I grappled with the unfamiliar feeling of giving a damn about someone, I picked up a bludgeon-sized plaster effigy of Saint Bartholomew from the priest's desk and went to the window to see what the hell was going on. The monastery courtyard was filling with bewildered-looking devil-dodgers, but my attention was drawn beyond the walls to what I assumed was the cause of the alarm.

I have no idea who named spew maggots, but whoever it was had a dark sense of humor or a poor grasp of scale. These demonspawn were between six and eight feet long. True enough, they were maggot-like in that they were eyeless and limbless and as pale as a bled corpse, but there was no spewing, quite the opposite in fact. Their round mouths were lined with three rows of serrated teeth, which were capable of chewing through rock. How they'd come to be on the streets of Appleton instead of miles underground was a mystery as much as it was a surprise, but there they were dozens of them.

The priest joined me by the window. “Sweet Saint Bart and all the angels.” He tugged the improvised club from my hands.

“Miners must have delved a nest of them or flooded their tunnels. Look there’s more coming up.” I pointed out where two more were breaking through the cobbles.

“It can’t be just one nest, or one mine come to that.” He pointed into the distance to a cloud of dust rising from a collapsing building. “They’re coming up all over.”

I grabbed the lintel of the window. The wood creaked but seemed sound. “Do you mind?”

He shook his head. I swung myself out and up onto the roof. It was good to feel the cool rush of the wind against my scales. I looked across the city, across the tiled rooftops that spread in rolling red waves to the rim of the horizon. I could go anywhere in the city from up here, one leap and I’d be free, but I didn’t leave. The magic bound me to the priest. I climbed on the shoulders of a statue to get a better look. It had been worn to an anonymous lump by decades of wind and rain, but it made an excellent perch from which to view the city.

“What can you see?” the priest shouted.

“You don’t want to know.”

“Actually, I do.”

"More spew maggots, all over the city. They're eating everything, everyone that comes near. Buildings are collapsing into tunnels. It's chaos."

The cry of 'demon' rang through the streets. Spew maggots were said to be demonspawn. They were supposedly created by infernal magic for the same reason that the Mage Lords created warspawn, which was to fight the battles that humans and demons didn't want to fight themselves. That had been over seven hundred years ago. Since then spew maggots had bred and lived relatively peacefully deep underground. They weren't harmless and were justifiably feared and avoided by miners.

Why they were here, eating the citizens of Appleton like it was the good old days of the Schism War was a mystery, at least I hoped it was. It occurred to me that it might possibly be my fault, given it had been just over a week since I'd released Shallunsard. I felt a small stab of guilt when I thought about my comrades of the Blade down in the sewers up close and personal with the maggots, but the feeling passed when I recalled how none of the bastards had tried to spring me from prison. Down below, the monastery gate cracked like kindling under the assault of a couple of maggots that were smashing their chitin armored heads against it like a pair of living battering rams. A sense of alarm rose within me as I realized that the monastery and the Order of Saint Bartholomew were in grave danger.

"If I had my swords I could do something to help them," I shouted. And then it struck me. The concern I was feeling wasn't mine. I didn't give a damn if my own Mother was being choked down by the maggots, so why did I care about these sanctimonious geese? I didn't, but the priest did. His anxiety was infecting me through the bond we shared, filling me with all manner of unwanted and hitherto unfamiliar emotions. And what was worse, it didn't even make me angry, just dispassionately aware of the fact.

"Everyone, get inside," Tobias shouted. "Dear gods, why are they just standing there? Move, damn you."

"Can't you do something?" I asked. A maggot reared up and bit a chunk out of a grey-haired sister. "Sweet salvation, they're fast."

Perhaps summoned to the feast by its kin, or drawn by the blood soaking into the earth, another maggot burst through the cobbled courtyard. The smell of burning filled the air, smoke ropes uncoiled into the lightening sky.

"Give me my blades and I can help them."

"I can't."

"Then you do something. They're dying down there."

"I just can't. The angles are wrong. There's nothing I can do," the priest shouted. Those members of the order who were able, ran inside while the maggots feasted on their unfortunate brethren.

"Fuck the angles. Those things will go through this place like giant flesh-eating maggots. You have to do something." I'd never heard me sound so concerned for anyone except myself. It was strangely moving, a bit like indigestion.

"Didn't you hear me? I can't."

I snorted. "I heard you. I just don't believe you."

He craned his neck and glared up at me as though I'd just called his mother a whore and then with a yell, he turned and gesticulated at the courtyard. There followed a moment of utter silence where it seemed that time held its breath, froze the world, and stilled the very beating of my heart. The next moment rushed in with the fury of a storm. The air was whipped to splinters as sharp as glass and the pre-dawn day turned to fire. The backwash of heat knocked me off my perch and onto the roof. My third eyelids flashed closed a moment before flames engulfed the courtyard and utterly consumed the maggots. The smell of cooked demonspawn was, unique.

The priest sagged against the sill. I grabbed the edge of the roof and swung back in through the window. He was out cold, drained by the spell. If that was what happened when the angles were wrong, I'd love to see what happened when they were right. The milksop had power.

I picked him up and tossed him on the bed before going back to the window to survey the damage. The courtyard, several outhouses, the remains of the gates, and a cart in the street outside the monastery were all blazing merrily. The fire would have spread to the monastery proper had not a dozen or so of the order rushed out and doused the blaze with a variety of small spells and a good quantity of water. By the time they'd finished, the suns were over the horizon and a fair portion of Appleton had been reduced to smoldering rubble. In truth, the city didn't look too worse for wear, perhaps a little blacker than the day before when it had mostly been grey.

While he was unconscious the priest's anxieties didn't reach me through the bond we'd been forced to share, so I could enjoy watching the god-mongers in the courtyard stumbling around in the bleeding light of dawn. As amusing as it was watching them flounder, I couldn't help wondering why the maggots had attacked the city. I looked to the west, beyond the black line of rooftops, towards the distant shadow of the mountains where Shallunsard's lair lay buried.

The priest moaned in his sleep. I slapped a damp cloth on his forehead and although I'd resisted temptation for almost a full hour, I finally gave in and searched him. He had a sweet rum-bung stashed in his pack which didn't surprise me as I'd never met a poor priest. I took a couple of the crowns and some pennies and put the still healthy pouch back where I found it. Taking the coins hurt. A stab of pain skewered me between the eyes, but it was nowhere near as bad as that which I'd felt when I'd given him a bit o' lip after the bonding. This pain settled into something akin to a hangover and I'd had plenty of those. Of course, I had to go and spoil the moment by fantasizing about smothering the whey-faced bastard with a pillow which caused an instant and blinding pain that dropped me to my knees.

The priest woke up about an hour after he'd cast the spell. Not long after he came round there was a knock on the door. Still groggy, he motioned for me to open it.

"What d'you want?" I asked the handful of slightly singed and pensive-looking heaven-peddlers.

A skinny little woman looked up at me, clutching the yardstick pendant around her neck. "We would like to speak to Brother Tobias. Is he, that is, we would like…"

I got bored listening to her and closed the door.

The priest glared at me. "For goodness sake, Breed. Let them in."

I shrugged and did as he bid. They shuffled inside. "Ah, Tobias," said the woman. I slammed the door behind them, put my back against it, and folded my arms. The weak-kneed culls jumped in unison. The priest shot me a warning glance.

"I've spoken to Benedict," the woman stammered. "He asked me to, that is, he'd like me to…"

"Say thank you?" I suggested.

The woman dared a scowl in my direction. "He wanted me to ask you when, er... well..."

One of the other priests, a portly fellow who looked as bored of listening to her as I was, stepped in as she choked on another mouthful of words. Tobias rubbed the bridge of his nose, dark circles ringed his eyes. "You destroyed the whole courtyard, Toby, not to mention the damage to the monastery. It was pure luck that you didn't kill anyone. Such a regrettable lack of control." The fellow sighed. "We've already had the city guard pay us a visit. To put it mildly, they are less than pleased."

"You're right, Alph, I don't know what came over me." Tobias scowled at me.

Alph softened. "It was probably shock. Nevertheless, it has left us in a difficult situation."

Tobias bowed his head. "I'm sorry. I'll go and explain what happened."

"Oh, no need. Benedict managed to placate them, for now." The group exchanged guilty looks. "He, that is, we were wondering when you were thinking of leaving? Only, sooner might be better than later, given what has happened."

Tobias sat on the edge of the bed. An uncomfortable silence fell over the room. Alph went over to him and put his hand on his shoulder. "I'm sorry, Tobias, but I'm sure you understand. Your use of the spell was, well."

"Impressive?" I offered. I was only trying to be helpful and speed up the painfully slow eviction.

"That's enough, Breed," Tobias's voice was graveled and weary. "Sister Lillian, Brother Alph, everyone. I did what I thought I had to do, but yes, I panicked. I knew the angles were wrong, but I did it anyway." He again shot me an accusing look. "I made a bad calculation. I'm sorry."

Rather than give him a kicking, which is what would happen in the Guild if you screwed up, the group closed around him and offered their deepest sympathies. Bad angles my arse, they were jealous and afraid. He had power that would make most sellspells weep, and they were making him apologize for using it to save their miserable hides.

After an hour or so of turgid theologizing and the recitation of many, many trite aphorisms, Sister Lillian led the group in a long-winded prayer. When they were done, the sorry crew filed out. Exhausted and downcast, Tobias sat and stared at the icon of Saint Bartholomew.

"I told you the angles were wrong," he said.

I shrugged. "They looked pretty fucking right from where I was standing."

* * *

The greenshanks finally cornered and slaughtered the last maggot just before midnight. The booming rapport of firelances heralded an end to the menace, but the damage had been done. The priest half-heartedly packed a few more things while I watched the city burn.

The next morning, after a breakfast of thin gruel we departed, waved off by a tired Father Benedict and a guilty-looking Sister Lillian. The three of them exchanged a few whispered words and said another prayer before we could finally be on our way.

I was loaded with the pig pizzle's baggage, but I didn't mind. Although he was in a somber mood, I was happy that we were leaving town and heading to Valen, which was exactly where I wanted to go. I didn't know a lot about Imperial history, that which was recorded seemed like the dullest, egotistical fluff; just a list of wars and the names of the kings and princes that waged them. What I did know was that the Hall of Heroes was in Valen and that the Hammer of the North and his blasted hammer were buried there.

I kept my head down and my eyes open as we made our way through the carnage. After Sketh's killing and the maggot attack, I was betting Jing and Mother would be too busy to worry about me. Of course, as soon as they had a grip on the situation one or other of them, both if I was unlucky, would come after me. Crime lords, like nobility, were a vindictive breed and it was bad for business to let a slight go unpunished. Until a few days ago I'd have been fighting with my fellow Blades against Jing and the maggots and whatever else fate threw at the Guild. Now the only family I'd ever known was lost to me. I cannot say I missed them.

A curfew and order for summary execution for looting had immediately been put in place and judging by the crop of makeshift gallows that had sprung up across town, the law was being enthusiastically enforced.

We fought our way along crowded streets, past the burned-out wrecks of buildings and yawning maggot pits. A column of bull-shouldered miners, candle lamps tied to their caps, passed us on their way to the mines. Instead of the usual resigned misery, today their grimed faces were rigid with fear. The boss of their crew was an ogren with a limp. She cursed and kicked those who dawdled but didn't seem overly enthusiastic about her work. I didn't blame her or them considering what might be waiting for them below ground.

"Why are they going to the mines today?" the priest enquired. "Surely it's too dangerous?"

"They don't have a choice. Look at their wrists. D'you see the jewelry?" I pointed out the bracelets marking them as indentured servants. "The mine owners' will make them earn their freedom even if it means sending them to hell. The Empirifex needs his calthracite."

The priest blanched. "It isn't right. Someone should stop this."

I laughed. He was ridiculously naïve. How this cull had survived to adulthood was a marvel. "You should go tell the patricians who own these poor culls' debts then.

I'm sure they'll take heed of your council, and while you're at it, you can spring me, seeing as how you're so set against forced labor."

He stopped and glared at me. The miners filed past. The tide of refugees heading in the opposite direction flowed around us. My head started to pound.

"How can you, how dare you make light when you've seen what those things have done?"

"What am I supposed to do? Cry? At least they're only bound by contract. They could do a runner if they wanted to, unlike me." The veins in my temples throbbed.

"No one made you break the law."

"In point of fact, they did, sort of."

"Enough. You've said enough."

Steel flashed in his eyes and just for a second it looked like he might forget his meek manners and burn me to a crisp. I stood my ground. Let him, I had little to lose. He shook his head and stormed off. Perhaps like me, he was getting a taste of how the other felt. Perhaps his flaring temper was mine. I hoped so. I hoped my anger was causing him as much confusion as his bleeding heart was causing me.

As we made our way out of the city, I heard all manner of grisly tale being spread like pox through the scared droves fleeing the mayhem. Wild-eyed street preachers lamented the end of days, drunks gave gory, unabridged accounts of what the spew maggots had done. Citizens bleached pale by fear told of entire streets that had been swallowed by sinkholes and their hapless inhabitants devoured by the beasts crawling below. Demons had apparently come to Appleton. My palm itched. I put my head down and kept walking.

Flooding in the calth mines had probably driven the maggots to the surface. Damn mine owners, scraping every last crumb of calth out of the ground. It was a surprise this hadn't happened before. That was what I kept telling myself as I forged a path to the gate. While I beat my guilty conscience into submission I kept us moving. I was carrying almost all the priest's belongings as well as dragging him behind me and shoving aside those laggards who got in our way.

Occasionally he insisted we stop and help some unfortunate cull whose cart was stuck in the mud or who needed a penny to buy food for their sick infant, blind mother, one-legged aunt twice removed. The priest was soft for all manner of con trick and sob story and slowed our progress considerably.

The closer we got to the Old Town gate out of the city, the more crowded the streets became. It seemed like the only folk not trying to leave were the bondsmen and women and their families. Huddled groups of the indentured watched as the tide of people flooded from the city, leaving them behind to clean up the mess along with the greenshanks who'd enslaved themselves with oaths of loyalty instead of debt. I shook my head. *Fools the lot of them.*

On Main Street an urux had sunk up to its shoulders in a pothole, miring the over-laden wagon it was pulling up to the axles and blocking the road. The animal wheezed pitifully as its lungs were slowly crushed and its frustrated owner lashed and kicked it in a futile attempt to get it moving.

The damage the maggots had caused was immense and still taking its toll on the city and its inhabitants. All over town buildings were collapsing, undermined by the maggots' furious burrowing, leaving both sides of the city a wreck. If they'd survived, the Midnight Court would do well out of this.

We reached the gate just after midday. The greenshanks on duty were in an ugly mood. Many had the ghostly ash-blasted features of those who'd been using firelances. The backblast from calthracite and zanthe crystal dust tattooed the skin of cannoneers with tiny silver-white pockmarks. The greenshanks eyed the crowd with the cold detachment of people too used to killing but we passed beneath their dead-eyed gaze without drawing attention.

Bursting from the city on the desperate tide, we joined the wave of dispossessed rolling north. I kept glancing over my shoulder, to see if I was being followed. As far as I could tell I wasn't, and so we made our way out with a group of refugees that swelled and contracted by turns as people joined or left the main road. Anxiety and tension permeated every conversation. Every knot of travelers was tied together by the fearful rumors that demons had returned.

"Off t' Shadowspite," a wide-eyed, grinning beggar barked at the priest. The maunder couldn't have been as old as he looked, given the vigor with which he was scratching his nethers and skipping along the road, but he was grimy, withered as kindling, and stank of pel and cheap drink.

"I'm sorry?" Tobias looked up for the first time in hours. He'd been quiet since our little argument, lost in whatever wearisome thoughts passed through his soft skull case. That he'd torched the monastery courtyard was probably also weighing heavily on his tender little conscience.

"Them demons." The old man cackled and gestured at me with shit stained fingers. "They're heading t' the mountains. Mark me, this is just the beginnin'."

"And you'd know, would you?" I made as if to backhand him. "Did you divine the truth in a ha'penny dram of bucket brew?" He skipped back, stayed just out of arm's reach. Beggars are good at gauging how much and from whom they needed to keep a distance.

"Don't like the rub o' truth, eh, demonspawn?" The old tosspot shot me a gap-toothed grin.

The proclamation caused several of our fellow travelers to give me the fish eye. I laughed it off but there wasn't a blasted thing I could do to allay their fears, not now that the old scrote had planted the seed of distrust in their fearful and superstitious minds. To attempt to deny the claim would have been tantamount to an admission in their eyes. In truth, any acknowledgment would have been divined like chicken guts and, given what I look like, probably taken as proof of guilt. People were afraid and looking for something tangible on which to hang their fears. Not to mention that in part, they would have been correct.

The demon mark in my palm itched, or perhaps I just thought it did because my conscience was pricking me. Whatever the cause, I ignored it. I didn't let on that I'd heard the whispered conjecture about my heritage, or that I could smell the pungent aroma of fear that bloomed like swamp miasma whenever the old pel-head stirred the travelers' doubts about me with his drug-fuddled insinuations.

That night, when the group we'd been walking with stopped to make camp, the unofficial leaders of the motley crew, a retired soldier, and a baker asked for 'a quiet word' with the priest. If I hadn't seen him turn the monastery courtyard into a furnace I'd have been concerned for his safety. As it was I just hoped the angles were right.

"People are afraid." I overheard the baker say and saw the heads of his crew nod in agreement.

“This is ridiculous,” the priest replied and proceeded to argue my case. It was a spirited, but ultimately futile effort.

The debate went on long after suns’ set. I had to admire the priest’s tenacity, but why he even bothered to argue with them was beyond me. They’d made up their minds before they’d come over to speak to him, the thing that made me chuckle was that, in this case, they were right. I was part of the problem. Not that they knew it, they were just ignorant peasants afraid of me because I didn’t look like them. I was dangerous to be around, trouble in tooth and claw, and on some level, the mad old beggar had sensed it.

In a purely practical way, we were better off without the rest of the group. I knew that if I was hunting this road, I’d go for the slow and helpless before anything that looked like me. Add to that the priest’s explosive gifts and we were far more likely to travel unmolested by brigands than a bunch of old folk, children, and merchants. The fools didn’t know it, but they were arguing to divest themselves of the best defense they had against demons and more mundane monsters.

When tempers began to fray, and voices grew louder, the priest walked away. I could see that he was used to losing by the way his face fell so easily into the sad little frown I’d seen so often in our brief association. It was the same look I’d seen on his face when Blackbeard was about to close his account. This seemingly habitual acceptance of inevitable failure, despite all the power he could wield baffled me.

“I don’t know why you bothered,” I said as we set off, leaving the camp of scared refugees behind us.

“Because it’s safer for everyone if we travel together,” he answered, restoring my lack of faith in humanity. “And because their ignorance had to be challenged, now more than ever.”

He had to go and spoil it.

“I’m not exactly a saint, you know.” I shook my left wrist, the silver cuff gleamed.

He rubbed his chin with his stump. “No, perhaps not, but neither are you a demon.”

I’m used to keeping a straight face, but I was sure I could feel the prickle of a blush touch my cheeks. I blame the human part of me, it always lets me down.

“Oi, wait,” someone behind us shouted. We stopped. I was surprised to see the old tosspot who’d caused the trouble skipping along the road, waving his spindly arms. I set off walking. The priest stayed where he was.

“I’m coming with you,” the beggar announced.

“I don’t think so.” I hunted around for a rock to throw at him.

The priest shook his head. “Why would you want to come with us? You all but accused my servant of being a demon.”

The beggar scratched his bony crotch and leered at us. “Better t’ run with the wolves than the sheep, eh?”

“Oh, no you don’t.” I said but the priest waved me to silence.

“You may come with us.” He smiled benevolently at the old scrote. “Perhaps when you get to know Breed better, you’ll revise your opinion.”

The old man slapped his thigh and danced on the spot. “I doubt it.”

“So do I,” I said. “Now fuck off.” I bared my fangs, but my aggression didn’t impress him. The beggar was smart enough to know who was in charge. He grinned back at me, his bloodshot eyes bright with mirth.

“D’you have a name?” the priest asked him.

“Tosspot,” I offered.

The beggar laughed and danced about some more. Like most hardened pel users, he struggled to keep still. “Tosspot? Aye, I’ve tossed a few pots.” He cackled. “Tossed in a few too. Tosspot, all right demon.” He winked at me. “That’ll do.”

Chapter Nine

When it became too dark for the priest and Tosspot to see, Tobias called a halt near a roadside shrine dedicated to the Pantheon. The All-Seeing Eye, the symbol that represented the dozens of officially sacred gods and hundreds of honored saints was painted on a roughly carved stone that was surrounded by flies, piles of rotting fruit, and dead flowers.

After the priest had prayed and cleaned up the shrine, we made camp, or rather, I made camp. Tosspot and the priest wandered off in opposite directions to void their bowels while I built a fire and prepared some food for Tobias. I wasn't hungry, I'd eaten my fill the night before at the monastery, which would see me right for a day or so. Humans were constantly eating, drinking, and shitting. It was a wonder they ever got anything else done.

Tosspot came back first. I could smell him before his grimy little monkey face emerged from the bracken. The fresh, smutty brown streaks on his ragged breeches confirmed his complete lack of hygiene or self-respect.

"Go wash before you sit by this fire, you stinking cockroach," I growled. Humans struggle to growl and talk, I have no such problem. He looked around for the priest, but he wasn't back yet. The grin faded.

"There ain't no rive—" he began.

I pointed in the direction of the stream that I could hear burbling in the woods north of where we were camped. Grumbling, he trudged back into the undergrowth. If I hadn't been stricken by a severe case of fuck it, I would have followed him in and drowned the disgusting old bastard.

When he returned, Tobias said a prayer and then without further comment, ate the burnt bread and cheese I'd prepared. At a time like this I'd clean my blades or wax my bow. I felt lost without them. When he finished, the priest took out a notebook and pen. He cursed.

"What's up?" I asked.

"I've lost the nib." He rummaged in his bags.

I laughed.

"Something amusing?" He gave up looking through his bag and resorted to using a pencil for his scribbling.

"I met a fellow who specializes in stealing nibs, at least, that's the story he told me. He was quite the rum cove."

He looked up, fixed me with a questioning stare. "Do you know anyone who makes an honest living?"

"Plenty. Why, priest, d'you want to meet some?"

"Are you implying that priests are dishonest?"

"Certainly not, master." I cracked a smile.

"It doesn't work on me, you know." He closed the book.

"What doesn't work on you?"

"Showing your fangs like that. I'm not intimidated or impressed."

You fucking well would be if I wasn't bound by a geas. The thought and accompanying mental image of me ripping his throat out was immediately followed by a spike of pain so sharp it made my eyes water.

The priest's attitude immediately changed from scolding to concerned. "Are you all right, Breed?" He moved over to me, rested his stump on my shoulder. "That was my doing, I'm sorry. I shouldn't be angry at you."

I blinked away the purple lights and almost laughed but managed to catch myself. The idiot didn't understand the nature of the bond as well as he should. “No, I deserved it.” I said, as contrite as a beggarly cur.

“No, no you didn’t. I’m sorry. Sorry for everything.”

“No need, master.”

He looked pained. “Don’t call me master. Call me Tobias, or priest, anything, but I am no one’s master.” That was the wisest thing he’d said all day. I smiled, tight-lipped, jaw clenched. He sat next to his pile of bags and picked up his notebook. That he felt guilty was good. It was a weakness I could work to my own end which was to get as far from Appleton as possible and as close to the tomb of the Hammer of the North as this fool could take me.

“Your hair, it isn’t like human hair, is it?” he asked, keen to change the subject.

“No, not really.” I resisted the urge to remark on his startling powers of observation.

“Does blood flow to the end of each shaft? Only, I notice some of them are pierced.”

“Almost to the end. They don’t bleed much when they’re torn.”

I got the feeling he was making notes about me, studying me like one of those things kept in the jars of vinegar that moldered in the apothecary’s window. A dull headache pulsed in the back of my skull.

He nodded and scribbled something in his book. “You have a third eyelid?”

Again I resisted the urge to congratulate him. “Yes, very useful it is too.”

“But no tail at all?”

“No, more’s the pity. Thoasa tails make excellent weapons and give them superb balance.” I scratched my nethers, sat back and grinned. “Anything else you want to know about?”

The tip of the pencil snapped on the page. He shut the notebook. “I, er…”

The undergrowth stirred. I could smell Tosspot before he emerged, spackled with loamy detritus, looking for all the world like a mummified turd. He stank less of shit than he had, but the smell had been replaced by another equally unwholesome aroma which explained the flush in his cheeks and the length of time he’d been away. He reached for the bread I’d left by the fire.

“Touch it, and I’ll break your arm.” I said. His hand froze mid-air. He looked at Tobias who frowned at me before turning to the beggar.

“Please, take it, eat your fill,” Tobias said.

Tosspot snatched the bread and tore a chunk off.

Uncharacteristically for a pel addict, he put half back.

"Don't feel that you need to ask if you want to eat anything, Breed," Tobias nodded towards the bread.

I looked at Tosspot gnawing on the chunk of bread with his blackened teeth. "Not hungry, thanks. You eat it before it goes stale." The priest finished the bread by which time the suns' red halos were being cut to ribbons by the saw-tooth spikes of the treetops.

* * *

We'd camped near the road. Carts, wagons, and people on foot passed by late into the night, all heading away from Appleton. I didn't sleep. I didn't need to, which was handy because I didn't trust that self-abuser Tosspot. I'd work out watch shifts with the priest on the morrow if he still insisted on letting the mad old goat travel with us.

The priest had rolled himself up in a blanket. Tosspot curled up beside the dying embers of the fire, his cheeks were dusted with ash making him look like a penitent on pilgrimage.

"One o' them maggots came up near Steel-Eye Square," he said. "Right under a big, old bull urux." His rheumy eyes shone in the firelight. "It ate right through it, came out its back and that old bull still alive." He shook his head, dislodging breadcrumbs from his matted beard. "Hole the size o' the suns right through it and it still standing, eyes wide as dinner plates. Took an age afore it realized it was dead. Now that's stupid, eh?"

"Speaking of stupid, how come you didn't get eaten when they attacked?" I asked.

He tapped the side of his rum swollen nose. "Could ask you the same, eh?" He chuckled. "I'm quick, used to be really quick. Quick as you."

Now it was my turn to laugh. "No human is as quick as me."

"Not now maybe, but once, a long time ago," he said.

"Before you got a taste for pel and cheap booze?"

"Oh, aye, back in my glory days." He hacked and spat into the fire. "Back when the road was scattered with rose petals and every step was marked by a ballad, back when we were heroes."

I laughed. Deep in the forest, something howled.

* * *

We'd walked for four days and had barely made it a hundred miles from Appleton. At this rate, I'd die of old age before we even reached Valen. I needed to put more distance between me, the Blades, and the Pearl. If they'd a mind, Mother and Jing could afford to send an assassin to just about anywhere in the Empire. I wasn't the praying kind, but I very much hoped Jing had been eaten by a spew maggot. It was simply too much to hope that a giant, carnivorous demonspawn had done for Mother.

We came to an old, pre-Schism bridge where the road split north and east. I knew it was pre-Schism because it was massive, well made, and decorated with grim-faced, human warriors. Centuries of neglect and robbery had taken its toll, and the once magnificent example of pre-Schism architecture was slowly crumbling into the gushing torrent. Even in its dilapidated state, it was far grander than anything I'd seen that had been built after the war.

The priest informed me that we'd be heading east to Valen. The more direct route was over the unimaginatively named Dragon Spine mountains that ran from north to south. We could have taken the road north, through the foothills and up as far as the coast. From there we could either follow the coast east or take ship to Valen. The easiest, but longest route was the one the priest decided to take. We'd take the road east, go around the mountains before turning north to Valen. If I'd been on my own I'd have gone over the mountains, but I was shackled to a one-handed priest and a stray lunatic. The priest could blow the giblets out of just about anything nasty we might encounter, but I still wished that I was carrying something sharp and pointy instead of a pack full of books and a skillet. I ask you, books instead of blades? Pointless. My comrades would, quite rightly, burst their bladders laughing if they knew what I'd been reduced to.

That eve, as twilight dimmed the day and tinted the world in shades of mauve, we came upon a village, and not a moment too soon. I had been forced to walk at a snail's gallop for hours while the priest blathered godly nonsense at the capering madman. The endless sermonizing made me wish I'd been born without ears.

According to the boundary stone, the village was called Little Lea. It was little enough, but I couldn't see a lea, just a dusty gash of road, and a three-legged dog mooching around the sign. If it had been named appropriately the place would have been called Little Shithole, which I'll grant was less lyrical than Little Lea but a touch more honest.

The inn wasn't hard to find. Other than a scatter of one-storey dwellings there were only a few other buildings of note. Standing back from the road was what looked like the village hall. Near the hall was a run-down guard tower that was marked by a tattered Imperial standard. Across the road from the guard tower, down by the river, was a mill, and beside the mill's tailrace was a turf-roofed forge. The mill's water wheel churned monotonously, each revolution marking the passage of time with a sodden creak. If I'd been given the choice of living a single day in Appleton or somcwhere like this for a hundred years, I'd choose Appleton in a heartbeat.

"There isn't a temple," the priest said like it mattered.

"There's a shrine." I chinned in the direction of a roadside shrine that was hung with faded prayer ribbons and piled with tattered offerings. The priest went over and knelt before the badly painted image of the All-

Seeing Eye. Tosspot pulled a broken pipe from his shirt and licked the sticky pel residue from the bowl.

"You're not going t' pray? Beg the gods to save you from your miserable existence?" I teased Tosspot, not just because I was bored, but also because I didn't like him.

"After you, Breed." The idiot grin was replaced by a facial tic. "Don't suppose you've got any coin have you?"

He didn't need to go on. He was an addict who spent every penny he got on pel or gut-rot booze. I had what I'd stolen from the priest and under normal circumstances wouldn't have given him so much as the stink off my shit, but perhaps if he got drunk the priest might cut him adrift. I tossed him a penny.

Despite the uncontrollable twitching that afflicted him, he snatched the coin from the air with the practiced deftness of the desperate. "Ah, yer an upstanding cove, Breed." He scuttled over to the inn, knuckles bleaching around his prize.

The priest spent the next half hour with his head in the dirt before the All-Seeing Eye. I spent it eyeing the traffic and getting the lie of the land for want of something better to do. There seemed to be a lot of business going on between the guard tower and the village hall, even though it was the time of day when all respectable types should be sitting down to their dinner.

Three uniformed greenshanks ambled back and forth between the hall and the tower. I doubted that there would be many more of them stationed here, perhaps two or three with maybe a captain or a sergeant. Although we were on a main road, the village didn't warrant any more protection than a handful of greenshanks. If there hadn't been an inn it wouldn't have had an outpost at all. Places like this usually deputized the locals to swell the lurchers' ranks when the need arose. I knew this from personal experience of having to leg it once or twice from the odd posse of pitchfork-wielding bumpkins when I'd pulled jobs out of town.

The priest eventually stopped praying and came over. "Thank you for waiting, Breed. I sometimes lose myself in contemplation of the holy scriptures."

"It's not like I have a choice, is it? If I wander too far, my brain'll melt and run out of my ears like tallow." I spoke without thinking. He frowned, I immediately regretted snapping. Not only did it hurt, but I had to win this cull's trust, and being sharp with him wasn't going to keep him sweet.

"No. Quite." He brushed past me and stomped towards the inn, head down, shoulders hunched. I sank a fang into my tongue until I tasted sweet iron. I did it to remind myself to stay focused. A year and a day. It wasn't long. If I was to get the hammer for the blasted demon or get hold of enough gold to pay a sellspell to break the bond, I'd need to get on the priest's good side.

From the outside the inn looked like a dump. It was even less inspiring on the inside. A string of half rotten, pipe-smoked hams was hanging above the bar, out of reach of what would have to be extremely hungry patrons. The cloying, sickly sweet smell of partially cured, partially rotten pig was overlaid with the odor of stale beer, piss, pipe-smoke, pigeon shit, and dried urux dung. It was the same olfactory tale told by every backwater tavern in the Empire. Bubbling on the hearth was a large pot of mutton fat and turnip stew. A dog was licking the oversized ladle propped in the inglenook. It was all very homely and utterly wretched.

“We don’t serve your kind,” the one-eyed innkeeper barked as she burnished a tankard with a spit rag. I looked around, as it was hard to tell where her eye was aiming. Out of habit rather than anger I reached for the ghosts of my blades. The priest strode over to the bar. Before the woman could open her mouth again, he flipped a silver half-crown on the stained counter.

“Don’t be ridiculous, that is my servant. I require a room and food, for both of us.”

The barkeep frowned and rubbed harder at the tankard. She was obviously thrown by the sureness of the priest’s demeanor, the absolute, ‘do not question me’ tone of voice he’d produced from gods only knew where. I was impressed, it seemed that the little pissweed had some orchids after all.

‘We don’t serve your kind’ wasn’t anything I hadn’t heard before, even in Appleton it was a common refrain and had lost its sting years ago. Under normal circumstances, I’d either teach whoever said it some manners or, if there were too many witnesses, I’d leave and return at a later date and rob them blind. I liked to think of it as an arsehole tax. However, this was a first. A human was speaking up for me. If it hadn’t been his fault that I was here I’d have been touched.

Placated by the coin, we were shown to a booth. While we waited for our food and ale to arrive we were surreptitiously scrutinized by a handful of bacon-faced and slack-jawed yokels. Happily, Tosspot was nowhere to be seen.

Eventually, the barkeep came over and slid two plates of congealing slop across the table, along with two tankards of grease-spotted ale. When she saw me looking at her stitched up eyelid, she turned her head away. I caught a whiff of something fishy with subtle undertones of overripe peach. It was her. The lank, greasy hair, the pasty complexion livened by cheap rouge. Her antipathy towards me made sense now.

I gave her the smallest of nods, an imperceptible acknowledgment that said, her secret was safe with me, which it was, so long as she played fair. She wasn’t warspawn, neither was she like me, a hybrid of two distinct species. She was probably one of the ‘touched’. A poor cull spawned a little too close to an old, Schism battleground who’d been warped before birth by the poisonous magic that still polluted those places after seven hundred years.

The shame of being touched meant good business for shankers who, for a price, would remove a touched babe's less than human feature with a snip here and a stitch there and no one would be the wiser save dear old mother and father. Eyestalks were a common Schism touch, so many a child grew up one-eyed or blind, but to some doting parents it was thought better to maim their children than have them called outcast.

Those parents who couldn't afford the discreet services of a shanker often tossed their ill-favored offspring into the nearest river rather than live with the shame. Some rare few kept their children as they came. It was no surprise that the innkeeper didn't serve warspawn, she didn't want anyone with a sense of smell like mine to rumble her. That she could 'pass' for human with just a few minor adjustments had probably saved her life. She didn't let on to me, she hurried away.

"What's the matter?" Tobias asked.

"Nothing, except," I chased a lump of gristle around my plate. "It's just that I've never been so far from home." I looked him square in the face, didn't blink, didn't blush. If there was one thing I could do well, other than fight and steal, it was lie when I needed to. He maneuvered his bowl with his stump and stirred the broth.

He looked down. “I never intended this to happen. You must believe me when I tell you that everything I do is because I have to. So much is at stake, so much depends on me.”

“I understand,” I said, the bile rising in my gorge. “Fate has conspired against us.” It was hard playing nice when all I wanted to do was grab him by the back of the neck and drown him in his stew. A swift, blinding stab of pain, so sharp it made my eyes water followed the murderous thought, which was good. I’d never cried in my life, but soft cull wasn’t to know that.

The priest put down his spoon and almost patted my arm with his stump but paused mid-air before awkwardly withdrawing. “I promise, I shall endeavor to make our time together as easy as I can. I’m not a tyrant, unlike some.” He’d left something unsaid, but I didn’t dwell on it. I had the fish on the hook.

Sometime in the early hours, I woke to find myself sitting on top of Tosspot with my hand around his throat, about to smash his head in with a chamber pot. Someone else was shouting. Sleep-fugged, I forced my brain to work back from there.

I dimly recalled that the door had creaked open while I was sleeping on a palliasse beside it. The priest had been snoring fitfully on the bed. Someone had crept inside, and I’d instinctively grabbed their ankle and dragged them to the floor. At the same time, I’d leaped on top of them and picked up the first thing that came to hand, ready to beat them to death with it. Then I woke up just in time to not kill Tosspot, which was regrettable.

"Sweet Saint Bart, Breed. Let him go," the priest commanded.

Reluctantly, I stopped squeezing the old scrote's neck and got off him. "Knock next time," I said and returned to my mattress. Tosspot made an unnecessarily dramatic show of coughing and gasping for breath.

"If that's how you greet a friend, I'd hate t' see how you treat your enemies," he mewled.

"You're no friend of mine," I said. "What did you think you were doing, sneaking around in the middle of the night?"

"I've been busy. I've been scouting the lay of the land." He got up close to the priest, and whispered breathily in the poor cove's face, spittle flying from the blackened stumps of his teeth. "I've been exploring the criminal underworld, for your safety, mind, and this is the thanks I get?"

I had to laugh at the idea that Little Lea could possibly have anything even approaching a criminal underworld.

"Well, er, thank you," the priest said while trying not to recoil from the old sot's mephitic breath. "But there really is no need and for Bart's sake, what's your real name? I refuse to call you Tosspot any longer."

"Rubin, your Holiness, and mark me, places like this can hold nasty surprises for unwary travelers, eh?"

"Thank you for your concern, Rubin, but I don't think we're in any danger here."

"Twat," I said. The priest looked shocked. I pointed at Tosspot. "I meant him."

Tosspot chuckled, breathed rum fumes and the stench of decay into the air. "Ah, well, you're right there, Holiness, but yon Breed might be, eh?"

"What do you mean?" the priest asked.

"This is a waste of time. You should just toss the old scrote out and let us get back to sleep." Tosspot's presence interfered with my plans to soften up the priest. They ignored me.

Tosspot cast a wary glance over his shoulder. "As I was about my business earlier on, I happened across a couple of bene coves."

"A couple of what?" The priest looked to me for clarification.

"Reliable types. Although I very much doubt it round here. Mark me, he'll have been pissed out of his skull the minute he left us." I beat a few lumps out of the mattress and lay down. "He's probably been sleeping in a ditch 'til now. You should have a word with old one-eye, you paid for privacy."

The priest waved me to silence. 'Go on, Rubin, tell us what happened?"

"Well, I went with these fellows to a humbler establishment, where the price of vittles is more suited to my pocket."

"He means a backroom bawdy hole where you'll be lucky if the bucket-brew doesn't make you blind, or the owner doesn't cut your throat when you're in your cups."

The old sot scratched his orchids. "While I was there. I heard that they're fixing to try and hang one o' them." He chinned in my direction. "On the morrow, so they say. They're making out that the cove is a demonspawn an' has been bewitching livestock, curdling milk, and cursing the locals. But my contact says that it's all a set up to snatch a claim to some land where calth's been found. That's cold work, if you ask me, hanging a cove for the price of some rock, even if it's a misbegotten, by-blow like Breed here." He looked expectantly at me.

I shrugged. "So?" I felt no bond of kinship with other warspawn just because they were warspawn.

"So, I'm sayin' people get a taste for this kind of thing, eh?" He pointed a crooked finger at me. "You best be on yer uppers, less they nab you for hexing their chickens, or whatever it is you demons do."

"Hexing chickens? Not I, Tosspot. I'm more your beggar-strangling type of demon."

"That's enough, Breed." The priest turned to Tosspot. "Tell me exactly what you heard, Rubin."

It was a long night.

Chapter Ten

The next morning, instead of leaving Little Shithole, the priest insisted that we follow the crowd of locals to the village hall, which was being used as a courtroom for the 'trial'.

"So what are you going to do?" I asked the priest. "Demand they let this cove go or you'll burn them to a crisp with your sorcerous might?"

Tobias pulled up short and turned on me. I sensed a lecture coming.

"What I do is not sorcery. It is, as discovered by Saint Bartholomew, the manipulation of latent energy contained within the angles and planes of existence. And no, I am not going to threaten anyone. The Empirifex's law is all that is required to ensure justice is done," he said without a whit of irony.

"So it's not sorcery, and Imperial law is the epitome of justice?"

"Correct."

"My arse."

"How dare you," he spluttered. "You know nothing, nothing of the enlightenment of Saint Bartholomew."

If he hadn't been capable of frying me in my own juices I would have laughed in his face. "I know sorcery when I see it. I also know there's nothing as bent as Imperial law. Trust me, I've bribed a lot of greenshanks and magistrates in my time." A little voice in the back of my head was quietly suggesting that I shut my piehole, but I couldn't help myself. I was annoyed that we weren't leaving.

The priest was shaking. I could feel his anger raging below the surface. "I am not a fucking sorcerer," he said quietly.

And then I tumbled it. Curse me for the halfwit I was, but it took until right then to realize that all this Scientician waffle was how he handled the Paradox. Using powerful sorcery put him on his arse, but his delusional belief in all this angle bollocks saved him from exploding or turning himself into a pool of living slime when he overreached himself.

I recalled a story about a sorcerer who'd done just that some years before. The story goes he'd been hired to kill Countess Orkazny, the Empirifex's cousin and favorite lover at the time. She'd come to Appleton to inspect the calth mines. Apparently, the Grundvelt Separatists had sent the sellspell, but as he was channeling enough power to wipe out half of Appleton, he lost control and the Paradox got him. Rumor had it that the Empirifex had the still-living slime he'd turned into poured down his co-conspirators' throats until they choked to death and that he kept what was left in a jar. Mother laughed hysterically whenever she told the story. Whatever the truth, it was time to heed the little voice.

"All right, all right, whatever you say, but Imperial law's put a lot of high-minded dissenters in the calth mines as well as rascally coves like me."

"They are nothing more than traitors and criminals," he said, with little real enthusiasm. Like everyone else, he knew the truth.

"Call 'em what you like. But if what Tosspot—"

"Rubin." His jaw tightened. "His name is Rubin."

"If what Rubin, says is true, you'll need more than the law to spring this cove. People have skinned their own grandsires for shares in calth mines. There's a lot of coin to be made from powder."

"Enough. We're going to the trial, and if I suspect there has been any underhanded dealing, I shall step in, as is my right as a citizen of the Empire." He fixed me with a watery stare. Pain needled my brain. Proving that just thinking about punching him into unconsciousness and dragging him away before he got us hung was also against the rules of the geas. He strode off towards the village hall.

"Aren't they expecting you in Valen?" I called after him. He stopped, turned, and narrowed his eyes at me. "Won't your order be expecting you?" I pressed hopefully. He looked like he was about to say something but instead turned and marched resolutely towards the hall with Tosspot in tow. "Miserable, whey-faced fuck," I muttered, somewhat foolishly as it turned out. When I recovered, I got up and followed them, mindful to direct my curses at the gods rather than the priest.

The hall was an unimposing, double-height, one-room affair, tied together by smoke-blackened beams that had probably been hoisted into place by the ancestors of the locals now gathering beneath them. The inheritors of this architectural marvel were elbowing and shoving each other, fighting to get a place by the railing that partitioned the chamber.

After listening to the gossip in the gallery it seemed that, in the opinion of the learned farmyard advocates, it was a stitch-up. Few seemed to care because from what I could make out, the accused was a freak and an outcast. 'Ratface', the alleged demonspawn, was by all accounts as good as hung.

"Why are we here again?" I asked the priest, who'd also been ear-wigging the general chatter. "I mean, I like a good hanging as much as the next citizen of the

Empire, but we're supposed to be going to Valen. Saint Bartholomew will be waiting."

"Don't be facetious, Breed," the priest said as we pushed our way to the front of the crowd.

"Aye, don't be facetious, demon." Tosspot deliberately spoke loud enough to draw the attention of those nearest to us. Some potato-faced locals glared at me. I glared right back at them. Some shuffled away, others made the triangular sign of the holy eye. I made a silent vow to strangle Tosspot as soon as I got him alone.

The accused was led into the courtroom by a bored-looking greenshanks. Ratface, unlike the town, was well named. I got a good taste of her smell as she was led past the gallery. She was probably no older than eleven, pre-pubescent for certain. The long dress she was wearing made it impossible to tell if she had a tail, but she certainly had the face, if not the physique, of a mostly shaved rat.

Her eyes were small and dark and set either side of a long, broad nose over a mouth of large teeth, and her enormous ears stuck out at right angles to her head. Nobody in Appleton would have given her a second look. The spectators crammed into the hall were all human and within the arbitrary limits of what passed for 'normal'. In Little Lea, the girl must have stood out like a turd on a pillow.

"What kind of warspawn is she?" the priest whispered.

"I don't think she is. She's probably just what Tosspot said, a by-blow of Schism magic, a lucky accident. Kids like her are usually done in when they're born. I s'pose Mummy and Daddy must have—"

"Hold your tongue," the priest snapped. I again found myself reaching for blades I wasn't carrying and was immediately lashed by a crushing pain for my troubles.

"Fuck's sake." I jammed the heels of my hands into my eye sockets in a bid to crush the pain that was trying to rip its way out of the front of my skull. "This relationship will not end well, priest," I growled. A grumble ran through the crowd and a space cleared around us. Tosspot giggled and hopped around like a frog on a griddle.

"All right, quiet down everyone, let's get this over with," said a self-important little burgher as he pushed his way through the crowd. "I said, shut up you lot." He squeezed behind the bench and claimed the center chair. There were ink stains on his lace-trimmed cuffs and fingers marking him out as a nib-tickler. He had the overblown airs of an Imperial lackey and was probably a tax collector or some other stripe of crown actuary.

He nodded to the greenshanks, who motioned for the girl to get into the rusting cage that stood in the corner of the room. It had no doubt been brought in to make the place look more like a courtroom although the chickens pecking through the rushes undermined the authoritative grandeur somewhat. Caging the girl seemed excessive, given she was less than five feet tall. I could tell the greenshanks thought so too. He was looking everywhere except at Ratface and an old woman who was giving him the evils from the public gallery.

For her part, the girl seemed blissfully unaware of the danger she was in. She sat on the stool provided, kicking her legs, dark eyes inquisitively scanning the crowd. When her gaze fell on me, she smiled. I looked around to see if anyone had noticed, which of course they had. The space around us got a little wider, the stares a little more pointed. I would have killed for a weapon, would probably have to before the day was over.

A couple of other worthies joined the nib-tickler on the bench. One was evidently the miller, given the light dusting of flour on her best Gods' Day smock. I guessed the other was the blacksmith as he stank of charcoal and fire and had a wiry cast to his skinny frame from days spent pounding iron.

"These are a fine bunch to judge if the girl's demonspawn." I said to the priest. "A smith, a miller, and a money-grubbing coin-counter." Tobias didn't answer, he was too busy scribbling in his notebook. Tosspot was leering at anyone who happened to glance in his direction while scratching his nethers. The earthy musk of the dung-dusted crowd was threaded with a volatile mix of anger, excitement, and fear. Our little crew were making quite the impression. Another couple of greenshanks muscled their way into the room, rust-pocked halberds in hand. They closed the doors behind them and hushed the crowd.

The three cronies on the bench put their heads together and had a quick confabulation. When they'd finished nodding sagely at each other, the nib-tickler rapped on the table. It was an unpleasant reminder of my own time before the beak and set me very much against anything they might have to say on point of principle.

"In view of the statements and evidence we've already received, it has been decided by the council that we shall proceed directly to sentencing the accused, Clary Bolliver, to, er, death by hanging, sentence to be carried out immediately. Costs incurred in the prosecution of this case to be paid by the family of the defendant. May the All-Seeing Eye have pity on her wretched soul." The miller elbowed him. "What? Oh. Case closed."

"Well, that's that. Shall we go?" I asked the priest.

Before he could answer the old woman who'd been glaring at the guard screamed as though she'd been run through. The girl woke from her daydream at that and thrust her scrawny arms through the bars in an effort to reach the old woman who was likewise straining towards the girl.

Some of the crowd looked away, perhaps ashamed. A few looked upset, but most were nodding, mouths set in troutish frowns of grim approval. It seemed the good citizens of Little Lea were as quick as their city-bred counterparts when it came to adorning the nevergreen tree. As someone who lived in a rough old world, where justice was summary and almost always fatal, I was unmoved by anyone's plight save my own.

"Just a minute," said the priest. The mouthy burgher tried to ignore him, but Tobias ducked under the rail and strode over to the bench, bold as you like. "Councilors, a moment of your time, if you please."

The councilors looked at the greenshanks. The two by the door didn't move and the one by the cage had his hands full trying to keep the old woman away from the bars.

"This is most irregular, er, Father," the burgher said.

"I hope it is. I would hate to think that trying children for their lives is a regular occurrence in Little Lea."

"That, Father, is not a child. That is a demon," the miller exclaimed while making the warding sign of the eye.

"That remains to be seen." The priest rested his stump on the table. The gaze of all three of councilors flicked to where his hand should have been. "I was led to believe that this was the first and only sitting of this court, am I correct?" They nodded in unison. "In that case, and with the greatest respect for your rank and office, I must draw your attention to the fact that witness testimony must be given in any capital case, brought anywhere in the Empire, as stated in Imperial law."

The nib-tickler pushed out his chest. "Ah, well, we've heard the evidence informally, there seems little need to go over it."

"Never the less, Imperial law states, unequivocally that you must. Sergeant." The priest marched over to the soldier by the cage. I would never have guessed he had this much mettle in him. It was likely to get us killed, but I had to admire his brass. "Fetch your commanding officer at once."

"I must protest, Father." The miller folded her arms. "Priest or not, you've no right to come barging in here, laying down the law."

The blacksmith, who had until this point kept his mouth shut, now stuck his oar in. "Neither you nor yer robes carry any weight here, priest."

"I'm afraid you're wrong on both counts." The priest straightened up, seemed to grow in stature. "As the first son of the Patrician house of Vulsones, I am within my right to demand that this trial is conducted in accordance with Imperial law. Furthermore, as an ordained brother of a sacred order of the Pantheon, it is within my remit to act as defense counsel for the accused. I take it nobody objects to Imperial law?" He looked at the girl who was oblivious, but the old woman wasn't.

"Please, save her. Save my granddaughter," she begged.

"That's settled then," said Tobias in a tone of voice that would brook no argument. "I need time to review the evidence and prepare a list of witnesses, so I suggest a short adjournment. Shall we say until the morrow?"

The nib-tickler looked at his colleagues. "I, er, no. I mean yes, that would be fine, I think. Court adjourned?"

* * *

The priest's little announcement made a marked and immediate impression on the citizens of Little Lea, and well it might. Everyone had heard of House Vulsones, one of the wealthiest noble houses in the Empire and a power in the Senate. I looked at the priest in a whole new light, the hypocritical little bastard.

By the time we returned to the inn with a bundle of court documents our bags had already been moved to a better room. This one had a fire burning merrily in the hearth, well-fitting shutters, and fresh rushes. No sooner had the priest sat down than the captain of the guard was shown in by the suddenly more deferential innkeeper. The captain was unshaven and wearing a uniform made for a younger and leaner version of himself. The silvery flick of an old dueling scar marked his stubble-roughed cheek.

He saluted. "Patrician Vulsones, my name is Nestor Reynard, acting captain of the garrison." He smelled of cheese and had recently splashed himself with rosewater to try and mask the odor of stale sweat. It had failed.

"You are aware of the trial, acting Captain Reynard?" The change in the priest's demeanor was as remarkable as it was sudden. Even Tosspot was stunned into silence. Tobias Vulsones had adopted the indolent weariness of a noble being forced to deal with inferiors, as though breathing the same air was an insult. I wasn't sure if this was an act or if I was seeing the real Tobias and the scholarly priest was the mask. Either way, it occurred to me that I'd been gulled for the second time in recent weeks.

Reynard looked uncomfortable. "Yes, my lord, of course. These are dark days, evil is—"

The priest cut him off. "Why weren't you present for the hearing, Captain Reynard?" Tobias faced the fire and clasped his stump behind his back. This pose didn't suit him, it looked contrived, but Reynard was too busy staring at his boots to notice. "Indeed, why weren't you sitting on the jury, Captain? Surely, as a representative of the military, it's your duty, particularly in a capital case?"

As much as I liked seeing a greenshanks sweat, I hadn't missed the dagger-eyed stares from some of the locals when the priest had spoiled their little party. He probably ought to throw the guardsman a bone, just in case the yokels got a taste for hangings. Killing a priest, a thief, and a madman probably wasn't the worst of what went on in a grubby hole like Little Lea.

"Yes, you're right, but I had other matters to attend to and, well, it seemed a straightforward case."

Tobias snorted. "That remains to be seen. I will, of course, give a full report to the Knights Imperial as well as to the Imperial Magistrates when I return to Valen. I'm an old friend of Commander Pretorius."

He was a pale human to start with, but at the mention of the commander of the knights, Reynard turned as white as a bled pig.

"Commander Pretorius? I see. Well, I came to let you know that the garrison and I are at your service, my lord."

The priest half turned from the fire, the flames cast his face in bronze, and I could well imagine that profile on a coin. "That's good to know, Captain and I'm sure from now on everything to do with this trial will be run in accordance with Imperial law."

"Of course, my lord, I'll see to it. Now, if you would excuse me, I must organize some patrols. We've had reports that there have been attacks on some of the local farmsteads." Reynard looked pointedly at me. "They say it's demonspawn."

I grinned. "They talk a lot of shit, greenshanks."

"Greenshanks? Only criminals call guardsmen 'greenshanks'."

I waved my cuffed wrist at him.

He narrowed his eyes and tightened his grip on his sword hilt. "Until the morrow, Lord Vulsones."

"Captain." The priest nodded.

Reynard spun smartly on his heel as though trying to prove he still could and marched out. When the latch dropped, the priest sagged into his usual slouch-shouldered stance. He went over to the table and began sorting through the court documents.

"You really shouldn't antagonize the local law. I might need his support," Tobias muttered, his gaze fixed on the ink-stained pages.

"Me antagonize? If you hadn't put your dainties in it there'd be no need to worry about upsetting the local ironsides and we'd be on our way to Valen, Lord Vulsones."

"And an innocent girl would be dead. And why are you so keen to go to Valen?" He'd dropped the patrician tone when the greenshanks left, but it returned with a vengeance now.

"Why do you care so much?" I said, the force of his anger beating down on me. "Innocent girls, boys, household pets, get hung every day. Why is this little ratkin so special?"

He slammed his fist on the table. "She's a child, damn it. She's just a child. And I will not ignore any injustice if it is in my power to prevent it."

"And what if she really is a demonspawn, what then?"

"I do not believe there is such a thing." He didn't sound convinced to me, whereas I knew for certain that demons and therefore demonspawn, were very real. I just couldn't argue the point too forcefully without getting into dangerous waters, waters that flowed straight to the pyre. "You're in the minority then," I said. "Because those spew maggots are infernal, everybody knows it."

"A lot of mistakes were made during the Schism, but that was centuries ago. Time has passed. We are what we do, not what we were born."

"Is that right, Patrician?" I grinned. "Even I know that which is born of infernal magic is demonic, and that which was created by the Mage Lords are warspawn. I have a soul, according to the Pantheon demonspawn are soulless and damned." I folded my arms. "Hey, I didn't make the rules, your lot did."

The priest shook his head as though he was arguing with a child. "There has been interbreeding and seven hundred demon free years since the Schism. Everything has changed. What would you call yourself, Breed?"

"Unlucky. But I'll tell you this, I'm not infernal."

"You show me your soul, Breed. Tell me in which organ it resides. I have seen all manner of creature inside and out, and I have never yet seen a soul."

"I'm no theologian, but that sounds like heresy to me."

"I am a Scientician, it is my job to question. Knowledge and learning are divine gifts." He sounded sickeningly sincere.

"It's a good job that you're a Vulsones," I said. I'm not sure what kind of look he gave me, something halfway between pained and angry.

"What do you mean by that?"

"I mean if you were a common cove you'd have talked your way to the gallows long before now. I don't know why you're bothering with all this, you could be living like a king."

"If we let this girl die undefended, word will spread and every Schism-touched, by-blow, everyone with so much as a snaggle tooth will end up burned or hanged by ignorant peasants or those with axes to grind. You know what people are like. They can be savage, particularly when they're afraid."

I laughed. "Oh, I know all right. It strikes me that it's us freaks who should band together. It seems like you humans are the real danger, not us monsters."

"That is also another reason why I, a human, must stand up for this girl. You're speaking in jest, which, by the way, is an irritating habit, but you don't know just how many powerful factions are searching for an excuse to wipe out everything they deem 'unholy' which to translate means everything that isn't human."

His words washed over me, I was already bored with the conversation. "You haven't won yet, patrician. These yokels are keen to hang someone. Tread carefully or it'll be us."

Chapter Eleven

At dawn, the priest dragged me over to the guard tower, so that he could speak to the girl. The court was due to convene at ten, which was apparently when milking finished. Heavy rain hammered home the promise of a miserable day as the peasants gathered outside the hall. Despite the inclement weather there looked to be more spectators today than there had been yesterday. News of the priest's antics must have spread to every den of clod-hoppers for miles around.

Tosspot had disappeared the night before with a penny the priest gave him and hadn't returned. If the miserable old piss-sack kept leeching coin off the priest we'd be as broke as a whorehouse pisspot before we got to Valen.

Tobias knocked on the guard tower door and entered unchallenged. Rain splashed into a bucket in the corner, socks and long johns steamed on a line slung above the stove. It wasn't exactly the best example of an Imperial military outpost. An old greenshank was snoring in an armchair by the stove. The grey-beard spasmed awake when the door creaked.

"Ah, I didn't hear you. Come in, come in, Father." He waved us in as he buckled his sword belt on over his patched tunic. "Early morning shift's always the worst, can't seem to keep my eyes open these days. If you've come to see Captain Reynard, you're too late. He's already gone over to the hall to, er, get things sorted."

"Actually, I came to see Clary. If you wouldn't mind?"

The guard shrugged and fished a ring of keys from his trouser pocket. "Her Nan's with her so watch out, she's a mean old goat."

"I'm sure she won't object to me visiting. I'm here to help her granddaughter."

"Aye, so I've heard. You're wasting your time, but I s'pose it's yours to spend as you see fit, Patrician. I'd leave well alone if I was you. A lot of folks have an interest in Halla giving up her place."

"Is Halla the grandmother?" Tobias asked.

The old guard nodded. "Aye. It's this way, mind yer heads when we get down there." He led us out of the room and through a hall, at the end of which was a short flight of steps leading down. A couple of off-duty greenshanks gave us the once over as we passed. It was reassuring to know that if the priest got himself locked up, busting him out would be child's play. I'd seen more secure chicken coops.

"There's not been a hanging in…" The greenshanks paused as though thinking while walking was a taxing matter. "Nine years. There isn't a lot of crime in Little Lea above a bit of cattle theft, rowdy drunks on Gods' Day, and the odd fight. That sort of thing, nothing serious. All this talk of demons has just blown up out of nowhere, people using it as an excuse if you ask me. Ah, here we are."

"I heard you," a trembling voice called from the darkness, thick with emotion. I could taste the salt of tears. "You know what they're after. They just want my land, that's what this is about. They're threatening an innocent child for the sake of what's under my farm, the greedy, spineless bastards."

The guard unlocked the door. "All right, Halla, that's enough. The father isn't here to listen to your theories."

"Actually, I'm very interested in what you have to say," the priest corrected, as he ducked around the guard and offered his hand to the woman. She pushed the girl behind her and looked at Tobias like he'd offered her a bag of eyeballs.

"If you've come to tell my girl to repent, you can be on your way. She's done nothing, d'you hear me? Nothing. Go tell that bastard Sandison and his cronies." She hugged the girl, who didn't seem like she needed comforting as she wasn't giving off any odor of fear. The tang of tear salt and anxiety that permeated the cell belonged to her grandmother.

The cell was more of a storeroom than a place of incarceration. It was piled with sacks and barrels of supplies. A small cot bed had been crammed into the corner.

"Leastways, we don't have to worry that she'll go hungry, she can just help herself." The greenshanks chuckled, nobody else laughed. "Right, er, just knock when you want out."

"Thank you. You might as well go with him, Breed, but don't go far."

"If they attack you, just scream and I'll come running." I winked at the girl, who gave me a shy grin.

When we were back in the entrance hall the greenshanks put the kettle on the stove. "Do you want a cup of chai?" he asked.

I looked around, surprised to find that he was talking to me. "There are only two other guards here, the rest have gone on patrol. I'm too old for running around in the wilderness. Did you say you wanted a drink?"

"Aye, thanks." I didn't, but it was such a novelty having a greenshanks offer me anything other than a beating, I felt I had to accept. He shoved a stool in my direction and poured a couple of mugs of chai that smelled like it had been stewing for a week. I sat and took the offered drink.

“I fought all through the Spice Wars,” the greybeard said. “For the last six months o’ the war my unit was in with a company of your lot,”

“My lot?” I didn’t think he meant Guild Blades.

“Aye. Thoasa, isn’t it? Although, I can tell you’re not just thoasa are ya?”

For a horrible moment, I thought he was going to shout “Demon!” and try to attack me with his kettle, but then I got what he actually meant. “Ah, no. My mother’s human.”

To my surprise, he looked more intrigued than disgusted. “Human, eh? That’s unusual. Thoasa are, well, they’re big folk, as you know. Your mother must be quite a woman.”

If only you knew. “Aye, she’s a singular individual that’s for sure.”

“One o’ them liz, er, thoasa saved my life when our ship was rammed by a Shen war galleon. I thought I was a goner. I was trapped below decks when the mast fell, an’ the ship was going down fast. One o’ them lads shifted it and swam me t’ shore. I’d broken my leg, see? No way would I have made it on my own, not with the brachuri swarming about the wrecks looking to pick off stragglers, the dirty sea scabs. See that.” He tugged up his trouser leg to reveal a silver scar running down his grey fuzzed shin. "Bone came right through." I nodded appreciatively, as that seemed to be what he wanted. To be honest, as scars went, it wasn't that impressive.

I spent the next hour listening to him tell me how terrible the Spice War had been and how much he missed it. I nodded when it seemed appropriate and drank his awful chai. Eighteen years after the Spice War, I was the beneficiary of his gratitude to the thoasa who saved his life. The funny thing was, he could remember dozens of tedious little details about the battle, but he didn't know the name of the person who'd saved him.

When the priest called for the guard he sounded as angry as all hell. He stormed out of the cellar and over to the door without saying a word. His writing scrip was pinned under his left arm and he was carrying a fistful of papers in his right. A wave of simmering rage rolled off him.

"What's up? She didn't have a go at you, did she? I told you to shout if she got nasty," I said and tried not to laugh.

"Enough. A child's life is in danger. Doesn't that bother you?"

"No, not really."

He looked pained as he stormed out like I'd just hoofed him in the nut-sack. I caught up and we walked to the village hall in half-arsed silence. I say half-arsed because priests, despite what you might think, aren't very good at silence. Preachifies like Tobias loved the sound of their own voices and so the short walk was punctuated with huffs, tuts, and sighs— all signs of the sermon he was aching to deliver. I could care less what he thought of me, but I was annoyed at myself. I had once again managed to alienate the person who could probably gain me access to Valen's holy of holies and the Hammer of the North's thrice-damned tomb. I had to try and make amends.

"Thoasa just aren't as…" I wanted to say soft. "As compassionate as humans."

He snorted. "You're not a thoasa."

This wasn't working. Every time he opened his mouth I wanted to punch him. "No, but I'm not a human either, thank the gods." I muttered through gritted teeth as hot barbs dug into my brain.

* * *

Across from the gawping masses, the three members of the council took their seats. They were joined today by Reynard, who looked uncomfortable, buttoned up in his patched and moth-eaten uniform.

The honest oak table they'd sat behind yesterday had been replaced by a much grander piece of furniture. Today they sat behind an elaborate, Shen-style monstrosity that had been inexpertly painted to look like leopard wood. I'd lay money on it that the ugly thing didn't purr when it was polished. If whoever had donated it to the noble court could have afforded the real thing they wouldn't have been within a hundred miles of this dung-burgh.

My money was on the nib-tickler, one Hubert Sandison. He'd been the mouthpiece yesterday, though it would be interesting to see who was in charge today now that Reynard was in attendance. Sandison looked particularly smug and had gone to extra effort and dressed in what must have passed for finery in the provinces. The garish ensemble of screaming blue velvet and cheap foil braid made him look like a sack of expensive shit tied with a bow. I didn't like him. Not only did he smell wrong, possessed as he was of a sour body odor, but he was a bully, and nobody likes bullies. His gaze met mine, and he narrowed his eyes. I bared my fangs. He looked away.

The priest had been given a small table near the council's bench, opposite the cage. He was busying himself sorting through the notes that he'd made, his face a study in concentration. After another twenty minutes or so the accused was escorted into the court. Her grandmother wasn't allowed to be with her, which the old woman complained about as she pushed her way to the front of the crowd. The blacksmith gave her a polite if embarrassed nod of acknowledgment. The girl didn't seem to notice or care what was going on.

Sandison turned to the greenshanks. "Er, right then, if you would be so kind, Captain Reynard."

The blacksmith looked pale and sweaty, the miller likewise. I focused on them, tried to taste what they were feeling, but there was too much going on to filter out their particular smells, especially as they were sitting next to old sour sweat. Perhaps, like me, they were anticipating the priest giving them a lecture that they'd never forget. He certainly looked like he meant business. I folded my arms. I was looking forward to the show. And then something familiar and altogether unwelcome brushed my elbow.

"Don't turn around and don't say anything." The old greenshanks from the guard tower whispered in my ear as he put the tip of a blade between my elbow and my ribs. I didn't move, I waited. The old guard had made the mistake of announcing his presence and his plan. I just had to pick the right moment to make him pay for it. My fingers tingled.

Captain Reynard stood up, tipped a nod to a couple of greenshanks who pushed their way through the crowd and stepped up behind the priest who was still going over his notes. When the crowd hushed, he looked up, confused.

Reynard snatched a piece of paper from the desk and pointed at the priest. "It has come to the court's attention that this man is an impostor. Guards, seize him."

"What? How dare you. Let me go." Tobias shouted as he was grabbed by the greenshanks. In the one-sided struggle the table went flying. The neat pile of notes scattered and swooped in slow, diving arcs across the floor. My hair spines bristled.

Any minute now.

Reynard turned to Tobias. “You, sir, are an impostor, sent to aid the demonic forces at work in this town by those who would see decent humans thrown down. You are a traitor to your own kind.”

“That’s a damn lie.” Tobias said loud enough for the whole courtroom to hear. “This is all because Halla found calthracite on her land and she won’t sell it.”

On a signal from Reynard, one of the greenshanks punched the priest in the gut to shut him up. It worked, Tobias doubled in pain as the wind was knocked out of him. I was an island of stillness amid the jostling crowd as partisan feelings were aired and scuffles broke out on all sides of the court. The blacksmith stared resolutely at the table, the miller’s dusty face was scarlet with guilt and Reynard nervously fingered the tarnished hilt of his saber. Only the nib-tickler was grinning like the world wasn’t about to turn to shit. He nudged Reynard.

“Clear the court,” Reynard ordered.

“No, not yet, you fool, call the witness.” Sandison hissed.

One of the greenshanks encouraged the crowd to get back with a few swipes of his halberd, many fled the building. The priest sagged in the grip of the other guard. The one behind me kept his hand steady and his blade poised. Halla scrambled under the barrier and locked her hands on the bars of the cage. Clary was paying attention to what was happening now. She leaned close to her grandmother and whispered something in the old woman's ear.

"Bring in the witness," said Reynard. The crowd surged like a wave in a washtub. The greenshanks with the halberd barged past me. I didn't turn to see where he was going, I didn't want to provoke the old bastard behind me before I had to. With any luck, he'd fall asleep before he got the order to finish me.

"This is a sham. Whoever you produce is a liar and you know it," the priest said to the council.

"You should have kept your nose out of our business," said the miller. The blacksmith's jaw tightened but he kept his gaze fixed on the table.

A few minutes later the greenshanks came back. Even before I saw him, I could smell Tosspot.

"Why are you even bothering with this farce?" the priest asked. "We all know the truth of the matter."

"Silence." Sandison slammed his fist on the table. "You are not the law in this court. I, that is *we* are. You, sirrah, will hold your tongue or lose it. Now, the witness will stand forward."

Tosspot staggered before the bench. He was patently in his cups but, with the fortitude of a well-seasoned sot, somehow managed to stay on his feet after no doubt drinking enough gut-rot to kill a bull urux.

"What's your name?" Sandison asked him.

Tosspot leered at me. "Tosspot."

The miller and the blacksmith looked at each other, shared in a glance the shame of a guilty conscience. Bloody amateurs.

"Hmm. As you say. Pray, tell the court what you told me."

"I don't remember telling anyone much of anything, but thanks for the grog."

"This very morning, you told me that this man." He pointed to the priest. "Was in league with demons."

"No, I didn't. You told me he was in league with demons, and I said I wasn't surprised." Tosspot belched. I could smell the hot, gingery fire of cheap brandy from across the room.

The priest folded his arms. "He's your witness? A beggar who'd sell his mother for a sniff of pel. Who are you trying to convince with this ludicrous charade?" He raised his voice, no doubt for the benefit of the locals who were pushing against the greenshanks' halberd. They didn't care what he said, they had their own scores to settle.

The rat girl let out a low, keening wail, as though finally aware of the danger she was in. Her grandmother tried to comfort her through the bars of the cage.

"Now see what you've done? You gutless bastards." Halla spat at the council.

Sandison surged to his feet. Reynard clamped his hand on the pig-eyed fool's shoulder and pushed him back down. The piss-and-iron stink of adrenaline-filled the room. The air sang with the promise of violence. Sharp work was afoot.

Reynard looked at Sandison with undisguised contempt before turning to his soldiers. "Clear this fucking room."

The guards shoved everyone out and barred the door. When it was done, Reynard turned on the priest. "You're right, my lord Vulsones, it was a poor plan and badly executed. I'm quite embarrassed." He sighed apologetically and drew his sword. "How about this. When they were unmasked, the impostor and his…" He cast a sidelong glance at me. "Demonic minion attacked the council and the hapless witness. In the ensuing battle, the brave guardsmen and women defeated the servants of evil. Alas, they were unable to save the witness, who was struck a cowardly blow by the demon. Is that more convincing, Vulsones? Oh, and by the way, it was Commander Pretorius who had me sent to this venal little shithole in the first place. She took a liking to my lover and wanted me out of the way. Suffice it to say, I will not be sending her a report regarding this incident."

"You mange-faced bastard," said Halla. "I'll tell her. If I've got to walk to Valen, I'll tell the world what you've done."

Reynard dug the tip of his sword into the table, eliciting a gasp from Sandison. "Hmm. You have a point." He cleared his throat, "The brave guardsmen and women defeated the servants of evil, including the old witch, Halla Grenfyle and her monstrous get. There, that should do it." He focused a meaningful glance about six inches behind me. The sword point that had been touching my elbow was withdrawn.

"Sorry," the old greenshanks said.

"Don't be," I replied.

Thoasa have something akin to a second brain that controls the body while the other brain, the one I oversaw, could relax, and think about just how I was going to rip the heads off the smug puke-stockings who had planned my demise.

Soldiers old or young make poor assassins. They tend to lack finesse and in this case, speed. I spun. The guard's blade thrust into empty air. I grabbed his hand and crushed his fingers into the hilt of his knife and twisted his wrist until it broke. He cried out, I relaxed my grip, and let the blade fall from his useless fingers and into my free hand. I turned and hurled it at the greenshanks who had hold of the priest. More through luck than judgment, I hit him and not Tobias. The guard staggered, clutched his ruined eye. Cackling like a madman, Tosspot somehow managed to avoid being stabbed by Reynard, who seemed most perturbed by the old scrote's capering antics. I can't say I blamed him.

"Get her out of there!" I shouted at Halla. She didn't need to be told twice. Thanks to the general ineptitude of the greenshanks the cage wasn't locked.

The blacksmith kicked over the table and pulled a knife. The miller fell off her chair in her haste to flee, although gods only knew where she was thinking of going. Behind us, the only door was being guarded by the greenshanks with the halberd, and she didn't seem inclined to move, not with half the town outside, hammering to get back in.

"You've made a proper arse of this, acting Captain," I said, trying to draw Reynard out. Scarlet with rage, he duly complied and leaped at me while the blacksmith circled round to my right. The greenshanks who'd had hold of the priest collapsed. The old greenshanks backed against the wall behind the railing, cradling his mangled hand. In stories, the hero always manages to fight on after sustaining horrific wounds. In reality, a smashed wrist is more than enough to take the fight out of even the bravest cove, particularly humans who break easily and have poor pain tolerance.

I grabbed the knife I'd sheathed in the downed greenshanks' face in plenty of time to meet Reynard's clumsy lunge. Although I prefer to use two blades I'm handy with one. I blocked and kicked him in the gut. He folded over and kindly offered his neck. How could I refuse?

The miller screamed when I finished Reynard. Tobias was bellowing at me to stop, but it was too late. I ignored the pain that was trying to push my eyeballs out of my skull and ducked away from the blacksmith who leaped at me, waving his knife with all the aplomb of a blacksmith unused to knife fighting. I swayed back and stamped down on his knee. As he dropped I ran him through. He curled around the blade and fell, mewling as he died.

"That's enough, Breed." Tobias grabbed my shoulder. I managed to stop the blade an inch from his neck. To his credit, he didn't flinch. "That. Is. Enough," he said. Almost killing my master caused an excruciating burst of pain to flare in my skull and I hit the floor beside the blacksmith.

"Sweet Saint Bart, what have you done?" Tobias asked as though it wasn't obvious. The townsfolk were hammering at the door, Clary was sobbing, as was the miller. Someone was choking on their own blood.

"I just saved your life, that's what. Fuck, this really hurts. I should have just let him stab me."

Sandison mumbled something inaudible. During the scrap he hadn't moved a muscle. He'd just sat, rigid with fear, watching his world turn to shit. Now, surrounded by the wreckage of his petty schemes he woke up to the nightmare his greed had created. "I wasn't going to let them hurt her, Halla," he bubbled. "I swear, I just wanted to scare you."

Halla glared at him and hugged her sobbing granddaughter. I got to my knees. "I'd shut up if I were you." I said and, still seeing double, turned to the guard with her back to the door. She shifted her grip on the halberd and braced. I stood up and weighed the knife in my hand. Stunned or not, I knew I could take a country greenshanks and so did she by the way she was shaking. "You might want to step aside, greenshanks."

"Best do it, Dana," the old greenshanks said from where he'd slumped against the wall. He turned to me, his voice thick with pain. "I knew your kind was tough, I should have done you quick, without saying anything."

"Next time, eh?" I answered. I felt anything but tough right then, but they didn't know that. I couldn't bring myself to look at the priest.

The miller peered from behind the table, Sandison hunched into his ornate chair. I tried to keep my eyes on them and the guard by the door.

"There is but one way you can redeem yourselves," the priest said.

"Anything, just name it. Any penance, any recompense," Sandison spluttered, his gaze fixed on the still blinking head of Reynard that lay at his feet.

Tobias raised his hand. "Just shut up and listen. I want you both to go out there and confess your crimes to the people of this town, and then tell them to disperse. You will then take yourselves over to the guard tower and surrender to whoever is left in charge. I'll send word about what has happened to the nearest Imperial outpost. Do you understand?"

Sandison and the miller nodded emphatically and stumbled to the door. I had to give it to the priest, despite being as pale as a fish belly, he was remarkably unruffled by what had just happened. If only he had a legion of Imperial knights behind him to shore up his words. In my experience 'authority' meant nothing without steel reinforcement. I just hoped the yokels didn't know that too.

The greenshanks unbarred the door. There was a sizable crowd waiting outside, some had armed themselves with clubs and other makeshift weapons. When they saw the councilors they backed off a few feet. Sandison raised his hands and patted the air to still their chatter.

"The holy father…" he stammered. "Is a demon. Kill him, kill them all!" he screamed and dived into the crowd. The greenshanks cursed and tried to hold the crowd back, but their blood was up. They'd come for a fight and one greenshanks wasn't going to deter them. The miller hesitated for a breath before running to join Sandison. I looked around for another way out.

The few windows were high and small, too small to get everyone out quickly. Even if we got out the villagers were just about bright enough to run us down before we got very far. I could leg it on my own and leave the others to their fate, but the thought of spending the rest of my short life in blinding agony because I was bonded to a dead priest didn't thrill me. The crowd edged forward.

"Step aside," Tobias ordered. He looked like he was about to pass out.

I stepped over to support him. "You can't talk this mob down, let me—"

He grabbed my shirt, sweat stood out like coffin nails on his pale forehead. "The angles are right, Breed."

I immediately backed towards Halla and the girl. The old greenshanks caught on that something was about to happen and shoved his comrade out of the doorway and back inside.

The crowd surged forward. Tobias went to meet them. The air turned sharp and a sulfurous petrichor rose like a storm was about to break. The priest raised his arms.

It was a strange feeling, being near to, but not the target of a huge discharge of raw, magical energy. The first thing that happened, after a heart-stopping moment of utter nothing, was that lightning arced from the priest's hands and leaped to the iron chandelier, showering the room with sparks before lancing a dozen jagged forks into the crowd. The second thing that happened was me being knocked on my arse by a percussive whump of hot air.

Lightning leaped from one member of the mob to the next, binding them in dazzling, azure chains. They jerked, spasmed and burned as the wreath of fire incinerated their clothes and melted the flesh from their charring bones. The acrid stench of storm clouds, combined with the fatty stink of burning human made my eyes water. Seconds later, it was over.

Black, fire-trimmed flakes of crispy human floated into the sky before gently drifting back down to earth as the intense heat dissipated. From what I could see through the smoke, none of the mob had escaped, including the two treacherous councilors. All that remained of Sandison was a leg that was strangely untouched by the magical fire. I knew it was his as it was still clad in a white stocking and a bright blue shoe. There was nothing left of the miller. Like the rest of the mob, she'd been reduced to charcoaled dust. A few errant flames idly licked at the doorframe, but the blast had been extremely well focused.

"I see what you mean about those angles," I said to the priest, but he didn't hear me, he was too busy fainting. I caught him before he kissed the dirt and carried him like a babe in arms, over the cindered remains of our attackers and out into the drizzle. The smell of death hung in the air, mixed with the gloom of late summer rain that was bleeding from the heavens. I looked up, let the water wash the ash from my face.

Although the sound was buried beneath the planishing hammer of rain, I heard the distinctive clunk of a trigger being pulled, but by the time I realized what it was, it was far too late.

My first and, as it turned out, only reaction was to drop the priest. A moment later I was hit in the chest with the concentrated force of a charging urux. The impact punched me off my feet, turned my ribs into jagged splinters that sliced into my chest and shredded my heart and lungs. I vomited a spray of blood.

I knew I'd hit the ground because all I could see was the sky. As I bled out, I lost all feeling in my limbs, and my consciousness retreated to a tiny point somewhere in the back of my skull. I looked out of the well of my being, through the rain-blurred windows that were my eyes.

"That was a damned risky shot. You could have hit Tobias," said someone I couldn't see. Whoever he was, he spoke like a toff, not unlike the priest save that it entirely lacked his humility and was instead replete with self-importance.

"No, it wasn't," another male voice answered. This one, by contrast, spoke in a soft, breathy purr; precise, but lacking the indolence of the truly noble. “He was never in any danger. I do this for a living and, if I may say so, I am rather good at it.”

Annoyingly, they both remained beyond the scope of my dwindling vision which was a pity as I was curious to see what my killers looked like.

“What in hell is it?” demanded the first. I assumed he was talking about me.

“Dead is what it is. Why yes, it was a bloody good shot, now you mention it,” the breathy one sniffed.

“You want praise? I’m paying you a fortune, isn’t that enough?”

“Not really, no. I am an artiste. Coin pays the bills, but praise feeds my soul.”

“What rot.” The toff laughed.

“You wound me, sir.”

“Don’t tempt me, Schiller. Now, if you wouldn’t mind, help me bind Tobias.”

“With pleasure.” Breathy tittered. “We don’t want him coming round and turning us into charcoal, do we?”

Someone nearby groaned. I guessed it was the priest. I knew it wasn’t me because, I acknowledged with a surprising lack of rancor, I was a breath away from being dead.

Chapter Twelve

After the initial excitement of dying, I learned something interesting. Nothing happened. One minute I was bleeding out beneath a suitably maudlin sky, and the next I was covered in dirt and someone was dragging me from the ground by my ankles.

In between dying and resurrection, nothing had happened at all. There hadn't been any flames of hell, no divine rivers of wine, no twelve-cocked thoasan love gods came to greet me, no holy winged vaginas, not even an army of sacred golden newts to show me the way to the source of all life. Just nothing. I suppose it could have been worse, but death was something of a letdown.

I tried to struggle free of the iron grip around my ankles, but I couldn't move. Panic gripped me, my nose, mouth, and eyes were full of dirt. Before I choked I was pulled from the ground like a turnip. Harsh daylight forced tears from my eyes. Whoever had dragged me from the hole released me. To my dismay, I found I still couldn't move but my vision quickly cleared. I spat out a mouthful of dirt, focused on my rescuer and immediately wished I hadn't. It was a corpse, or more accurately, one of the restless dead.

It wasn't fresh, but it was still recognizably male. A noose was hanging around its twisted neck, its shriveled muscles creaked like hawsers as it grabbed me under the arms and hauled me over to a tree. Its empty eye sockets wept grave dirt and grubs as it leaned over and propped me against the trunk. And there was me thinking there was nothing worse than being shot. It seemed that like life, death was full of unpleasant little surprises.

The corpse shuffled back, canted its head to one side and tried to smile with its atrophied facial muscles. "Breeeeed," it hissed. It spoke with Shallunsard's voice. "You are, without doubt, the most amusing creature I have met in centuries." The demon laughed.

I didn't. Something to do with being shot to death had quite muted my normally robust sense of humor. "I'm the only creature you've met in centuries." Air whistled through my shredded lungs. "Am I dead?"

The corpse nodded. "As good as, save that thing you term a soul has not yet left your body."

I never thought I'd miss him, but I really wished the priest was here. "Soo, I am, or I aren't?"

"You am, but that can change." The corpse demon plucked a grub from its chest and stroked it with a rat-gnawed finger.

"Ah." I sensed another deal looming. "What do you want?"

"That which is mine. You owe me a hammer, remember?"

"How could I forget, and why the corpse?"

"Why not? I could have come to you as a cloud of flies, a flock of ravens, a gaggle of vengeful chickens, but none of those are much good at digging stupid breeds out of graves."

"If you'd come a day earlier, there wouldn't have been any need to dig."

The demon squeezed the bug and flicked the remains in my face. "I find your priestly friend rather irritating and besides, I don't have time to drop everything and rescue your pathetic carcass, I have civilizations to destroy, cities to level, that kind of thing. The damned make perfectly able minions." He sketched a bow. "You don't have to pay them, they don't answer back, perfect."

"I'm still dead, though."

"Don't sulk, Breed, I can repair the damage, for a price."

"Now why doesn't that surprise me?"

"Because I'm a demon?"

"Aye, that'll be it. So, what do you want, other than a holy relic that belonged to one of the greatest heroes of the Schism War."

He growled at that and fire blazed in the empty eye sockets. "Someone regarded by ignorant fools, as one of the greatest heroes of the Schism War."

"Whatever. Other than his blasted hammer, what else do you require of me?"

"Your immortal soul."

"Really?"

"No, of course not, stupid." The fire faded. "Souls are ten a penny, why would I waste a bargain for yours when there are people eager to give them away for nothing? There are a lot of stupid, bitter people out there, Breed. No, I want you to kill the priest."

"If I kill the priest before my term of servitude is up, I'll die a slow, painful death. I'm not seeing anything in this deal for me."

The demon corpse's eyes glowed blue. The cuff around my wrist became ice cold and rimed with frost. A moment later, a hairline crack raced across the polished surface. The glow in its eyes subsided. Just like that, the bond was broken.

"There. Do we have a deal?"

"Yes, we have a deal, but I need him to get me into the tomb, that's if he's still alive."

"He's alive. You may slay him when he's no longer of use to you."

"Right you are."

The corpse attempted to frown, atrophied muscles creaked. "Ah, Breed, your lack of scruples is heartening. If all mortals are as craven and self-serving as you, the war will be over before the battle has begun."

"You might as well send your spew maggots home now then because I'm a paragon of loyalty and compassion compared to most." I had no intentions of killing the priest, at least not in the foreseeable future, and certainly not at the behest of the demon. Shallunsard's contempt irked me, and for that reason alone I was going to thwart him. Mother was the only person who could treat me like an idiot and get away with it.

"Are you ready?" the demon asked.

I grunted.

"Good. Now hold still, this is going to hurt." The light in the corpse's eyeless sockets flared again. It reached a hand towards me. I wasn't a stranger to pain, but what happened next was a singular experience.

My ribs had been blasted into my heart and lungs. Now every tiny splinter of bone was pulled from the substance of my pulverized organs before knitting back into ribs, right before my eyes. Not only could I see the demon's infernal powers at work, but I could feel them, acutely. I felt every torn vein slither through my ravaged flesh, every fiber of my shredded vitals grow anew. When my lungs were whole again, I screamed to the limit of my breath.

When it was over, the corpse demon lowered its arm. The light faded from its eyes. I rolled around on the ground, reliving the agony of being shot for about ten more minutes until it finally stopped hurting. My chest was whole again, covered in a mass of scarred pink flesh and orange scales.

"Sweet salvation, did it have to hurt so much? My head feels like it's going to burst."

"You should thank me, Breed. Pain is life, only the dead feel nothing. The headache will last until you are reunited with your master."

"What? But you just. I thought you'd sorted that, I thought the bond was broken."

"It is, more or less. I have ensured that you won't die and that you can function, but a little pain will, I feel, lend a measure of urgency to the performance of your task."

"You bastard."

"Demon." He grinned. The corpse shambled off, its head lolling on its broken neck.

Now that I could move again I saw that I was on the edge of a neglected cemetery, overgrown with ivy and crooked saplings. It looked like something that had belonged to a much more prosperous settlement than Little Lea. Cracked tombstones and bleached wooden plaques poked through thick clumps of whiptail grass and grey billows of grand dame's mantle. Although there were no recent burials that I could see, it was probably still used for suicides, murderers, and the occasional warspawn who happened to die in the village.

The corpse stood a moment on the edge of its own grave, staring into the unmarked pit as though contemplating the eternity it would spend rotting in the ground. It turned to me, looked at me with its sightless eyes. Its mouth opened and closed, it reached out to me in a silently pleading gesture as it collapsed into the hole.

* * *

It took me a few attempts to stand up and gain full control of my leaden limbs, but once the blood started flowing again, I let my nose lead me back to Little Lea. It wasn't a hard trail to follow, the smell of ozone and burnt meat clung to the trees in clotted webs. I'm not one to dwell, not even on my own death, so I didn't.

When I reached the edge of the wood, I climbed a warty old fir and took a look-see at the town. From my vantage, I could see a few people milling uncertainly outside the village hall around the semi-circle of blackened ground. Another group had gathered outside the guard tower. If they were still alive, that was where Clary and Halla would probably be holed up. As much as I never wanted to set foot in the miserable dung pit of a village again, I felt invincible now that I knew Shallunsard was looking out for me. I didn't like the idea as such, but as I had more enemies than friends, I was grateful for what help I could get and I was alive, and that was good, particularly after experiencing the alternative. Thus, emboldened and with a new-found zest for breathing, I headed for the village to look for that soft cull Tobias.

I was spotted on the outskirts of town by a pig-eyed plow-boy. I waved all friendly like and he shrieked and ran to his companions. Before I could say 'risen from the dead' they scattered which was terribly rude but that's country folk for you. I headed over to the guard tower and knocked on the door. "Let me in, it's me."

No answer.

I knocked again, louder this time. There was shuffling on the other side and a spy hole opened a crack.

"You're dead. I, I buried you," the old greenshanks croaked.

"You were a bit premature there, but it's the thought that counts. Now let me in before the yokels grow some spine and come back."

I heard snatches of muffled conversation before the bolts were thrown and the door opened. I made sure my shirt was tied to cover my unnaturally healed chest before I went inside. The greenshanks called Dana and the greybeard were waiting with their halberds leveled. Halla and her granddaughter were sitting by the stove. Everyone was giving me the fish eye which came as no surprise.

"Is this it?" I asked. "Where's Tosspot and the priest?"

"How are you standing?" Dana demanded. "You were dead, I saw you. There was a hole in your chest the size of my fist."

I sighed. "You have small fists, and you obviously don't know anything about warspawn. Thoasa can heal just about anything faster and more efficiently than any other race."

"Oh, aye? So, if I run you through you'll be able to heal that will ya?" She set her weapon.

"You, run me through? That's a bit optimistic, don't you think?"

"That's enough, Dana," Greybeard said. He looked tired and his hand was heavily bandaged.

They all looked tired and confused, except for Clary. She was sitting by the fire, swinging her legs, and gnawing a chunk of bread. Tosspot ambled in from the other room clutching a brass-buttoned uniform jacket in his grubby paws. "Can I borrow this?" he asked the greenshanks. "Only, yer Captain won't be needing it no more."

“No, you damn well can’t. Put it back,” Greybeard snapped.

I snatched the jacket from Tosspot and put it on.

“Get your own, demo—” Tosspot began.

Short on patience due to the whole being shot to death incident, I grabbed him by the throat. It would have been so easy to snap his scrawny neck there and then, but I let him go. At least his drug and booze-addled brain accepted without pause that I was back from the dead, and the sooner I could move everyone away from that awkward topic the better.

“I need some weapons, preferably swords, and I need to know who and where they took the priest.”

Greybeard squared up to me. “Now, just you wait a minute. Why should I help you?”

“Because you’re outnumbered.” I gave both greenshanks my best, killer stare. “And I’m in a very bad mood.” I hoped they understood how sincere I was about that. As useless as human senses were, I hoped they both had the wit to realize that I’d end them if they made a wrong move. They relaxed. The woman put up her weapon. I nodded. “Excellent choice. Now, what happened after I was k… shot?”

It turned out not a lot had happened after I went down. Greybeard kept the girl, her grandmother, and Tosspot inside the village hall until the ambushers had thrown Tobias in the back of a wagon and headed off north. The leader of the crew of four sounded very much like the cove who'd attacked the priest in Appleton, the one Father Benedict had called Marius.

When they'd left, the old greenshanks had quite rightly taken me for dead. It was Halla who'd insisted they bury me in the unconsecrated graveyard, given that I was a warspawn which was a lucky escape. The old man thought thoasa should be burnt, as was their custom.

The only noteworthy information I could garner from the greenshanks' and Halla's accounts was that the four humans, one of whom had a firelance, had headed north on the main road.

"Are you going after them?" Greybeard asked while I tried the two swords he'd brought me. They were well balanced, standard issue short swords. I sheathed them and buckled on the scabbards. It felt good to be armed again, splitting headache aside.

"Aye."

"Well, good luck to ye, but I think you're going to need more than a couple of blades to deal with that crew."

"You volunteering?"

He laughed. "Holy Eye, if I hadn't promised to take Halla and Clary to Middleton I might do just that. I don't like what Reynard had us do, not one bit, but I'm near retiring, see? I need my pension." he shrugged.

"Next time then, although there is something you can do, as payment for not killing you." I grinned.

He frowned. "What?"

"Keep Tosspot here until after I've gone. I don't need him following me."

Greybeard nodded. He looked relieved. "All right, I'll do that for ye. Anyway, I'll need him to be a witness when I explain this mess to the area commander. Although, I've no idea how I'm going to explain how you came back from the dead."

"I'd skim over that part if I was you."

He scratched his chin. "Aye, maybe you're right. So, what are you, really?" Given that he was smiling I got the impression that he was more curious than fearful, but I knew that no matter what I said, he'd make up his own mind.

I shrugged. "Just another breed."

* * *

It was dark when I set off north. I ghosted the road, careful to stay in the trees in case any of the denizens of Little Lea still fancied hanging someone. As the ambushers were humans, I was counting on them resting up somewhere after a few hours on the road. They might have even dared an inn this far from real civilization and without any fear of pursuit. About twenty miles from Little Lea, I came across such a place. There weren't any carts outside, just a few journeymen and women inside, huddled around their ale.

I asked the innkeeper if he'd seen my 'friends'. Despite the heavier than normal traffic on the road, he remembered them. They'd stopped briefly and much to the innkeeper's surprise had headed east, away from the main road to Valen. He'd been glad to see the back of them on account of their sick companion who'd stayed in the cart. The innkeeper suspected he had the plague, or worse given how secretive they were about him and how they wouldn't let anybody near the cart.

I dropped him a couple of coppers from Tobias's purse for his trouble. I'd taken the money from the priest's gear. I'd hidden the books in the old graveyard, in the same hole as my rescuer. He could perhaps read them to alleviate the boredom.

My head was pounding, but after a mug of ale and a bowl of something hot, I felt refreshed and eager to track down my killers. I hoped they were enjoying themselves, I hoped they were squeezing every ounce of amusement from every single moment because these were the last few hours they'd be spending this side of hell.

The tree cover and scrub became sparser the further east I went. The ground lay in balding folds that rose into humps and hummocks crowned by fangs of sword thorn bushes. The road dwindled to little more than a scratch in the landscape. My headache was now a rhythmic pulse, a regular thud that kept pace with every step.

I stalked the road, following the faint impression of cart tracks. After a couple of hours, the ground took a sharp, upward sweep. The higher ground had been scoured clean of greenery by rain, harsh sunslight, and freezing winter frosts. It hadn't always been a wasteland, I could see the ghostly outlines of terraces glittering in the moonlight. Here and there the remains of walls scarred the barren landscape, hinting at what had once been. Another mile further on, with the road still climbing, I came across a cart. Nearby, an urux stopped chewing a silvery grey shrub long enough to give me an appraising glance before returning to its meal.

I let the shreds of a lazy headwind roll over my tongue. It had a peculiar taste, a cross between acid and fire. It called to something in my blood, something ancient. My hair spines bristled, the demon mark in my palm itched. I crept over to the cart. It was empty, but the priest's soapy peachy smell clung to the boards. Five sets of footprints vanished over the brow of the hill about twenty feet away. The urux hadn't just escaped, its harness had been unbuckled. Whatever they were planning it didn't seem to involve coming back this way.

Mindful that I might be close to my quarry, I crawled up to the crest of the ridge. The ruffled breeze shifted, drenching me in the strange smell. It was hard to decide if it was the denatured air or the sight that greeted me that made me gasp.

I was on the lip of a vast crater. Level with the rim, the sightless eyes of a huge stone face gazed through me to the west. The face was that of a human woman which had been carved on a tall spire. The spire had snapped across the neck, but it hadn't fallen.

I blinked, unsure if my eyes were playing me false. But they weren't. The tip of the spire had started to fall, to separate along a jagged fissure, but some force held it at an impossible angle. I couldn't guess how long it had hung suspended like that, but there it was, frozen in the gelid air, surrounded by clouds of dust that glittered beneath a sky of serried stars. I dragged my gaze away and peered into the depth of the crater. The face was one of four on the pinnacle of a pyramidal building that looked like the world had risen around it. The crater was littered with other similar, but smaller structures. The civilization that had once flourished here was still dying, caught in the moment of its destruction, probably during the Schism War. The base of the giant stepped pyramid before me was lost in a well of shadows two hundred feet below.

A frosty mist filled the crater, made ghosts of ruins and islands of spires. As I looked more closely I could see shattered columns, porticoes, and statuary hanging in the air around the pyramid and just like the face, they weren't falling. The core of the building was shot through with ragged cracks. Chunks of masonry, some as small as a fist, others as big as an urux, hung at odd angles up to a foot from the main structure, as though locked in the first burst of an explosion. I had no idea if the pyramid had been a palace or a temple. Whatever it was, every tiered level was intricately carved with friezes depicting human figures dancing across the walls. Fantastical winged beasts, the like of which I'd never seen, anchored every corner of the wedge-shaped edifice.

Whatever force held the building in thrall didn't seem to extend more than a few feet beyond the main structure, but it was still unnerving to be so close to something that was in the process of exploding, albeit extremely slowly. That it was Schism-touched was beyond doubt, but I hadn't a clue why the ambushers would have brought the priest here. Five sets of footprints plowed a trail down the ashen slope. Scree marked the places where one or other of them had slipped. Far below, I spied a flicker of light that might have been a campfire.

"Demon," someone behind me hissed.

Tosspot had crept up from downwind and, lucky for him, was beyond the range of my blades. An inch closer and I'd have vented him.

He gave a rasping laugh as he squinted at my sword tip. To add to my profound joy on seeing him, I noticed that he'd brought a friend. Clary gave a shy wave. Cursing, I bundled them both away from the edge of the crater. "What the fuck are you doing here?" I asked. In truth, I was more annoyed that he'd managed to sneak up on me than the fact they were here.

Clary stepped forward. "We've come to help."

"You can't. Go away, go home."

She folded her arms. "No. We're here to help Father Tobias."

"I'll kill that fucking greenshanks. You, take her home," I said to Tosspot. I should have known better than to waste my breath.

He folded his arms. "We're here to help the priest, not you."

I resisted the urge to slap the filthy little gobsnot. "Listen, the priest needs your help like he needs a second arsehole. Now, go away." Clary giggled. Tosspot muttered. Neither of them made any attempt to leave.

"You can't handle these coves alone. They've already killed you once," Tosspot said.

"Wounded. They wounded me." I corrected. They both grinned. "And they caught me by surprise. I can't for one moment imagine what help you think you'd be against a rough crew like these. Now get lost."

"We can keep watch," Clary said.

I was running out of time. A faint band of light was already bleaching the horizon. "Just stay here." I loomed over Tosspot. "I swear, if you follow me, I'll beat you to death with her." The urux let out a massive fart. "Fuck's sake, even animals are mocking me now." They both laughed. If I'd had any reputation left worth keeping, I'd have killed them both and buried them in a shallow grave.

Chapter Thirteen

The steep slopes of the crater were knee-deep in soft dead earth. When I reached the bottom, I avoided touching the unnaturally tilting slabs of stone that were peeling away from the building. I didn't want to wake them from their slumber and remind them that they were supposed to be collapsing. As I edged around the structure, I stepped over a fallen column and roused a cluster of beetles the size of cats. They took to the air on iridescent wings.

I waited to see if their flight had drawn any unwanted attention. The heavy blanket of silence fell again, marred only by the occasional, mournful gust of wind. I continued to make my way round the ruin until I could see the fire I'd spotted from above. Whoever had set it had gone, leaving a couple of packs propped beside it. I was about to go over and search them when the wind shifted, and I caught the faint whiff of something that I couldn't quite place but knew that I probably should. I pressed myself against the wall and tasted the air. Amid the many strands of scent, one stood out, but it took me a minute to recognize what it was. When I did, I almost laughed. The stink of Calthracite was so common back home that I almost ignored it out here, which could have proved fatal, *again*. I made a note of where it was coming from, which if my nose led me right, was somewhere above and to the right of me. I ducked back around the corner out of any possible line of sight and started to climb. The instant my hands touched the wall I knew why nothing grew down here. As well as being freezing, the stone vibrated upon contact as though the pulse of my blood had quickened some latent energy locked within. The intense, low-level thrum made my fingers tingle.

I ignored the strange sensation and followed the trail of scent to its source. The gunner was sitting cross-legged, overlooking the campsite. He had his back to the building and a sleek-barreled firelance resting in the crook of his arm. His shoulder-length, black hair was curled into a mass of glossy ringlets, and he smelled of expensive perfume that was musky-sweet and spicy. He was wearing an elegant, black velvet coat and breeches to match. Silver buttons winked in the darkness. I climbed up to the next tier and carefully inched along until I was directly above him. When I was in position, I dug my feet into the stonework and lowered myself down until I could feel the slight wash of body heat rising off his wiry frame. In one swift movement, I grabbed the barrel of his gun and a fistful of his silky tresses and yanked him off his arse.

He let out a high-pitched shriek and reached for the rapier sheathed at his hip. I ripped the firelance from his grasp and bashed his head against the wall before throwing him off the building. I should have been more careful, the last thing I wanted to do was alert the other three, but this foppish bastard was probably the one who'd shot me, and I was still a tad annoyed about that.

The gunner lay groaning, face down in the dirt. I waited a while but when nobody came rushing to his aid I jumped down. The footsteps I'd seen led to what must have been a balcony but was now a ground-level entrance into the pyramid.

The gunner rolled over and opened his entirely black and glittering eyes. "Urgh. Holy Eye. Didn't I kill you?"

I kicked him in the gut, doubled him over. "Not enough, puke-pail. Although it was a damn good try, I'll give you that."

He rolled over, groaned some more before pushing himself up on his elbow. "I aim to please if you'll pardon the pun. I pray you, would you allow a fellow to take a pinch, I've come over all queer."

"What?"

"Snuff, old thing. Would you mind if I took a pinch of snuff?"

"Help yourself," I said and checked that the lance was primed and loaded.

The gunner sat up and reached inside his coat. A thread of blood dripped from his pointy little nose onto his immaculate, white silk shirt.

I gave him the dead eye. "Finger and thumb, prickling, or you lose the arm." I had every intention of killing him as I felt it only fair to return the compliment he'd paid me, but not before he'd answered a few questions about his crew. He dabbed at his bloody nose with a lace cuff and, with finger and thumb only, tugged a silver snuff-box from his coat pocket. "Tell me about your friends and who hired you?"

He plucked a pinch and sniffed. His fingers were long, pale, and slender and hardly looked strong enough to pull the trigger of the lance, let alone lift the thing. "That's better," he said when he'd passed the point at which he might sneeze. "I believe introductions are in order." He made to rise, I shook my head. He inclined his head and remained seated. "Schiller, Sebastian Schiller, at your mercy, it would seem."

There was a burr to his voice, not quite a buzz, but his entirely black eyes and the cottony body odor lurking beneath the smell of perfume marked him out as something other than merely human. I wasn't sure what, so I kept my distance.

"Breed," I said.

He gave a tight-lipped smile. “Charmed, I’m sure. As to my comrades, we’re honest mercenaries, hired to apprehend the patrician priest. That’s all I know. Do you mind if I stand?”

“Lose the sword, same drill.”

He carefully unbuckled his sword belt and let the weapon drop. “If it’s any consolation I only shot you with a third of a load.”

“Er, no, it’s not. Who hired you, what’s the job?”

“Cassia got me the job, she and I have worked together before. Father Marius hired her, and she found Richter in some dive in Valen. As to why he hired us, who knows? Perhaps they’re having theological differences.” He shrugged elegantly. “I’m just doing what I was paid to do. You really need to ask Marius, but you’ll have to be quick.”

“What do you mean?”

“They’re off to Valen. There’s apparently an apportation device inside.”

“They’re apporting? Why the hurry to get back to Valen?”

“Marius mentioned something about a synod meeting. Look, I honestly don’t pay much attention to the man, he’s a terrible bore. Do you mind if I take off my coat? I feel faint.”

"Very well. How come you're not apporting with them?"

He took off his coat, folded it neatly, and laid it next to his sword. "I'm not going back to Valen because I have business elsewhere."

"*Had* business elsewhere. I don't take kindly to people shooting me." As much as I was itching to see how he took to being shot, I didn't want to alert the others. I drew my sword.

The gunner smirked. "Snuff?" he said and threw the box at me. Although I looked away and held my breath as the cloud of spicy dust enveloped me, the distraction worked. With an impressive display of agility, the gunner leaped into the air and stayed there.

Wings. That explained why he wanted to take his bloody coat off.

As fine as silk, two wings unfurled as he leaped. I dropped my sword and aimed at him by which time he was thirty feet up, gossamer wings beating furiously. If I shot him the others would hear, but if I didn't, he'd get away and maybe ambush me again. The feather-boned bastard laughed. He understood my dilemma.

"Don't worry my scaly friend, I really do have to be elsewhere. I was only contracted until daybreak. But I will want my lance back at some point, so make sure to oil it regularly." He flipped a salute and soared up and out of the crater.

And that was my introduction to Sebastian Schiller, also known as the Mosquito.

I watched him along the length of the barrel, but I didn't pull the trigger because if what Schiller said was true and they apported, I was going to have a very bad headache for a very long time.

The Mosquito's sword was a thing of beauty. A master-crafted weapon, sharp as a needle and absolutely no good to me save as a toothpick. I snapped it in lieu of its owner's neck. After a quick search of the bags for more calth powder and zanthe crystals, I set off to find the others. By the time I'd tucked a few more loads into my belt the stars were fading into the grey gloom of dawn. I hopped over the balcony, sidestepped an eternally falling stone lintel and entered the building.

Daylight would have been cruel to this age-scraped ruin, but night painted grand swags of shadow across the walls that lent the room an air of poetic grandeur. As I explored further I discovered that the strange relic of another age was a labyrinth of dark passageways and rooms. It was a veritable kingdom of darkness and therefore home to me, a noble of the Midnight Court.

I followed the trail of footprints down a broad flight of stairs and was soon rewarded by the echo of voices winding up out of the darkness. I counted a further ten subterranean levels before I found them. One of the kidnappers, a bald cove who I took to be Richter, decided to make my task a little easier by choosing the moment I came upon him to relieve himself with his back to the stairwell. The first he knew that he was not alone was the last he knew of anything. I snapped his neck and let the body lie where it fell.

The doorway at the end of the corridor was flanked either side by slowly crumbling statues. The chips of stone flaking off the granite warriors were, like the building itself, falling over eons instead of seconds. My skin tingled, the air was alive with magical energy. I stole a quick look inside the room, ever mindful that the Mosquito might be behind me, waiting for his chance to strike.

To my great relief, the first person I saw was Tobias and he was alive. He was bound and gagged, sitting on the floor with his back to one of the dozens of the dark glassy menhirs that ringed the room. The fangs of stone were veined with gold and no two were alike. Tobias was glaring at the bastard who'd tried to kill him back in Appleton.

A woman who must have been Cassia was pushing one of the stones. I saw now that they were bedded into metal grooves that were set in the floor. Bearing set in the grooves allowed the stones to be slid with relative ease around a series of concentric circles.

"Now move the 4th of the 2nd to the meridian of Canuta," the bearded fuck ordered the woman. He was pacing and reading from a scroll. "Ah, no, correction, move the 2nd of the 4th to the meridian of Canuta."

"Are you sure?" she asked.

"Of course, I'm sure."

"You said that last time."

"I know what I said last time. Just do what I say now. Where's Richter?"

"He went for a piss."

"What, now? I need him in here."

"When you have to go you have to go."

"Just hurry up and move that and then get him in here. Or we're going without him."

Tobias shook his head. He seemed to be laughing behind the gag, something that did not go unnoticed. It earned him a hard slap across the head from the man I guessed was Marius.

"I'm glad you think this is funny, brother. I wonder if you'll be laughing when father sees you. Cassia, go find Richter, the circle is almost complete."

The woman shot Marius a filthy look before she left the room muttering to herself. "Move the keystones, Cassia, find Richter, shove a broom up your arse and sweep the floor."

She was still grumbling when I hit her in the face with the butt of the firelance. There was an audible crack, her head snapped back, and her nose exploded in a burst of crimson. I caught her before she fell and dumped her beside Richter.

I checked that the zanthe crystal was secure in the firing claw and, just to be on the safe side, poured another charge of calth down the barrel.

"Cassia! Cassia? There's one more stone to align. Cassia where the—"

Marius didn't finish his sentence because I stuck the barrel of the firelance in his face as he stepped into the corridor. After this brief introduction, I backed him into the room and prepared to spray his brains all over the stones. I waved at Tobias and took careful aim.

The priest shook his head violently and yelled something through the gag. I lowered the gun. Marius opened his mouth to say something. Just in case he was a sorcerer I cracked him on the side of the head with the butt of the firelance. He went down but was still conscious, and made to get up, so I hit him again. This time he lay nice and quiet. Tobias frowned and although I couldn't make out what he was saying, he was unhappy about something, despite having just been rescued. There was just no pleasing some people.

"What?" I said to Tobias, knowing full well that he couldn't answer. "I didn't want him to do to me what you did to those villagers now did I?" I went over to where he was sitting in the innermost ring of stones. The air was different here, it stank of blood and steel and felt heavy as though a storm was about to break. I untied his hands. He had a black eye but seemed no worse for his ordeal. Now that I'd found him, my headache vanished.

He scowled at me. "Marius said they'd killed you." He got up and went over to Marius.

"You're welcome. No, please, don't mention it. Oh, you didn't."

"He said they shot and killed you and yet here you are like nothing happened." He rolled Marius over. The side of his face was swollen but he was alive and moaning, more's the pity.

"They lied to you. So, why are they after you, priest?" I asked in a bid to change the subject.

"Nothing. A misunderstanding." He turned to me. "Who the hell are you, Breed?"

We stood there for a long time, weighing the lies we were telling each other against the truths we were keeping to ourselves.

"I met the gunner, Schiller. He said he used a light load so that he didn't catch you in the blast and so that he could get extra range. He shot me, just not enough." Satisfied that my story was convincing, I leaned on the firelance and waited for him to spill.

"Marius is a priest of the Order of the Sanguine Shadow and a fellow member of the Synod. Our respective orders had a theological dispute."

I waited some more.

The priest flipped Marius on his front, bound his hands behind him and, with a deal of relish, gagged the semi-conscious man. "There's a prophecy that says the demons will return. This much was accepted by all, and indeed, seems to be happening as predicted. Some factions within the Synod are using the prophecy to push for all non-humans to be removed from the Empire. It's a populist tactic, designed to win votes."

I shrugged. "It's not the first time. The 'Send Them to Shen' campaign reached Appleton. Bunch of crackpots, nobody paid them any heed."

"This is worse, much worse."

"Tell me later. Right now, we better get going. I don't know if Schiller's still hanging around." I made to leave but Tobias grabbed my arm.

"No, we're going back through the angle gate." He gestured to the stones. I didn't see any gate, just four concentric rings of six-foot-tall slices of stone set in steel and marked by symbols.

"Ah. yes, this is the apportation device," I said as though I knew what I was talking about.

"Oh, you're familiar with the concept? The magic is pre-Schism. Saint Bartholomew understood that there was a vast web of interconnected—"

"Yes, I'm sure he did, he was clearly a very clever fellow. But do you have to use it? I've heard some old Schism magic isn't safe."

"It isn't, and I do, I'm afraid. I need to get back and deal with the trouble Marius and his faction are trying to foment. There's no time to waste."

"How many can go through?" I asked, hoping the answer was two.

"As many as can fit within the inner ring, a dozen or so in this case. Why?"

"Just wait here, I've got to go pick a few things up."

* * *

An hour later, just as the suns were rising, I returned with Tosspot and Clary.

"What are they doing here?" Tobias asked. Marius and the woman were conscious, bound and gagged and propped against the wall by the door. They glared venomously at me. I resisted the urge to kick them as I passed.

"Because some aching-heart holy man thought he could make the world a better place by adopting any waif and stray that crossed his path, without any thought to what might happen to them in the future. Do you want me to turn them loose? I can dump 'em back on the highway for the wolves if you like."

Tosspot reached out to touch one of the stones, but Clary slapped his hand away. "We had to hide from the Dandyman," she said in the matter-of-fact way children spoke. “He killed the urux and sucked its blood, but I’m good at hiding, aren’t I, Rubin?”

Tosspot nodded. “Yes, Clary, very good.”

Tobias looked like he’d just received a blessing from the angel of guilt. “We can’t leave them. I just have to make sure I get the angles right with this thing.”

I’d already decided they were coming with us, but I let him think the decision was his. “As you wish. So, where will this thing take us? Only, I’d rather not appear in the middle of Valen’s high street.”

Tobias grinned. “Don’t worry, Breed that won’t happen.”

Chapter Fourteen

I'd never been able to apport. Mother is a master of that particular sorcerous art, but all I could do was boil water and make light. It's the thoasa in me, warspawn can't use magic. That I could cast any spells at all was an aberration, and a testament to what excellent tuition and sound, regular beatings can achieve.

This was something different to what Mother did. This was an apportation device, a sorcerous machine from the time of the Schism. Looking at the gleaming slices of calthracite crystal it was hard to imagine a world where these things were common, and my sire's ancestors didn't exist. For all that their palaces were grand, their civilization mighty, and their magic powerful, I couldn't help thinking that it must have been a dull world with only humans around.

Schiller hadn't shown his face again, but I kept a weather eye out for him, just in case and set Tosspot to keep watch over Marius and Cassia. We'd had to truss them up because, apparently, it would be barbaric to slit their throats. Tobias set to work adjusting the stones, taking copious notes, and doing a lot of muttering and head-scratching. Clary seemed happy to sit and watch what was going on.

"Is it nearly ready?" I asked. I was bored and more than a little disturbed by being in a building that was collapsing around us really slowly, even dust particles caught by our turbulence drifted across the room like threads of smoke. "I said, is it ready?"

The priest hurled his notebook across the room.

"I'll take that as a no then."

"I just." He sighed, rubbed his head with his stump. "If I've miscalculated I could send us miles, even continents off course, or worse, send us somewhere that no longer exists."

I waved away his insecurity. "Don't worry, you're good at all this angle stuff. It'll be fine, I'm sure, I've got a good feeling about this." Right then I was feeling supremely confident of my ability to survive anything having escaped death's mean grasp once. I was also eager to be in Valen and one step closer to the Hammer of the North's tomb.

"That's easy for you to say, but if I get an equation wrong…"

"Your head will explode. Yes, I know all about the Paradox of Power, or whatever you've decided to call it. You'll be fine."

He stopped what he was doing, the look on his face hardened. "Marius and the others were adamant that they'd killed you. How did you survive, Breed?"

I sighed. "Not this again."

"How?"

"Why does it matter, sorcerer? Just be glad that I did."

Marius gave the mercenary a knowing look. Damn the man, but he was enjoying this.

"Don't you understand? They don't want to hurt me, Breed. It's you and your kind they want to destroy."

"Yes, I got that impression when they shot me, but, and correct me if I'm wrong, didn't he have a knife at your throat the first time I saw you? This cove just has a taste for killing."

"Marius and his faction want to be rid of people like you and Clary; all warspawn, all Schism-touched. The demons' return was prophesied, and he and his cronies are seeking to make capital from it."

"That's ridiculous," I laughed half-heartedly.

"Which part, Breed? Do you dispute that demonic forces are at work? Is that even possible after what you've seen?" He folded his arms and gave me a measured look.

The urge to slap him was once again upon me. Given his abilities, I refrained. "Yes, I do. I think it's a steaming pile of urux shit."

"I have proof that it isn't." He cast a triumphant glance at Marius, who was shouting through his gag and kicking his heels like an angry child. The mercenary elbowed him in the ribs.

"Go on," I said, dreading what Tobias was going to say. My palm itched.

"The prophecy," he said.

I breathed a quiet sigh of relief.

"The one I found while researching the life of Saint Bartholomew."

"You need to get out more."

He poked me in the chest with his stump. "This is serious, Breed. You know what you saw in Appleton. It is happening, the demons have returned."

"A few big maggots don't prove anything."

"The prophecy I found was written by the Red Witch herself."

I pretended to stifle a yawn.

He gave me a look laced with fury. “It speaks of a time when the demons will return, and it infers that the warspawn will aid them.”

“Might I remind you of my earlier comment with regards to urux shit? Warspawn were made to fight against demons, not with them.” I ignored the nagging little voice that suggested my association with Shallunsard could be construed as aiding demons. That the Red Witch might have scryed my malefaction, might have seen me, sent a shiver down my spine.

“Indeed, they were, but the wording of the prophecy is ambiguous and has been used by some within the Synod to make political capital.”

“By ‘some’ you mean this cocksnot?” I pointed the lance at Marius, who tried to hide behind a disgruntled-looking mercenary.

“Lower the weapon.” Tobias sighed. “Marius is a greedy halfwit, but the blame for this mess lies with me.” He scratched his close-cropped pate. “At first, I only discovered part of the prophecy. I shouldn’t have told the Synod anything until I’d found the whole of it. I should have known it would be used for base, political gain.” He tucked his stump into his sleeve. “I was just so excited. So few texts survive from the time of the Schism, and it was written and signed by the Red Witch.”

"I understand, I do." I tried not to sound too pleased that he'd failed to connect me with the infernal disaster that had befallen Appleton. "Why, only last month a colleague and I were lamenting the lack of good books." The conversation I'd had with Wulf had gone more along the lines of what was better to wipe one's arse upon. We decided that thin-leafed books of poetic whimsy and fanciful tales were much nicer than dry old texts, but weighty tomes stuffed with history, philosophy and other fantasies were much more absorbent. It seemed that a lot of old shit soaked up a lot of shit.

"I've been terribly naïve, to the detriment of all," said the priest. Marius sniggered. "If you don't shut up, I'll let Breed shoot you." Marius stopped laughing. "Come, Breed, walk with me."

It rankled that I had to pretend that I was still bound to the soapy cull, but I had to tickle this fish carefully. I still needed him, and he could turn me to cinders without breaking a sweat, so I followed him from the chamber.

"I knew the manuscript was incomplete, but the Synod immediately debated what I'd found, as though that was the whole of it, despite my protestations."

"Well, that's all very unfortunate, but why are you telling me? Why aren't you back in Valen arguing with the Synod or, you know, turning them into a smoking pile of charcoal?"

He scowled. "I'm going to pretend you didn't say that. I couldn't go back until I'd found the missing part and I did, in our chapter house in Appleton, just before I met you. I sent word back to Valen to try to halt the Synod vote until I got back. That was my second mistake." He leaned against the wall, his gaze drifting to the cooling carcass of Richter. "Seems everything I do turns sour. Maybe father's right, maybe I am cursed."

"Sorry?"

"Never mind. Suffice it to say, I told someone I thought I could trust and he told his son."

"What does the second part say?"

"That we will be saved by a warspawn."

"Well, that's wonderful. You should go back and tell the arch mumblers in the Synod."

"I'll most likely be arrested before I get to the Synod. I was accused of theft of the original document, a total fabrication."

"You're a Vulsones, who'd dare swear falsely against you? Who'd dare swear against you at all, come to that?"

"My father."

"Why would? Ah. He's the one you told, the one who betrayed you."

"Aye, to Marius and his faction."

"Marius isn't just a religious 'brother' is he?"

"No, he's my actual brother, not that there's much love lost between us."

I had to laugh. These so-called nobles were no better than us sewer-dwellers when it came down to it. They just smelled sweeter. "Do you want me to kill him? I'm an only child and it's never done me any harm."

"No, absolutely not. I forbid it."

"He was fixing to kill you back in Appleton, or have you forgotten?"

"No, he wasn't, he was just threatening me. He wanted the part of the prophecy that I'd tracked down to our monastery in Appleton."

"Did he get it?"

"No."

"Well, that's a relief."

"I sent it to our father for safekeeping before my brother arrived."

"Oh."

"Quite. Father sent Marius to keep me out of the way until after the Synod votes."

"Why not sit on you out here?"

"Because Marius wanted to get back for the Synod meeting. The leader of Marius's order is going to stand for Eklesiasti. If she wins, she'll make sure that warspawn are banished from the Empire."

"Oh."

"Is that all you have to say?"

I shrugged. "Oh, shit?"

It took another hour of scribbling, handwringing and pushing stones back and forth before myself, Clary and Tosspot were invited to join Tobias on the central platform within the rings of stones.

"Remember, Breed, just shoot the stone. Do not shoot my brother."

After a long and tiresome debate, the priest had agreed that I could destroy one of the stones to stop Marius following us when he eventually got free. I played along to keep him sweet. Death and the demon had freed me from servitude to the priest, and now I needed the priest's help to free me from the demon.

I turned to Tosspot and Clary. "You two sure you want to come?" I wasn't overly bothered what they decided. A big city like Valen had rich enough pickings to keep a couple of coves like those two alive. Clary nodded.

"Got to see the city, demon, got to see the city one last time." Tosspot coughed. He looked in worse shape than the restless dead Shallunsard had possessed. His skin was sallow and drawn as tight as rawhide over the fleshless planes of his face. I wasn't surprised he was keen to go to Valen, it had been days since he'd had any pel or drink.

"Is everyone ready?" the priest asked. I nodded. He gave me one of his sad-and-disappointed smiles and raised his hands. "Remember what I said, Breed."

"Trust me." I pretended to aim at one of the stones. As soon as the priest turned his attention to casting the spell, I aimed up on Marius.

Luckily for him, the shock of apportation caused me to miss. When the spell was cast, it felt like I was being dragged backwards into the teeth of a calthracite grinder. Through the ghostly sandstorm of a disintegrating world, I saw the flash blaze from the lance's muzzle and a million, shining points of light erupt in another place and time.

By the time the roaring echo of the shot died, we were somewhere else. The scintillating air turned black and jarringly solid. For a moment it felt like I'd just stepped into my skin and it didn't quite fit. I decided that apportation by device was the most unpleasant thing I'd experienced other than being killed.

I was about to step forward when I sensed something in front of me. I tucked the lance under my arm and cast a light spell. The pale globe grew into a ball of diffuse light which revealed a jumble of stones that had partially fallen and jammed against each other to form a low roof of jagged angles. Unlike the one we'd just left, this room had not been warped by Schism magic and had fallen wholly into time's withering grasp. The rings of stones had survived but crumbling masonry crowded around them like a pack of hungry dogs. It was pure luck that we hadn't apported into rubble. I took a breath, tasted fresh air.

"Dark in here, innit?" Tosspot giggled.

Tobias leaned heavily on one of the stones.

"Sit down before you fall," I said to him.

Tobias sat. "Where did the light come from?"

"Me. I think I see a way out." I ducked past the jutting blocks and set off towards a paler patch of darkness that I could see in the distance. "Stay here and keep quiet while I take a look."

The taste of fresh air grew stronger, the kiss of a breeze brushed my skin and stirred cobwebs that draped the shadowed exit. Cracked and at a rakish angle, a carved bloodstone door lintel still held, but the rich veins of scarlet had bled from the stone and streaked the canted uprights with rusty tears. I loaded the firelance. Priming the pan and ramming a charge home was easy, though it took a few attempts to lock the zanthe crystal into the tiny claw. The weapon wasn't designed with hands like mine in mind.

A locked iron grille sliced daylight into rust-framed rectangles. We weren't in a city, we were in a cemetery and an old one at that. I smashed the lock off with the butt of the firelance and took a look-see outside. The cemetery had been built on a steep-sided valley. Ancient tombs jostled for space and climbed in tiers one upon another. Some had been robbed of bloodstone and gold-veined marble, others were rigged with ropes and blocks, ready for dismantling but the thieving tackle had been abandoned decades ago and left to rot. Down below on the road, an old cart was laid on its side like a dead drunk, its axle crushed under the weight of broken statuary.

It was a typical human cemetery. Mausoleums thrust spires to the sky, oversized porticos sheltered flattering statues of the wealthy dead. Warspawn don't go in for this kind of thing. It seems we weren't bred to think overmuch about how we'd look or what people would think of us when we were dead, which is handy as most warspawn in the Empire are dirt-poor.

The ghostly outline of the disused road snaked out of the valley. The spires of the necropolis walled the world from view, but I guessed we must have been near a big city, given the size of this place and the smell of sewage and wood smoke that rolled down the valley on a lusty breeze.

"The cemetery was built on the site of old Valen, part of it anyway," Tobias said when he got his wind back and joined me by the entrance. "I thought we'd come out near the Halls of State, but of course, they weren't built until after the War."

"How far is it to the new city?" I asked.

He half smiled. "That sounds so odd. Er, a little under an hour on foot, I'd say. I must confess, I've never walked here." The priest leaned against a wall, he was still as pale as pastry that had been rolled too thin.

"The suns are setting. We should stay here the night," I suggested. "We can decide our next move on the morrow."

"The morrow. Yes, good idea." Tobias slid down the wall. "In the old days, they had six dedicated technicians to control translocation." He threw up.

I stepped back. "I can see why."

* * *

I sent Clary and Tosspot to collect firewood while I found us a nice tomb to hole up in. I chose a grand, old mausoleum that still had its heavy bronze door hanging from a single hinge leaving just enough of a gap for me to crawl inside. According to the name engraved on the lintel, the occupant was a merchant called Amari Geran. His massive, bloodstone sarcophagus stood in the center of the empty chamber. A person-sized hole had been chiseled in the side causing the veins of liquid scarlet ore to bleed out. I had a shufti inside, just to make sure the occupant wasn't the animated kind waiting to jump out and surprise us. He wasn't. Amari's bones lay scattered amid shreds of faded grave clothes. His coffin had been smashed open and his remains roughly plundered for what gold and gems his family had decided to donate to the grave-robbers. The wind whistled under the bronze door, but it would serve us well enough. I half carried, half dragged the priest inside Amari's grand, corpse crib and propped him against the sarcophagus.

"Tell me about the demon," he asked without preamble when he came round.

I poked around the tomb, affected a casual air of disinterest. "Which one would that be? I've known a few in my time."

"Listen, Breed, there comes a time in everyone's life when they must make a choice. For some few, the choice they make can affect hundreds, sometimes thousands of peoples' lives."

I picked dirt from under my claws with one of the greenshanks' blades. "Have you ever considered that they might not give a shit? Have you considered that option? They might think, 'Fuck everyone else, as they have fucked me over the years.' They might be so used to being crapped on that they cannot ever imagine a circumstance where they would give a flock of flying-monkey arseholes about anyone, other than perhaps a tiny handful of people. Even then, not enough to stir their conscience above not actually stabbing those lucky few to death for a bent penny piece."

"I can only imagine the life you've had and how difficult it's been." He propped himself up on his elbow.

His breath smelled of peaches. "You have a choice. I've read the prophecy. I've seen the mark on your hand."

"What mark? What are you talking about?"

He beckoned me closer. I went over, knelt beside him. "That night in Appleton, when you saved me, that's when I saw it." He lowered his voice. "I knew then that you and I were meant to meet. It took me a while to find the right official to bribe, but eventually, I had you released into my care."

I had to laugh at that. "Released into your care? Funny, I thought you had me bound to you as a slave."

"The bond goes both ways."

"No, it doesn't."

"Well, all right, it doesn't, but it was the only way I could think of to get you out. I had to pay a lot of money, there were other interested parties who wanted you to go to the mines and die there."

I stabbed my blade into the crack between flagstones. "Well, I've quite literally died for you since then, so I think that more than makes up for your misguided attempt to 'help' me. And for your information, I wouldn't have spent longer than a week in the mines."

Exhausted, he leaned back against the sarcophagus. "No, probably not. Not with the bounty on your head. Don't worry, I paid that too."

This was the first I'd heard about an actual bounty, although I should have guessed there would be one. "How much was it?" I asked, my professional pride getting the better of me.

"Five hundred crowns, plus one hundred for the inconvenience and hurt caused."

I laughed. Five hundred was a good price. Such a high bounty wouldn't do my reputation any harm at all. "'Inconvenience and hurt.' Pork Chop has a sense of humor, I'll give him that."

"It wasn't Jing, it was someone called Mother Blake. Apparently, she's the head of another den of thieving murderers. I dread to think what you must have done to gain her enmity, but it's not too late to change, Breed."

Right at that moment I found a whorl of sandy grit on the floor to be the most fascinating thing in the world. I ignored the priest's prattle in favor of studying how the tiny peak curved so precisely that it might have been cut by a scalpel blade instead of the breeze that snaked inside the tomb and drew patterns in the dust. It was quite remarkable. "Five hundred's a good price," I said and meant it. "I know a fistful of coves who'd do me for free."

"Only a fistful?" Tobias smiled. "Tell me about the demon."

After his latest revelation, I was more than happy to shift the topic of conversation away from bounties and who'd issued them. "It's called Shallunsard. It tricked me into freeing it, and for my trouble I got a mark in my palm to dog me the rest of my days. There you have it. The simple, embarrassing truth. Happy now?" I knew my patter was sweet. I could blend truth and lies with the skill of a master alchemist when I had to.

The priest thought about it a good while before nodding. He looked disappointed. I didn't give a shit. Wrapped in our own thoughts the only sound in the tomb was the wind. Eventually, the priest broke the silence. "Let me tell you about the prophecy."

"Actually, it's six hundred, which is a *really* good price. She must give a damn to put that much up." The more I thought about what Mother had done, the less bad it seemed. Tobias cleared his throat. I looked up. "Yes. Sorry. The prophecy. Please, tell me a story."

"You can be very irritating sometimes."

"It's been mentioned. Do go on."

"The manuscript I discovered spoke of a time when the demons and their infernal minions will return. I believe this is happening now. Some of my colleagues in the Synod have interpreted the wording of the Red Witch's prophecy to mean that warspawn are among the ranks of the infernal. Particularly one paragraph that says warspawn will aid the demons. I think it refers to one warspawn, not all warspawn." He paused as though waiting for me to confirm what we were both thinking. I didn't, I kept my mouth shut. He shook his head. "I think that part refers to you."

"Now wait a minute, I didn't plan on freeing the demon. It tricked me."

"I believe you," he said, which surprised me. "Gods help me, but regarding this, I believe you." He waved his stump at me. "Do not think I extend that faith to every word that falls out of your mouth."

I laughed. "Fair enough. Now, supposing Shallunsard and his cronies are planning on laying waste to civilization again. Surely, having warspawn fighting for the humans makes more sense than kicking them out of the Empire?"

"Those who own calthracite mines disagree, for obvious reasons. People like my father. He's backing the imbecilic racial purists out of greed. It's sickening, and he is not alone."

"Well, nothing we can do then, is there?" I was still thinking about the bounty Mother had put on my head, trying to angle the cold deed in a light that showed she cared about me, in her own twisted way. It wasn't easy. As for the prophecy stuff, Tobias was talking about, I gave not one shit for what a bunch of robe wearing, knife-tongued coves in the Synod were plotting. I wanted nothing to do with the schemes of princes.

"Is that all you have to say?" He looked shocked.

"What do you want me to say? I'm not the official representative of all warspawn, you know. I speak for one, me. So it'll go badly for the warspawn, nothing new in that is there? Some will live, some will die, life will go on."

"I don't understand you, Breed."

"That much is obvious."

"Listen," He leaned close. "The second part of the prophecy, the part I found in Appleton, said that a warspawn will lead the fight against the infernal forces. One who is cursed by demons and blessed by gods." He looked at me expectantly.

"I'm only half what you're after. Sorry, priest, but I've not been blessed by any gods."

He shook his head. "I prayed, Breed. I sought the guidance of Saint Bartholomew. When I was in Appleton I prayed for a sign, and you came."

Now I felt sorry for him. "It's just coincidence. I'm not who you're looking for."

"It also says, 'Only the one who has been blessed and cursed shall wield the hammer of the North'. We can find out if you're the one and at the same time silence the malcontents in the Synod."

I was instantly converted. "Sorry, what was that you say? The who can do what with the what?"

"According to the parchment I found in our library in Appleton, only one blessed by the gods can wield the hammer. You must have heard of the Hammer of the North?"

"Of course I have. Despite appearances, I don't live under a rock."

"Good. Now listen. I have a plan, it's very simple, but if it works, it will prove that the prophecy is genuine and not even my father would dare gainsay the gods. We can stop this travesty before it goes any further."

"Let me guess, we find the hammer, I wield it and we show the Synod, thus verifying the prophecy?"

"I told you it was simple." He beamed, the ever-present furrow in his brow softened.

I couldn't believe what I was hearing. "What's in it for me?" I tried to sound cool about it.

"You get to be a hero, demon," said Tosspot as he crawled through the gap under the door.

"Aren't you dead yet?"

"Not yet." Tosspot's red-rimmed eyes shone like beetle backs in the narrow slice of sunslight. "Got to see the city one more time. See the Hall o' Heroes."

Chapter Fifteen

At dawn of the next day, the priest went alone to the city to contact his order. I climbed one of the tombs to keep watch on the road and wait for his return while Tosspot and Clary busied themselves hunting rock rats for the pot. Nailed above the rusting cemetery gates was a makeshift sign promising harsh penalties for anyone other than those entering with rightful business. The sign was as old as the bones that lay scattered about the place, scavenged by dogs and rats from the plundered tombs of the ancient great and good.

It occurred to me that I spent a lot of time in cemeteries these days. I wasn't sure if it was a step up or down from sewers. What was a step up, was owning a firelance.

From my vantage point, crouched between the turrets of one of the larger mausoleums, I could see the walls of Valen to the east. Slick and shining grey against an iron sky, they were imposing even from a distance. A highway skirted the cemetery, but further west I could see the faint outlines of other, long-abandoned roads leading from nowhere to nowhere, stretching across the scrubby fields that were studded with the plowed rubble of old Valen.

It started to rain again, but I was as mindful as a tyrant's wet-nurse about the care of the firelance and made sure to keep the barrel and the pan covered with an oiled cloth that Schiller had thoughtfully left with his gear. Until recently, I'd thought there was some skill in using one of these beasts, but truth was any fool could do it, as I had so ably proved. An army equipped with firelances would be devastating. And whoever supplied the calth powder and zanthe crystals to that army would be rich indeed. All you needed was a nice, bloody war, and now thanks to me that looked likely.

I also realized that as villains went, Mother was an amateur compared to the powerbrokers in the Synod and the Senate. I looked to the south where storm clouds were gathering and thought of Shallunsard. I was sure that I could hear the distant growl of thunder or perhaps it was the sound of an army of demonspawn baying for blood and vengeance.

It was late in the afternoon when Tobias wandered into view. He was leading a jacanta. Like urux, the scaly beasts of burden were slow and dependable but about half the size, and far more tractable. The jac trotted along, saddlebags bouncing. I sighted Tobias down the barrel, just for practice and waited until I was sure he hadn't been followed before hopping across tombs back to our temporary home. We were not alone in the ruins, wild dogs, human flotsam, and plump rock rats eyed us suspiciously from the shadows but wisely kept their distance.

"Ah, Breed there you are." Tobias tossed me a brown robe when I got back. It was much like the one he was wearing and those that Tosspot and Clary were examining.

The two of them were laughing at the garments. They'd formed an inexplicable friendship in the short time they'd known each other, Tosspot entertained Clary by making up nonsense songs and she made sure he ate and drank. It kept them out of my spines, something for which I was grateful.

"It might be a little tight across the shoulders, but it should be long enough," the priest said as I eyed the garment doubtfully.

"You've seen your people then?" I asked and tried on the robe. It was tight and didn't cover my feet. "Do you have any thoasa acolytes? Only my feet are a dead giveaway that I'm not human."

"And they stink," Tosspot added. Clary laughed.

"You could wear a necklace of urux arseholes and not smell any worse for it, you old turd-mangler." I snapped.

The three of them sniggered. "I'm glad I amuse you all. What's your plan, priest?"

"We take Clary and Rubin to the mission house, and I'll speak with the order, after which I imagine you and I will be able to go to the Hall of Heroes and the tomb of the Hammer."

"That's it? They're just going to let us in, let us open the tomb, nick his hammer, and walk out again? If you don't mind me saying, it sounds a little optimistic."

"Why wouldn't they let us in? The hall is open to all citizens of the Empire," he grinned.

"What, that really is your plan? I was joking. It won't work."

"Have a little faith, Breed."

"No amount of praying ever sprang a lock."

"A debatable point. Just trust me when I tell you that the matter is in hand. Now, first things first, we need to get into the city." He scowled, stepped back, and rubbed his chin with his stump.

"What is it?" I inspected myself, keen to discover why he looked like he was trying to shit a porcupine. "What's wrong? Is it the color? Doesn't brown go with orange? What is it?"

"Although I'm sure there aren't any restrictions, I've never met any warspawn in the order and, well, you're right, your feet are very distinctive. Your hair we can hide beneath the cowl, your hands are human enough to pass in gloves. Hmm, but then there's your feet. Can you wear shoes?"

"You ever met a thoasan cobbler?"

The priest sighed. "We need to think of something else."

And so, it came to pass that the three of them traveled to the city dressed as members of the Order of Saint Bartholomew and I got to lead the jacanta, dressed in my own worn breeches and shirt, silver cuff on display to show that I was bondservant to a parcel of fools. My beautiful firelance, my swords, and the stolen jacket had been wrapped in the robe that didn't fit me and strapped to the jac.

"It smells bad," Clary said as we approached the towering gates of Valen which were flanked by two carved reliefs of gods with the bodies of lions and eagle wings fifty feet wide, spread across the implacable walls.

The gods, one male, one female, gazed at each other across the copper-clad gates that outshone the suns when the clouds fleetingly parted. Towers as big as castles anchored the hundred-foot-high walls which were patrolled by entire companies of spear-wielding knights.

Before we reached the gates, we passed through a tented encampment that must have been as big as Appleton. Clary was right, it smelled, but no worse than any city on a summer's day. As a born thief, I knew that where there was shit, there was gold, and by the smell of it there was a lot of wealth in Valen. On the hour, the gates were slowly pulled open by two teams of four urux. The All-Seeing Eye etched into the gates gazed down on us and a hundred other travelers who were waiting to enter.

I wasn't convinced that the main gate was the best way to enter the city, given that the priest's enemies were looking for him, but he assured me it was safer than trying to sneak in through the sewers or over the walls that he said were heavily guarded and warded by sorcery.

Once we got through the outer gates, we were funneled along a walled road that was also heavily patrolled. At the end of the road there was a second set of gates, plainly decorated, but equally sturdy, and two ramps leading into a city the like of which I'd never seen.

One ramp rose fifty feet above the ground and widened into squares and avenues which were supported by massive towers and arching columns that stretched above and below the walkways. The other ramp sloped gently down into the shady, stone and steel underground of the city. Iron grilles spanned the spaces between the higher roads and frilled the edges of the raised plazas. The grilles allowed light and air to filter down and no doubt stopped careless citizens and heavy debris falling into the busy undercity. It was the most incredible thing

I'd ever seen. Sure, it lacked the beauty of pre-Schism architecture, but the ingenuity and scale were impressive.

When Tobias and the others shuffled past the guard at the ramps the priest offered a benediction. The guard nodded and smiled politely until she saw me. As I passed, she eyeballed the cuff and her expression hardened but she waved me through after the others.

"Durstan the Third was afraid that if his feet ever touched the ground he'd turn to stone, so he had those areas of the city he frequented raised up," the priest said, anticipating my question.

It struck me as odd how madness and power seemed to go hand in hand at all levels of society. "Makes you wonder how there ever came to be a Durstan the Fourth." I mused aloud.

Tobias shot me a wry smile. "He killed his father."

"Now why doesn't that surprise me? I take it the poor folk live down below?"

Tobias gave me a pointed look. "No, we kill all the poor folk and use their bodies for fuel."

"I hear patricians burn better, all that fat."

He laughed. "Some of the less well-off live down there, aye, but it's also where the markets are. We have to stable the jac here, they're not allowed on the highways."

"What about our gear?" I asked.

Tobias grinned and took the jacanta to a stable that was just beside the gate, where he exchanged it for a token. I then became the pack animal, like a dozen other poor culls waiting by the gate, only they were getting paid for their labor. When I was loaded with our belongings we took the high ramp into the city. As we walked, I looked down through the grille to see a whole other city stretched out beneath us. The stink rising from the depths was intense, not just of filth but of animals, spices, and smoke from a hundred ovens. My nose started to run, beset as it was by so many new aromas.

The highways that linked open plazas and elegant courtyards and were thronged with culls and coves of every stripe. The only animals that were allowed were defanged uxatzi. The docile giants made slow progress around the city, pulling huge covered wagons. Due to a lack of animal traffic and several public latrines, the streets were amazingly clean. There were even culls going around with carts whose sole purpose seemed to be shoveling up the uxatzi dung and trundling it away.

When a wagon slowly rolled past us, I could hear music and laughter coming from inside. Sweet-smelling smoke curled from a copper chimney poking through the wagon's rear wall. The six-legged uxatzi pulling it was brightly painted, its capped horns were garlanded with silk and hung with silver bells.

“What the hell are they?” I asked as we followed the beast into a massive plaza studded with squat towers.

“They’re stair towers. They’re for access as well as support.”

“No, I mean the wagons. What’s in them?”

He smiled, clearly amused by my ignorance. “Taverns, chai houses, gambling dens, and brothels that cater to every taste. It’s best to avoid those with black silk tied to the uxatzi’s horns unless you like pain.”

I laughed. “Pain’s more an occupational hazard than a pleasure.”

I’d just about stopped sneezing by the time we were halfway across the plaza as my nose became accustomed to the host of new and exotic smells. The eastern section of the city was dominated by the palace of the Empirifex that rose above Valen like a gilded mountain. Tame dagori glided in lazy circles around the highest levels of the palace, their gossamer wings shimmered crimson and azure, their ululating song rang out across the city.

Tobias led us north. As we traveled, I realized Valen wasn’t just on two levels but here and there the ramps dipped into wide basins and open marketplaces, and where the city feathered out at the edges, neat streets of modest dwellings sheltered beneath the mighty walls.

Upper and lower city came together in split-level markets and gardens. Tall, skinny trees speared out of brick-walled valleys, eager to reach sunslight. Their upward sweeping limbs were hung with lanterns and signs proclaiming the type of goods being sold below.

From what I could tell, the different markets specialized in one type of merchandise, from silks to spices, meat to livestock. One of the ramps we took dipped into a flower market where vendors sold their wares from houses on stilts that lined the road. Polished mirrors reflected light onto terraced gardens that were crammed with potted plants and watered by small, shallow pools.

I was drunk on the smells, blinded by the profusion of colors and shapes of what seemed like every flower that had ever bloomed. Intoxicated, I floated along on an ocean of perfumes too numerous to unpick one from another.

It seemed that all of life existed in Valen, every shade of cull and cove strutted like kings and queens, knowing they lived in the greatest city in the world. I felt like a shadow, lost amid the sheer bullish exuberance. I was convinced the dips must swank about with gilded fingers from the sheer bump and crush of wealth brisking along the ramps and streets that were awash with the riches of the Empire.

A hobbling cove scurried along beneath the gaze of ordinary citizens. She tipped me a nod and made the sign of downturned horns with the fingers of her right hand. I hid the same gesture in a casual brush of road dust from my leg, also using my right hand, thus ensuring it was a friendly gesture both ways. There was no crime in a cove passing through another gang's manor, the crime was working it without permission or without giving the local chief their due.

I had bigger fish to fry than dipping silks and, to be honest, I was a little irked that I'd been taken for a common bung-nipper. I'd mastered the art of picking pockets and moved up the slippery pole of criminality almost before I was weaned.

* * *

It was suns' set when the priest led us down a quiet side ramp. Until then I'd have thought it was a major thoroughfare, but in Valen, the clean-swept avenue lined with slender trees was little more than a back alley. A dark arch wrapped itself around the end of the road, where I could see robed figures coming and going.

We passed beneath it and into a gated courtyard where a fountain topped by a slime-covered statue of Saint Bartholomew burbled in the center. On the far side was a mansion house that I guessed must be the order's headquarters. A skinny priestess with a nose like a ship's prow paced the steps of the building. Tobias waved to her. She smiled and beckoned us over, all the while casting nervous glances behind us.

"So, these are your friends," she said, and enthusiastically hugged Tobias. She gave me, Clary, and Tosspot the sly-eyed once-over and said 'friends' like she was talking about cock lice. When she let him go she turned to us. "I'm so very pleased to meet you all. Toby has told me all about you."

"Never mind, eh?" I said. It was a joke, but she looked at me like I'd just threatened to strangle her.

Tobias took her by the elbow. "Ignore Breed, Sister Kyra. That's what passes for a sense of humor in Appleton."

"Oh, I see." She forced a laugh and brushed a swag of light brown hair away from her face. I don't know how humans put up with the stuff. If I had hair like that flopping all over the place I'd shave my head. Sister Kyra was obviously very fond of her tresses and her appearance in general. Rather than rough homespun, her robes were silk. Expensive but subtle gold and diamond studs sparkled in her earlobes. The yardstick pendant around her neck was also gold. It seemed the Order of Saint Bartholomew attracted a better class of cull than your average cult.

"Can I pee in there too?" Clary asked. "I'm bursting." Everyone looked round to see Tosspot pissing in the fountain.

Sister Kyra gave Tobias a look that was composed of equal measures of horror and bewilderment.

"Best hold your water for a bit, Clary," I said.

When Tosspot finished pissing, we were taken inside where a ruddy-faced housekeeper appeared and took

Clary off with the promise of somewhere to pee and a slice of fruit pie. Tosspot wandered off on his own, trailed by a fearful-looking acolyte.

Tobias and I were led into a large office that was so elegantly appointed it looked decidedly plain. The building itself was the grandest I'd ever been in, either by invite or to rob, although drab compared to many we'd passed to get here. A silk rug had been placed on the floor, right where everyone could walk on it, and indeed bald patches marred the scrolling leaf design in several places.

The vast desk was oak and carved with such skill that it must have taken years. The walls were paneled, the sideboard dressed in silver ewers and goblets of plain but solid manufacture. The silver statue of Saint Bart standing on a plinth in the corner had sapphire eyes and I'd bet my arse the yardstick in his hand was made of gold. I tried not to drool.

Kyra politely guided Tobias towards one of the windows that looked out onto the courtyard. They bowed their heads together in whispered conversation. I could hear every word, but feigned indifference.

"Are you sure, Tobias? Are you sure this is the one? So much is at stake, it doesn't look, I mean this isn't what I expected."

"I'm as sure as I can be, Kyra. The question is, are you sure you want to get involved?"

There was more nervous laughter. “Of course, I support you, it’s just that if Augustra finds out about what we’re planning she’ll stop it, and that will be the end of us, possibly the whole order. The Empirifex favors the Sanguine Shadow. He apparently admires their devotion, and red is his current favorite color.”

“He admires them today, who knows what the morrow will bring?”

Until I met Tobias I’d never heard of the Order of the Sanguine Shadow, or the Scienticians of Saint Bartholomew come to that. There were so many religious cults and sects, so many gods and saints in the Pantheon it was hard to keep up, even if you tried, which I didn’t. Every Empirifex since before the Schism had elevated friends and favorites to the status of saint or demi-god, it was a time-honored reward for arse-kissing. I believed in the All-Seeing Eye of the Universe, uncaring, unblinking, just watching and keeping its own counsel, but that was as far as my beliefs stretched.

“If Breed can use the Hammer, we will have irrefutable proof that the prophecy is true and Augustra’s support will evaporate. Not even the Empirifex himself could deny such evidence. There are those in the Senate who’ll stand with us.”

“Hmm, that’s true. Augustra has made some powerful enemies, just a pity your father isn’t one of them.”

“I blame Marius for that, but I’ll deal with them when the time comes.”

"As you say. At least finding the hammer isn't going to be a problem." Sister Kyra turned and looked at me, probably to make sure I hadn't taken a shit on the carpet. I smiled brightly. She blanched, forced a thin-lipped smile of her own and looked away. "Are you sure you want to do this by stealth, Toby? Perhaps we should speak to our friends in the Synod and do this openly and with permission?"

"No. The Sanguines are too strong at the moment. They'd vote down any legitimate attempt and then we'd never get near the tomb. Once we have it, it'll be too late for anyone to argue."

Oh, but their schemes were dull. They were mice trying to run with dog rats. I had the strong feeling that it would end badly for them, not least because as soon as I had my claws on the hammer, I was gone.

"Breed?" the priest called. I didn't need to feign surprise, I'd stopped listening to their prattle and was instead planning on how I was going to get out of Valen once I had the weapon. My plan involved robbing them blind in order to pay a sellspell to break what was left of the geas binding us. I was already taking an audit of the goods I'd liberate to fund my escape. For once, everything was going my way. I went over and bowed to the woman. She smiled but couldn't quite stop herself taking a half step back and wrinkling her nose.

"I'm pleased to meet you, Breed. May Saint Bartholomew bless you and keep you in the right angle of his wisdom."

"Thank ye kindly, Holy Mother. I hope I'm worthy of his grace."

Tobias narrowed his eyes. "This is serious, Breed. The fate of all warspawn may depend on you succeeding in this task."

"What do you want me to do?"

They looked at each other, their faces knitted into patterns of worry as they worked up the courage to ask me to do that which I already intended to do.

"As we've already discussed, we want you to steal the Hammer of the North's Hammer," Tobias said.

I nodded with, I hoped, just the right level of contemplative anxiety painted on my face even though it was all I could do not to burst out laughing. "Well, priest, you know I don't go in for all this prophecy stuff. It's..." I was tempted to say, 'too clever for me' but I knew that wouldn't wash with him anymore. "Suffice it to say, there comes a time in everyone's life when they have to make a choice. Count me in."

That was it, I'd cracked him. The lock on his trust sprang open like the arms of all heaven's whores. Tobias smiled. There might even have been a tear in the soapy cull's eye. He thought he'd saved me, and so he had, just not the way he imagined.

Sister Kyra was obviously not one to be left out and ran over to the statue of Saint Bart and flung herself on her knees. "Saint Bartholomew has shown us the way. We will prevail, we will not bow down before tyrants. We will stand against both men and demons in His Holy name. No matter the obstacles, no matter the dark road we must travel, we stand in the right angle of his love. Praise be to Saint Bartholomew."

* * *

Sister Kyra spent an hour or so explaining at me in laborious detail why it was going to be necessary to break into the Hall of Heroes, instead of gaining permission to rob the tomb of one of the Empire's most revered heroes. She and Tobias then excused themselves and I was shown to another well-appointed chamber where a bath, a bed, and a table of food were waiting for me.

As soon as the acolyte left, I set off to find where Tobias and Sister Pain-in-the-arse had gone. It was dark now, the windows were shuttered, the corridors dimly lit, and mostly empty as good prayer-mongers were early-to-bed types.

Tobias and Kyra didn't look like they were going to bed when they left. They had the look of sneaking coves about them. Deep recessed doorways and alcoves full of maudlin statues of Saint Bart were perfect shady nooks for me to duck into as I followed the silken thread of

Tobias's scent. The ghostly skein led me down to a chapel that was buried in the bowels of the mission house.

I say 'chapel', it looked more like a workshop with pews. A knot of brown-clad figures, Tobias and Kyra amongst them were gathered at the far end of the room. Before each pew was a workbench. While they talked, the priests measured and sawed, hammered, and welded metal, wood, and leather components for sculptures that spun with flywheels and turned with cogs. Interlocking plates of copper, brass, wood, and steel wove abstract angles that vexed my eye as I tried to follow their intricate movements.

Sister Kyra's workbench erupted with light. I ducked, unsure of what was happening. A chorus of 'praise be to Saint Bartholomew' followed. The light died, and Kyra stepped forward and bowed before the semi-circle of workbenches. Another of the priests' machines emitted a low droning hum and more praise was offered. Tobias's machine vented tiny jets of flame, and lightning chased across the surface of a polished steel ball suspended at the apex of his pyramidal creation. After they'd all done their party piece, I decided that Tobias's show and mastery was the best.

I wasn't sure, but I think they were praying and honing their magical skills while strengthening their resistance to the Paradox of Power. After watching a repeat of the elaborate and somewhat ridiculous ritual, I slipped out of the chapel workshop, no wiser than when I'd entered.

* * *

Back in my room I stripped off my filthy and threadbare clothing, snagged a chunk of meat and climbed into the bath. I lay in the pleasantly cool water until my scales softened and I was able to clean a month's worth of grime from under my claws and out of the roots of my hair spines. The room smelled of camphor and cedar, redolent of temple incense. A mournful chorus of religious singing echoed along the hallway.

I felt a twinge of guilt, knowing that I was going to double-cross Tobias at the earliest opportunity. A plaster Saint Bart gazed sadly at me from a cobweb-draped shelf as though it knew what I was planning. Time passed, and I dozed off. Sometime later, I was woken by a knock at the door. Tobias entered. I got out and dried myself with the robe that was too short.

He froze by the doorway, looked anywhere but at me. "Oh. I, er." He closed the door. "Kyra and I have just spoken with the senior members of the order. We have their blessing to go ahead."

"That's wonderful." I stretched, I was tired but relaxed. The bed looked torturously soft, but the deep pile carpet felt just perfect for a quick nap.

"Are you sure you want to go ahead with this, Breed? I realize you only have my word that any of this is true."

"I trust you, priest," I smiled. "And you can trust me when I say this is as important to me as it is to you."

He looked up, blushed, and looked down again. "I'm certain that the Empirifex will not look unkindly on anyone who brings him one of the greatest weapons from the Age of Heroes."

"Why hasn't anyone dug it up before now? The Hall of Heroes must be stuffed with magical weapons."

"Dear gods. You're talking about the greatest heroes of the Empire. You can't just plunder their graves for treasure."

"You've lost me, isn't that exactly what we're planning to do?"

"No. Well, yes, in a way but it's not the same as theft. It's complicated."

"You're telling me, because from where I'm standing it looks like theft, or is it only stealing when someone like me does it?"

He rubbed his head. "Of course not, but there are circumstances when such actions are necessary."

"Feeding your family is necessary, but poor culls still swing for it."

"Will you do it, or not?"

“I said I would, didn’t I? When do you and your friends want me to do it?”

“Tonight. The Synod is meeting in two days. I want us to be there to tell them about the prophecy and to present you with the Hammer’s hammer.”

Highly bloody unlikely. I smiled. “As you wish.”

Chapter Sixteen

I can't say that I expected much but 'the plan' was less than reassuring. It involved Sister Kyra using some trusted contact to bribe a couple of guards to look the other way while we sneaked into the hall. Tobias assured me that there was nothing to worry about which, naturally, caused me worry. Apparently, there was no need to break in and absolutely no need to kill anyone. We were going to be let in through a side door and, more importantly, the tomb itself would be left unlocked for us.

I wasn't convinced, but I kept my own counsel and went along with it. I was a sharp cove, well able to improvise should the job go topsy. So long as I could get within strike of the hammer I'd work the rest out on the fly. As a kindness, I'd tell the demon that I'd done for the priest when I handed over the drubber. I figured once he had what he was after, he'd be too busy to hunt down either me or the priest. In truth, I didn't care. I just wanted to lose the mark and go to ground.

The Hall of Heroes was south of the order's mission house. I didn't see Clary or Tosspot before we left but I knew they'd fare well as they were both more savvy than the sop-souled preachifiers I'd left them with. The priest and I set out alone and headed along a road that snaked away from the spectacular heart of the city out to a broad, spoon-shaped valley. This time I was wearing a robe that covered my feet. Although older, the buildings we passed were even more lavishly decorated than those I'd already seen, lavish but tasteless. Many were lit up by great flaming torches that burned the night to amber and sheened the sandy facades in shades of bronze. Tobias explained in hushed tones that this was the administrative district and that most of the offices of state were located here amid parks and temples dedicated to some of the more prominent gods of the Pantheon.

Night seemed hardly less busy than day in Valen. So, cowls up and heads down, we hurried on until we reached a square on the other side of which stood the Hall of Heroes. Beyond the hall, the lip of the valley swept up to a grand parade of buttressed mansions, their shuttered windows picked out by faint rectangles of rosy gold. The Hall itself was laid out like a gigantic, seven-spoked wheel. A magnificent rotunda with a copper-tiled dome formed the hub. If I hadn't had such a pressing need to get inside and rob it, I might have spent a minute or two being awed. The size alone was intimidating, made a body feel small, insignificant. That humans lavished such wealth on the dead while beggars huddled in doorways said more about their contrary nature than anything. No poem, song, or tale could better sum them up than follies such as this.

"Each of the seven spokes is a chapel dedicated to one of the heroes of the Schism War," Tobias informed me as we skirted the square. "Their tombs are in their chapels, except the Red Witch. No one knows where she was buried."

"Or cares, I'll wager," I muttered under my breath.

"What?"

"Nothing. Lead on."

We passed the main entrance as we made our way around the building. Standing triumphantly on the necks of fallen demons, a pair of giant basalt heroes flanked the bronze doors. The plaza outside of the hall was deserted. One of the knights standing guard tapped out her pipe on a dead demon's horn, the other leaned against the sandaled foot of a giant warrior queen. Tongues of torchlight licked at the smooth contours of giant shoulders and gilded the manes of heroically flowing hair.

"This way," the priest whispered.

"You don't need to come with me," I offered hopefully. "Just tell me where the tomb is, and I'll be in and out before anyone knows."

The priest shook his head and hurried off along a side street dripping with vines. "The guard we bribed knows to expect two of us. One alone would arouse suspicion."

I suspected that the real reason he was coming was that he and his friends didn't trust me. I wasn't offended, they were right to be suspicious.

"Over here, hurry," he said unnecessarily. I was sticking to him like a louse on a dog until I had that hammer.

I adjusted the shoulder strap of the firelance. The long barrel lay comfortably snug between my shoulders under the robe. Tobias had tried to insist that I leave it, but there was no way I was going to trust it to the care of the priests. Truth be told, I was looking forward to using it again. He wouldn't understand that. He had power at his fingertips, or maybe he did know that for coves like me, barking irons leveled the field.

The vine-draped street tapered out behind the Hall of Heroes. Surprisingly, there were no high walls or spearpoint railings. A simple cobbled path led through a grove of lemon trees to the rear of the hall. The nearest chapel, one of the seven spokes, rose fifty feet above the street. Just below the roof, soft light embellished a narrow strip of stained glass that ran the length of both sides of the chapel. The walls were covered with flamboyant carvings in basalt and marble.

I think Tobias was trying to sneak, but the soft cull couldn't lift his feet clear of the ground for more than two steps. His scuffing gait was erratic, the way his shoulder brushed the wall irritating. He was not the person I would have chosen as a lamplight comrade. A small side door was nestled into the wall of the chapel, just before the point where the spoke met the hub of the atrium building. A city guard was loitering nearby and stepped forward when she saw us.

"Who goes there?" she asked.

"The night watch," Tobias replied.

Without saying another word, she shouldered her spear and marched off around the building. Tobias tried the door. As promised, it was unlocked.

The atrium was lit by a fire bowl held aloft in the middle of the chamber by a quartet of thirty-foot-tall angelic beings. Its radiance was reflected off the painted dome and spread fingers of gold into the surrounding chapels. Rather than illuminate, the wavering firelight merely served to add variance to the depth of shade that bathed the hall.

This chapel, if the frescos painted on the walls were anything to go by, was dedicated to a flaxen-haired sorceress. She was shooting ice spears from her fingertips, cutting down swathes of demonic hoards that looked more than a little like me. As far as I could see, the only non-humans represented in the sprawling frescos that covered the walls were the hordes of demonspawn. The side of good was entirely human.

"Magnificent, isn't it?" Tobias whispered.

"Words fail me."

Hugging the walls, we crept into the atrium.

"There are no guards within the hall and all the priests and visitors have left by now. The guard won't return for an hour," Tobias whispered.

The Hammer's chapel was directly opposite the entrance to the hall. I walked on the balls of my feet, but now and then Tobias scuffed the marble. It sounded loud to me, but he didn't seem to notice. His shoulders were hunched, and his head was down. I could tell he was cowed by this place, overawed by its sanctity. I could smell his fear but there was no going back now whether he wanted to or not.

* * *

An openwork iron screen separated the chapel from the atrium. Inside, the walls were painted with the heroic deeds of a hammer-wielding man-god. Swathed in furs, the golden-haired, square-jawed hero was smiting vicious demons with his overly large hammer.

He looked familiar, probably because he looked like every picture of every hero I'd ever seen. All that was brave and noble was lovingly reproduced in the image of the giant. It meant nothing to me, but Tobias bowed his head and said a quick prayer as we passed.

The entrance to the crypt was at the far end of the chapel. Beneath the murals were rows of verdigrised plaques bearing the names of fallen warriors who I assume our hero had led to their glorious deaths. The tomb door was set in the plinth of another giant, black basalt statue. It portrayed the Hammer smiting a horned and scaly demon with his stupidly large weapon. I waited for Tobias to open it, while I kept an eye out. Minutes passed without a key being turned.

"What's wrong?" I asked.

"I can't do it."

I went over. "What do you mean you can't?"

"I thought this was the right thing to do, but I'm not sure it is." He looked at me with eyes brimful of accusation.

"Come on, priest, spit it out."

"I can't trust you, Breed. What if you betray us?"

"You incinerate me with your holy, fucking calculation of smiting that's what." I didn't want to hurt him, but I wasn't going to let him stop me, not now that I was so close. I folded my arms, mostly to stop myself strangling him. "Now listen to me, patrician. We either get on and do this, or you work out how you're going to explain to your friends why you let them and everyone else down."

"This is sacrilege."

"Only if you decide it is." I don't know why I said that. It didn't mean anything, I was just trying to distract him from over-thinking or I'd have to knock him out. For some reason, the empty words struck a chord with him and he opened the door. The sound reverberated through the building. I took off the robe, unslung the firelance, and shoved the hesitant priest inside before quickly and quietly closing the door behind us.

It wasn't as dark as I'd expected it would be inside the tomb. Glow stones the size of my fist had been embedded in the walls and bathed the flight of stairs in an eerie, grey-blue light. We descended cautiously with me in the lead. The air was cold and tasted of dust but again it wasn't as stale as I'd imagined it would be. There were also the faint ghosts of other smells down here and the steps were swept clean.

"People have been down here recently."

Tobias nodded. "Yes, the tomb is maintained by priests of the Order of the Hammer."

"Ah, of course. I should have guessed there'd be a sacred order of tomb sweepers."

"Just shut up, Breed. Now is not the time for levity."

"Who said I was joking?"

The stairs came out in a chamber lined either side with statues of the Hammer in a variety of heroic poses. In the middle of the floor was a massive catafalque atop which was the hero's effigy. I shouldered the lance, grabbed the edge and started to push.

Tobias slapped his stump on my hand. “Breed, for gods’ sake, wait.”

I shrugged him off. This wasn’t the first tomb I’d robbed and although the covers were heavy, if you were strong enough, or had enough leverage to lift the male lid out of the female box they slid easily. I lifted and pushed. It growled, stone ground against stone. The priest started praying. When I’d turned it almost entirely at a right angle I stopped. Dust tickled my nostrils. I looked inside, expecting to see the Hammer of the North. Other than a rusted suit of armor, the sarcophagus was empty.

“He’s not here.” Surprise turned to dread as I searched amid the armor and rotting furs for the hammer. “The hammer’s not here either.” I couldn’t believe it. I searched again, in case I’d somehow failed to spot a body and a dirty great hammer.

Nothing.

The priest grabbed my arm. I shrugged him off. “It’s not here.” I slumped against the edge of the tomb.

“It’s not your fault, Breed. I should have guessed this might happen.” He muttered something under his breath and a ball of golden light bloomed in his palm.

“I might as well climb in and close the fucking lid,” I muttered. As well as still being indebted to Shallunsard, a small part of me was disappointed that the Hammer wasn’t there. I admit it, I was curious about the prophecy. I’d not paid much heed to the priest’s insane ideas, but for a brief spell, I'd let myself believe that I might have been part of something important. Mother was right, I was an idiot. "Come on, let's get out of here."

After he'd had a good rummage, I put the lid back on the sarcophagus. To say I was disconsolate was an understatement of epic proportions. I still had time left before the demon came after me, but no blasted idea where I might find the damned hammer.

"I wonder if he's ever been here," the priest mused as we made to leave the tomb.

"Does it matter?"

"No, I suppose it doesn't, not anymore."

We retraced our footsteps through the hall to the side door. I let the priest go ahead of me, while I considered my next move. As he reached for the door handle I caught a whiff of body odor and heard shuffling from outside. It was more than one person. I grabbed Tobias and tried to pull him back as I unslung the firelance. Both were mistakes. I should have just run.

The door was blown off its hinges and the hall lit up. The priest staggered, I shoved him out of my way and leveled the firelance at the door a heartbeat before a blast of magical energy hurled us across the chapel.

I hit the wall like a wet rag. Tobias hadn't been in the direct line of the blast, but I heard him wheeze like broken bellows when he landed. Dozens of armored knights swarmed through the door, their shouts reverberated around the chapel, the clamor of their armor bounced off the walls. I'd managed to keep hold of the firelance and once I'd stopped seeing stars I got to my knees and took aim at the first knight I laid eyes on.

"Drop the lance, demonspawn, or I'll blow you back to hell," a woman standing in the doorway called out.

I switched targets to her. "Then you'll be coming with me, fustilugs."

The knights put themselves between us. This was going to get messy.

"No, Breed," Tobias pleaded. "It's over, drop it. Don't give her an excuse. Surrender, live to fight another day."

I looked at the priest, saw a broken man. I don't know why, but I did as he asked and dropped the lance even though I was sure that he was being a mite optimistic about the whole 'living' thing. My assumption appeared to be correct as, when I dropped the lance, the knights piled me. In the process of binding my hands behind my back, I was kicked with rib-breaking gusto. The woman, who until now had been little more than a silhouette, came forward into the light. She was wearing crimson that perfectly matched her hair and the stripe of color painted across her eyes. It was not her appearance that gained my rapt if watery-eyed attention but the hammer slung over her shoulder.

"Looking for this?" She tapped the dusty shaft with henna-reddened fingers. "Well, Tobias, you are in a spot, aren't you? Having heard rumor of your villainous plan to steal this holy artifact, I gained permission of the Senate, your father included, to take it into safekeeping and help the knight captain here apprehend you, should the rumor prove true." She walked over to the priest who was being held at spear point by the nervous knights. "Surely, a Vulsones has enough personal wealth that you don't need to steal our nation's treasures to pay your order's debts?"

Tobias looked as angry as I'd seen him and yet he didn't turn her into a smoking pile of ash. "You know damn well that's a lie. I know Marius told you about the prophecy."

The wench rubbed her chin as she paced around him. "Now, which prophecy would that be, Toby? There are so many, I lose track. Your father is going to be very disappointed."

"Please, Augustra there's more at stake here than winning the approval of the Senate. Thousands of lives are at stake."

"Oh, please, Tobias, enough prattle I pray you. All this, being right and saving the day has given me a terrible headache. You'll have chance to say your piece when you go before the Synod. I'm sure they can't wait to hear why you desecrated our holiest shrine. Until then, the captain here will escort you to the temple of the

Sanguine Shadow." She indicated one of the knights with slightly more gold embroidery on his cloak than his fellows. "And unlike your soft-headed brother who came crawling back this morning, I'll make damn sure you don't escape." She turned to the knight-captain. "Gag him and bind him with the chains I brought and be careful, he may look like an imbecile, but he is not entirely without power."

"There's no need for that, Augustra. I give you my word as a Vulsones that I won't try to escape."

She laughed too hard. "I don't trust the rest of your family, so why the hell would I trust you? Bind him, and in the name of all that is holy, don't forget the gag. I can't bear to listen to him for another minute, let alone the next few days."

"Yes, Holy Mother." The knight saluted. "What shall we do with this?" He head-tossed in my direction. There was no actual malice in the look he gave me, just bored contempt.

The woman, however, gave me a look brimming with hate.

"Throw it in the dungeons."

Chapter Seventeen

Tobias was bound in warded chains and gagged before being carted off by the red-clad bitch who had my hammer. Shortly thereafter, I was dragged from the hall and thrown in the back of a prison wagon. I didn't resist, I was grateful for the chance to lie down as every breath I drew elicited a stabbing pain in my side that told me all was not as it should be in my giblet sack.

The journey to the lock-up gave me time to consider just how deep I was in the arsepickle. I concluded that I was up to my eyes in the nasty stuff. And thus began the recriminations, the wishful thinking, the torture of examining paths not taken, and the indignant self-pity of a life-long recidivist. Time flies when you're feeling sorry for yourself and before long the wagon stopped. The knights were nothing if not consistent and I was dragged from the wagon with the same casual brutality as I was thrown in it.

Upon first sight, I had high hopes that my lockup lodgings would be of a higher standard than I was used to, but the prison's dramatically theatrical façade belied its joyless interior.

Whilst being promised all manner of unpleasantness, I was dragged inside and hauled past the nice airy cells where wealthy coves could languish in comfort and taken down to the lightless dungeon. Even with my hands bound I know how to protect my vulnerables from casual jibs and culps, but no amount of acrobatics can shield a body from a concerted effort to give it a damn good kicking.

The tepid contents of a slop bucket brought me round after I so rudely fell unconscious before the knights had finished trying to kick the tar out of me. The poor fellows quite wore themselves out giving me the beating of my life, not to mention the hours it was going to take some unfortunate cull to clean all that blood off their nice, shiny armor. I don't remember losing consciousness again, I just remember thinking I was going to die and how, on balance, that didn't seem like such a bad thing.

As it turns out, I didn't die. I only wished I had. I woke up some time later in a cell. There was no light to give me a clue as to the time of day, but the blood on my face had dried to a tight crust, so I guessed some hours had passed since the beating. My head felt lumpy and swollen. I managed to prise my right eye open, but the left remained resolutely closed.

There was enough chain between the manacles that I was able to bring my swollen hands from behind my back to in front of me. After feeling my way through this latest collection of cuts and bruises, I surveyed my domain.

The cell was no more than eight feet long by five feet wide and about five feet high. Knights occasionally peered through the slit in the door to assure me that I wouldn't be in here long. They were very pleased to inform me that the pyre was already being built on which they would burn my partially strangled body after my guts had been torn out. That they were going to such efforts for a humble cove like me was rather flattering, and given how rough I felt, almost welcome.

As well as my ribs, my right hand was particularly painful due to being stamped on, but still, it just about worked. The knights had done more than enough to maim or even kill a human, but even half thoasa are made of tougher stuff. Even so, every time I moved a couple of ribs grated against each other. As I sat in pain and near pitch blackness, contemplating my grisly fate, a fly buzzed close to my ear. I swatted at it. "You can fuck off too."

Someone banged on the door. "Keep it down, you fucking animal," he shouted. "I'll flay your fucking hide if I've got to come in there."

Tempting though it was to tell him what I told the fly, I refrained. I'd had my fill of pain for the day and quietly fell into an exhausted and dreamless sleep.

* * *

I awoke to the sound of the fly buzzing near my face. I opened my eye to see that the end wall of the cell was covered in flies, thousands of them. How they'd managed to get in here was a mystery as there wasn't a window and the peephole in the door was closed. Perplexing though that was, what was really strange was their behavior.

The only one making noise was the one that was buzzing around my head. The rest were hardly moving at all. It was as though they were being deliberately quiet. Confused, I watched the glittering black mass crawl across the wall. I coughed up a lump of something slimy that I hoped wasn't lung. I don't know who the bigger idiot was, Tobias for trusting Kyra, or me for trusting him. I should have known better. There was only one person I'd ever been able to trust and that was me, and even then I quite often let myself down.

As if I wasn't sore enough, my palm began to itch. As I watched the flies an idea slowly wormed its way into my brain. I dismissed it, it was stupid, desperate and stupid. The itching grew more intense. I tore off my glove and had a good scratch. I could just make out the dark outline of the demon's sigil embedded in my flesh.

I looked at the flies on the wall. I looked at my palm. I laughed.

The flies had formed the same pattern as the sigil.

I crawled over to the wall. “Shallunsard, is that you?” I whispered. Of course, flies being flies, they didn’t respond. “What the fuck am I doing? I’m talking to flies.” I punched the wall, crushing a cluster of the bloated corpse-pillagers into the brick. The rest didn’t move, didn’t take to the air in an angry fizzing cloud of black like normal insects should. The wall was stained with blood and mashed bodies, broken wings glittered like diamonds in my hand. The idea, half-formed and utterly insane, wriggled deeper into my brain. I crushed all the flies forming Shallunsard’s sigil and waited.

After half an hour of staring at the bloody mess nothing had happened. In desperation, I concentrated on the pattern of smashed bodies and poured what little sorcerous energy I possessed into the bloody sigil.

Nothing.

Disgusted by my foolishness, I crawled away from the wall. At least there was nobody around to see my descent into madness. I rolled over in a bid to find some way to lie that didn’t hurt and as I did, I saw it.

The sigil was still on the wall, but the wall wasn’t where, or what it should have been. A portion of it had opened like a door, but one that was so thin it could only be seen from a sidelong angle. In the darkness the break was all but invisible and had I not laid down, I might not have seen it at all.

"That angle's right." I chuckled until I coughed and then crawled through the gap.

* * *

I don't know who decided where I'd end up. Perhaps it was me, perhaps it was the demon or perhaps it was just chance. I didn't care. I fell out of the cell into familiar territory. The perfume of the sewer filled my nostrils as I sank up to my elbows in the thick sediment of a sewage channel. I scrabbled back and managed to stop myself falling face first into the flow.

I was on a tiled walkway, a glazed tiled walkway at that. I guessed that I must be in Valen's sewers. I looked at the wall that I'd just fallen through. It didn't appear to be different to any other section of wall. I touched it, just to make sure it was solid. I didn't want to be followed by the guards because I certainly couldn't run or fight. I tasted iron, felt a rib dig into my giblets. I probably couldn't even walk.

"That isn't good." My voice was a whisper. I lay back to try and ease the pain. As if that wasn't bad enough, something nearby growled, low and threatening. Whatever it was, it sounded big. I tried to get up, but that simple act was now beyond me. Falling through the wall had pushed the broken rib deeper into my vitals and I was feeling it acutely.

Fuck it, I thought. I was tired. I decided to lie there and wait for whatever it was to try its luck. I could probably still deliver a nasty bite if the beastie came too close. The growling turned to snuffling and was soon accompanied by the click-skitter of claws on tiles. As it drew closer I got a noseful of its scent, the unmistakable aroma of wet dog rat. I'd escaped hanging, drawing, and burning, only to be eaten alive by rodents.

Something sniffed my hair. I opened my eye and saw twitching whiskers, a wet, brown nose and a pair of huge yellow fangs swam into view. This is it. I thought, and then a familiar face loomed out of the darkness behind it.

"Breed!" Clary exclaimed.

Content that I was among friends, I relinquished my grip on consciousness.

* * *

I wasn't sure if I was dead or dreaming, or both. After my previous experience I was reasonably sure that the dead didn't dream, but then there are probably as many ways of being dead as there are of being alive. I felt like I was floating on a river of velvet, drifting through underground grottos lit by exotic, spongiform blooms of fungi. Something was dragging me, guiding me through miles of passageways and tunnels. Warm brown eyes stared down at me and a soft, wet nose sniffed my face.

"Breed, wake up," Clary said, too brightly and too loud.

I coughed blood into my mouth, tried to sit up, failed.

"Stay, stay," Clary ordered. I was in no position to argue with an eleven-year-old, so I stayed put.

"Clary's right. Don't try to get up. I've sent for a healer. Rowan will fix you up or kill you. Hopefully, it won't be the latter, but I make no promises on her behalf."

That little nugget of information didn't perturb me overmuch, I'd grown inured to death threats. I did find the flash lad who'd spoken intriguing, even in my battered state. I say 'lad'. It was hard to tell if it was a boy who looked like a rat, or a rat that looked like a boy.

Whatever he was, he wasn't your average Schism-touched cull. Hovering behind Clary the boy rat was wearing fine breeches, silk stockings, silver-buckled patent shoes, a white linen shirt, and an embroidered silk waistcoat. That I felt so wretched but still noticed his finery was a testament to the skill of his tailor. His fur was sleek and dark, his tail as thick as my arm, and restlessly active. His front teeth were long, but nowhere near as long as those of the biggest dog rat I'd ever seen, which was sitting at his feet, eyeing me like I was the main course of a Gods' Day dinner.

"Where?" I managed to say in between gasping breaths.

The boy rat came over with the dog rat padding at his heel like a faithful hound. "You're in my home in Nightside. I am Leopold, the Duke of East Point."

"Clary, priest, Rubin?"

"Rubin, is it now, eh, demon?" Tosspot cackled.

I hadn't noticed him until he spoke. The mangy old sot was sitting on a watermarked silk divan, stroking a fat, white rat that was sleeping on his knee.

"Bet you're wondering how we got here, eh? How you got here." He took a pull on his pel pipe.

I nodded.

"Not sure I should tell you." He chuckled again. The rat on his knee stirred and draped the tip of its tail over its nose.

Drawing breath and trying to talk was like trying to suck an egg through a penny whistle. I lay back and focused on breathing.

"You're no fun today, Breed," Tosspot muttered, sulkily. "When you and priesty boy went off gallivanting, me and Clary were in the kitchen of the big house, weren't we, Clary?"

"Yes, Rubin, we were. We were told to help with the washing up. Which I thought unfair and so I curdled their milk, a whole churn." She laughed, and Leo laughed with her.

Tosspot's eyes lit up. "You'd been gone a spell when we heard a right ruckus. Knights kicked the doors in, the demon-dodgers were all yelling and crying." He grew animated, the rat on his knee woke up and started preening. "Me and Clary sneaked out the back and into the sewers."

"Into my domain." Leopold bowed.

"Heard you got arrested for trying to steal something and was all set to be hanged." Tosspot coughed. "How did you get out of that?"

"Apported." It wasn't exactly a lie. "How long since me and Tobias set off?" I had no idea how much time had passed since our ill-starred venture.

"Two nights ago," Clary said. I noticed she was making eyes at rat boy and that he was giving her coy come-hithers in return. "We came down here and Leo found us and took us in."

The Duke of Wherever bowed. "It was the least I could do."

"The Synod must have met," I said. Tobias had failed and if I wasn't much mistaken, I was dying, again.

The next hour or so I spent fighting to breathe as the right side of my chest swelled like a dead pig's belly. I discovered that if I lay perfectly still, it only hurt a lot instead of too much, which was a relief because I hate crying like a babe in front of strangers. At least the couch on which I was expiring was comfortable. The room was windowless as was only to be expected but had surprisingly good ventilation and was brightly lit by dozens of beeswax candles. Unlike Mother's lair, Duke Leo's audience chamber was elegantly appointed. No expense was being spared for my death watch, but I can't say I was grateful.

I must have dozed off again but woke in the sure knowledge that Rowan had arrived. The air in the room had turned crisp and smelled of frost-rimed loam, flint, and ghostberries. I opened my eye and tried to balance what one sense told me against the evidence of another and I couldn't. It smelled like an autumn morning in the mountains and yet I was most definitely in the sewers of Valen, staring at a myth made real.

I'd seen some strange things in my time but nothing like Rowan. It wasn't that her appearance was outlandish. Compared to coves like Ludo she was positively ordinary. It was more that Rowan appeared to be made of the unreal fabric from which dreams are woven. Her presence served to highlight how tawdry the world was, how lacking. Tall and slender, she had a pair of violet eyes, translucent skin, and hair like fine strands of spun glass that absorbed and reflected the colors in the room. She was wearing a long coat over breeches and a linen shirt and vest. The first thing she did was tip Leo a polite nod. The second was to look at me like most people looked at me before rushing across the room faster than a thought, whereupon she grabbed my hand and tore off my glove. The world around us receded into shadow. If she was going to kill me, there wasn't a damn thing I could do to stop her. Rowan was an Annurashi. Just as the humans had made warspawn, the Annurashi had made them, or so they said.

She held my face and stared into my eyes. Up close, I saw that hers were flecked with gold and silver and her pupils were purple and far from round. Her breath was as fresh and sweet as snow dusted apples. Why it would almost be a pleasure being killed by her.

"Did you choose this?" she asked. Her voice was many-layered, it reminded me of Ludo and was utterly compelling.

I knew my continued existence depended not only on giving the right answer but an honest one, two things that didn't often go together in my world.

"No," I croaked. "Tricked."

She didn't take her eyes off mine while I talked. My jaw throbbed where she had it clamped in her bony, four-jointed fingers, but I didn't have the breath or guts to complain. I heard the distinct sound of a blade being sheathed as she let me go.

The most disconcerting thing that happened next wasn't having an Annurashi tending to my wounds, nor was it the way she mixed sorcery with actual doctoring which was just confusing. It was when she stuck a long, hollow needle into my swollen chest and the air whistled out. The pain in my lung lessened immediately. It didn't vanish altogether, but I could breathe easier. She hovered her hand over my chest. Her eyes shone with a cold, blue light and the offending rib wriggled out of my lung and realigned itself. It was disconcertingly similar to the way Shallunsard had brought me back from the dead and just like then, it hurt like hell.

Without another word or second glance, the Annurashi packed up her things and went over to talk to Leo, who'd been loitering near Clary while the Annurashi worked. His faithful giant rat was cowering in the corner of the room. I had to give it to the Duke, he showed remarkable composure when dealing with Rowan. After a brief conversation, he clicked his heels and bowed. She acknowledged it with the slightest of nods.

"Keep your head down, Leo," the annurashi counseled. "Trouble is coming. I'm going to go and speak to the other Dukes. You need to prepare." She flicked a bladed glance in my direction.

"Yes, I know. Take care, Rowan, and thank you," Leopold said to the closing door.

I felt better than I had done in hours, if somewhat drained. My eyes started to close and then my palm began to burn as though I'd stuck my hand in a fire. I rolled over and tried to smother the intense pain but only succeeded in falling off the couch. The giant dog rat yapped. A dozen of its kin bounded into the room. I thought of Wulf and wondered how long I'd last.

Death by dog rat was averted by the Duke who calmed them with a wave. Clary and Tosspot actually looked concerned. I looked at my hand. Overlaying the demon mark was another sigil. Unlike Shallunsard's which was as black as squid ink, this one was pale, silvery grey. The two did not sit well together and as I looked, actually seemed to be writhing under the skin like eye fly larvae, fighting for dominance.

"I am so sick of pain." I gritted my teeth and repeatedly slammed my open hand against the floor, trying to beat the pain away.

Tosspot came over. His pipe was hanging out of the corner of his mouth. As usual, he was scratching his nethers. "Best stop all this mucking about, demon and get some shut-eye if you're going to rescue priesty boy."

"Who said I was going to rescue him?"

"I did." Clary beamed. She was cuddling the fat white rat. "I asked Leo to save you, so you could save Father Tobias because he saved me. That's fair, isn't it?"

Leo gazed fondly at Clary. "I think so."

I didn't need to ask what was in it for Duke Rat Boy. The soppy way Clary was looking at him spoke volumes. I crawled back on the couch and buried my face in a cushion. As I said, I hate strangers seeing me cry.

* * *

Clary told me it was morning when she woke me by sticking a bowl of stew under my nose. I ate the lot and asked for more, I was starving. While she went to see what she could find, Duke Leo turned up. He was reading a letter. He smiled.

"She's too young for tumbling," I said without thinking.

The Duke's smile faded. His tail twitched. "What do you take me for? Some foppish cull who'd tup a bud like Clary?"

"I don't know anything about you. All I'm saying is she's a nipper." I got up, stretched my legs. The dog rat growled.

"And all you need to know is that I'm the nib of this manor, and a gentleman," Leo replied, polite and threatening in the same breath.

Those big dark rat eyes were unreadable, but that twitching tail and tone of voice told me I was on dangerous ground. I put my attack of concern down to the lingering effects of the geas and wondered how anyone with integrity ever survived long enough to go grey. Maybe they didn't. Maybe all old folk were selfish bastards and, as the saying goes, the good all die young. I tipped him a nod, his due as a prince of the Midnight Court.

"Point taken, Duke."

He inclined his head. His tail curled around the missive and tucked it into his waistcoat. The giant dog rat set about grooming, so I fancied his master wasn't planning to do me a mischief, not now at least.

"Tell me, Breed, how old are you?"

Seemed a mite personal as questions go, but this was his manor. "I don't know, twenty? Something like that."

He nodded. "The oldest thoasa I ever met was thirty-five."

I snorted. "I'll be happy if I live that long."

"And not a little surprised, I'll wager." He gave a knowing smile. "Doesn't it bother you that your species is so short-lived?"

I shrugged. "Thoasa aren't much given to introspection, and anyway, I'm only half thoasa." I was all too aware of the short lifespan of thoasa. It was the price they paid for their incredible strength, speed, and stamina. Thirty-five was actually five years older than any thoasa I'd ever met, or indeed had heard of.

"So how is it you know an Annurashi?" I asked, intent on steering the questions away from my mortality.

"Rowan? It is more that Rowan knows me, knows everyone with pretentions in Nightside Valen, and a fair number in Dayside too."

"I didn't think they bothered with mortals."

“I don’t think they do as a rule.” He snorted. “Nor can I blame them. My guess is that Rowan is an ambassador for her kind. The Annurashi’s eyes and ears in the Empire, here to keep an eye out in case anyone starts another Schism War, or releases a demon, that kind of thing.” He gave me a pointed look.

I laughed.

Clary came back with a full pot of stew, and I ate until my stomach felt like it was going to burst. She’d changed out of her filthy homespun and was now wearing a peach gown embroidered with pearls. Her hair, such as it was, had been expertly curled and tied with a bow. She seemed more than pleased with her transformation from country peasant to fashionable young lady and took every chance to flounce and swish her skirts. I found my gloves under the couch. I was tempted to beg a clean shirt, but there didn’t seem much point. I was about to get all unnecessary with the base culls who’d taken Tobias and my hammer.

Duke Leo excused himself on an urgent matter of business and Tosspot had wandered off somewhere, probably on the hunt for more drugs. This left me and Clary kicking our heels. After listening to the girl prattle breathlessly about how wonderful Leopold was and how marvelous his domain, I asked her to show me around, something she was only too happy to do. I cared not one whit about how pretty everything was, I needed to know how to get out of here quickly should the need arise.

* * *

I thought I knew sewers until I found myself wandering the halls of Nightside Valen. The place was enormous, labyrinthine, built over centuries on many subterranean levels. From what I could see, each previously buried incarnation of the city became part of the fabric of Nightside. The whole history of Imperial civilization was here, layered in a dozen slices, hundreds of years thick.

Barrel vaulted halls were lit by antique glowstone chandeliers and waterfalls cascaded beneath suspended bridges. Nature, as well as magic and ingenuity had also been harnessed, and glowing fungi clung to the inside of colored glass domes, lighting side streets and alleyways. Other, wilder varieties clambered unfettered up the walls, their luminous polyps hanging like fat lanterns above the denizens of Nightside as they went about their daily lives in much the same way as those above ground. It was a whole other city beneath the dayside streets of Valen. The two had to interact, nothing this big could go unnoticed and I guessed a lot of money flowed between greasy palms at both ends of the pipe.

"I need some cutlery, Clary."

"Knifes and forks? What do you want them for?"

"What? Ah, forgive me, I mean blades. I forget you don't know what most kinchin coves ought."

"Come again?"

"You weren't born in the shadow of the nevergreen tree." She gave me a blank look. "You're not a cove like me, leastways, you weren't."

She chuckled and skipped across one of the swinging bridges that spanned a foaming underground river. "You'd be surprised. I've done a bit o'sharp and shady work in my time."

"Oh, aye? And what nefarious deeds should we credit your slate with?"

"Hexes mostly, only on them what wronged me, mind you. My ma taught me manners and some fine dark tricks before the fever got her."

Despite the gloom hanging over me about the priest, the demon, and everything else, Clary's confession was the funniest thing I'd heard in weeks.

"So all that cunning work they were accusing you of in Little Lea?"

"I done it." She dipped a curtsey. "Anyone who messed with my gran, I fixed 'em. I killed their cattle, poisoned their wells, and curdled their milk. They deserved it though, they'd been after gran's land for years, ever since she found calth in the stream."

"So why did you come with us? Why not stay to look after your gran?"

"Father Tobias solved all our problems, didn't he? Burnt 'em all up in a nice, tidy pile. Gran said I needed to broaden my horizons, so here I am, and a good thing too, eh? Saved your life."

It was a good job my ribs had been mended because I just about broke another laughing. Culls passing by looked at me like I was moon-touched, but their censuring stares only served to make me laugh more. I managed to stop eventually before I did myself another injury.

After scouting out a few boltholes and rat runs, I returned to Leopold's mansion which was located in the heart of his domain. Compared to this Darkling Court, Mother was a peasant, a country squire at best. And I thought she was the queen of the world.

When we got back, Leopold was waiting for us in what I now knew wasn't his audience chamber but was, in fact, a modest side room. The Duke was deep in conversation with an arch rogue if ever I saw one.

The cove looked and smelled human, he was tall for their kind, broad in the back, narrow in the waist and wearing dark, shadow friendly clothing. His soft soled boots were made for climbing or sneaking rather than marching, giving a hint to the type of trade he practiced, as did the hooded cloak he was wearing. It was traditional attire, favored by many a bladesman and woman who fancied themselves a night-blessed bravo. This one certainly did. When he turned around I saw that he was wearing a brace of knives bandoliered across his chest and a matched longsword and dagger sheathed at his hip. The only thing missing was a sign around his neck saying, 'I am a rogue'. Going on what he looked like, he was either very good at his job or very bad.

"So, this is Breed." He was well-spoken, but there was a hint of an accent under the judgmental sneer. He gave me a cursory once-over. His cold grey peepers were nailed deep into a hard, lean face. He folded his arms. "I don't know, Leo."

"Please, Cyrus. I wouldn't ask, but the priest is dear to someone who is dear to me." He was pleading, but the Duke's tail swished lazily. Despite his words, the lad was confident of the outcome, making me think this was a show for my benefit.

The hooded man rubbed his bristle-sprinkled chin. "The monastery will be heavily guarded, and even if we get in this Tobias is most likely dead already."

"Nevertheless, I would like you to try, Cyrus."

"I wouldn't," I said, as now seemed to be the time to offer opinions. "No offense. But I work alone."

They both looked like a turd had just recited poetry and then carried on their conversation, more quietly this time.

"I'm going to look for Rubin. I'll see you later, Breed," Clary said. She cupped her hand to her mouth and whispered, "Leo's only trying to help, he doesn't want you getting caught by the Imperials again." She smiled as though that little bit of wisdom would make me feel better and then left, but not before stopping to drop a coy bow to the Duke. The fat white rat followed her out. The big dog rat remained at its master's heel, smoothing the hair on its tail. It glared at me, which was actually quite heartening. At least something was taking me seriously, even if it was only an overgrown rodent.

"Then it's settled. Cyrus will help you find the priest. Are we all agreed?" Leopold looked at me. "Breed?"

"Do I have a choice?"

Cyrus eyed me disdainfully. "No, you don't."

I was impressed. The cove managed to pack a lot of contempt into few words. If he wasn't so matey with rat boy I'd have said that he didn't like warspawn or the schism touched but given their obvious friendship, I surmised it was just me he wasn't keen on for some reason.

Duke Leopold stepped in and smoothed the ruffled air before things got all unnecessary. "I think it would be best if Cyrus went with you. He knows the city better than anyone."

The only thing I was assured of was that Cyrus wasn't coming along to help me or the priest. He was coming to either quietly kill me or, at best, keep an eye on me. The Duke didn't trust me running around his manor without an escort, I understood that. I also understood that he might have paid Cyrus to vent me somewhere nice and quiet, where Clary would never find out about it. If I was someone like him, in charge of a fief with a reputation to maintain and peace to keep, I'd want a trouble causer like me out of the way, I got that. I just wasn't going along with it.

"Could I borrow a couple of blades? Only, I mislaid mine."

Cyrus snorted. "You won't need blades while you're with me."

I ignored him. The duke's tail swished thoughtfully. He smelled of rosewater and just a hint of mousy sweat, but only a hint, the lad was a cool cove.

"Of course," he said. "And perhaps a change of clothes?" He wrinkled his nose. "Those are rather distinctive. If you have to go abroad in Dayside it's best not to give the clanks a reason to stop you, especially now. As you know from firsthand experience, Imperial knights hit first and then hit again, just to make sure."

"Yeah, thanks. I take it the Sanguines won the vote in the Synod?"

Cyrus and Duke Leo exchanged knowing looks. I'd bet my shirt that they had a stake in this business. That they seemed surprised that I did was just another indication of how stupid they thought I was. I decided not to attempt to disavow them. I'd take the easy road and play the idiot, see if I could work their underestimation to my advantage.

"Aye, they did, in the main. They verified the legitimacy of a rather awkward piece of prophecy, which in turn has led the Senate to consider drafting new laws." Leopold's tail flicked angrily from side to side, belying the placid expression on his face and the calmness in those dark eyes. "They have yet to be voted on, but there seems little doubt they'll be passed. How do, what do you know about the Synod and the Order of the Sanguine Shadow?"

I shrugged. "Just what the priest used to babble on about. In truth, I didn't pay much heed. He talked too much for my liking."

I was given a couple of cheap old knives and a pair of breeches and a shirt. The clothes were dark grey and made of soft leather. They were also the finest clothes I'd ever worn. For the first time in weeks, I actually felt good, which was due in no small part to the Annurashi's healing. I was still weak, but I could see out of both eyes, my various aches had diminished, and my lung felt almost as good as new. I didn't know what significance the new mark in my palm had, or how kindly Shallunsard would take to being usurped, but I could tell him what I told her, with the same confidence. I didn't ask for what she did to me.

Chapter Eighteen

Leo and Clary bade me farewell before scampering off somewhere, leaving me alone with Cyrus. I wasn't sure what to make of this garlanded wolf. He looked too much the bravo for me to take him seriously. What I couldn't dispute was the map he owned detailing the main routes through Nightside and the sneaky sewer entrances and exits up to Dayside Valen.

From snatches of conversation I'd pieced together, and a few casual questions here and there, I'd found out that Nightside was divided into four quarters, each ruled by a duke. Like above ground, the dukes sat in council and made citywide decisions together.

"Are you paying attention?" Cyrus snapped. It was a fair call. I hadn't been paying much heed while he droned on about patrols and rock falls, and all the usual, petty inconveniences that seemed to worry humans.

"Of course," I replied.

He grunted. "Good, because I won't be going over this again."

"Pity. You have such a lovely speaking voice." I have to say, he was quick for a human. To be fair to myself, I was still recovering from my injuries, but credit where it's due, he was on me like a fly on shit as soon as the words left my lips. Without giving the slightest indication that he was going to move, he did, and I was pinned to the table with a blade across my throat before I could say— "Fuck, you're quick."

"I am." He assured me. "And while we're about the truth saying, let me tell you this, I do not like you." He pressed the knife a fraction harder against my throat. "You traffic with demons, and like the cold-blooded, fucking lizard that you are, you don't give a damn about anyone but yourself. Worst of all, *for you*, is that you have brought trouble to the house of my friend, which really pisses me off." The pressure on my throat increased a notch. He held the blade there for an uncomfortably long time before letting me up. "Now don't speak unless I tell you to because I find your lisping voice irritating, and if you so much as look at me askance I will end you. Is that clear?"

I might be a touch on the impetuous side, but contrary to popular opinion, I'm not a complete lackwit. I nodded and promised myself that before this game was up, I'd close this shitstain's account.

According to my new best friend, the plan was to avoid the sewers by going up through a storm drain that fed into the underground river which ran through Nightside. Apparently, the main sewer routes in and out of Nightside were being more heavily patrolled by the clanks since the attempted robbery at the Hall of Heroes. This was said with emphasis as if I might have forgotten I was the idiot who'd made a turnip out of what should have been a peach of a job.

He told me that the storm drains had an inlet near the Sanguine Shadow's monastery, but that it was difficult to get through. Again, I kept my mouth shut and didn't express my doubts as to the veracity of his claim, or its lack of importance to anyone save a soft, human pus-sack like him.

I was informed that once we were inside the monastery, we'd still have to locate Tobias if he was there and alive. How I'd managed to survive all these years without Cyrus there to point out the blindingly obvious was a mystery. One useful piece of information he offered was about the woman who'd stolen the hammer and thrown me and the priest across the Hall of Heroes. Her name was Augustra Octarius. She was the leader of the Sanguine Shadow and as of three days ago, the favorite to become the next Eklesiastis of the Pantheon. As much as I needed the damn hammer, I wasn't looking forward to dancing with her again.

After finishing the threat peppered briefing, Cyrus led me into the bowels of Leopold's sprawling holding. The more I saw of Nightside, the more I was convinced that it could only exist with the knowledge and approval of those above ground. There was no doubt the cement that bound the two was gold, which made me wonder whose side the royalty of Nightside would stand on should war come to the city, particularly as Leopold was touched. It made me curious about his fellow dukes. I caught myself. I was starting to think like a schemer and that never went well from what I'd seen.

The gutterhaunt led us to some smugglers' tunnels. The rough-hewn passageways smelled of urine and seeping water but were dimly lit by a few cracked and covered glowstones. The floor was smooth and firmly compacted from the passing of many feet over many years. In dingier side tunnels, I glimpsed the ghostly outline of barrels and sacks and lurking amongst them the bright beady eyes of dog rats and the occasional splatter of luminous fungus. Cyrus moved confidently and quietly. I was reasonably confident that I could beat him in a fistfight but blade to blade might be interesting. He didn't talk much, save to point out holes, low ceilings, or how noisy I was, which was bollocks. For the most part, we walked in near silence. I still had a headache but felt better to be up and moving, even if it was with someone who might try to kill me at any moment. In fact, it was that aspect of our otherwise dull trip that kept me awake. The question was, did I wait until he made his move, or pre-empt him?

The cove was carrying enough blades to open a shop, and his assault upon my person told me that he knew how to use them. He even smelled mean, his scent being comprised mainly of meat, hard liquor, and blade oil. I felt better than I had, but I wasn't at my best by any means, and my head was a constant aching reminder that I needed to find Tobias. I'd have to give killing this cove some thought and in the meantime, keep my guard up. About an hour into our little excursion, I heard the unmistakable sound of rushing water.

"Almost there," he said and lengthened his stride.

A little further on, the tunnel widened to a crescent-shaped ledge. The ground had been worn away by the water pouring from a drain above us and into the underground river that flowed below. Cyrus stood on the edge, hands on his hips, watching me with measured disdain from beneath his hood.

"Over here, Breed," he said like I might decide to go somewhere else. Dutifully I went and stood beside him.

"I take it we're climbing up there?"

He sniffed. "Aye." He pointed to the outlet of the drain some twenty feet above us. "We need to—"

Without over-thinking the deed, I straight-armed him off the ledge. I got the impression he turned his head, but the hooded cloak cut down his peripheral vision so that he didn't see me move until it was too late. He grappled with air ropes as he plunged into the muscular torrent and vanished.

“Threaten me, will you?” I demanded of the raging water. It didn’t answer.

Had I been inclined to feel a crumb of guilt over settling Cyrus’s account, the climb up the wet wall and into the drain would have rid me of it. A few feet beyond the opening the tunnel was sealed by a grille and had been for about a century if the rust was anything to go by. I checked for cunning levers or false locks, even had a quick feel with magic to see if there was a glamor cast upon it, but no. Unless you were very thin or made of water, it was a dead end, and would have been my dead end, had I not beaten the cunny-bucket to the kill.

Relieved, annoyed and soaked, I climbed down and sat on the ledge. I had to go back, but I couldn’t return to Duke Leo, given he was the one who’d probably paid the late and unlamented Cyrus to scratch me. As I pondered my next move, I heard soft footsteps in the tunnel behind me. I leaped to my feet, blades in hand. Of all those I imagined it might have been, Tosspot wasn’t one of them.

Even though he’d bathed and was wearing clean linen, he still looked grubby, the grime he’d accumulated over years had been tattooed into his pel-poisoned flesh.

“Got yourself lost, eh, Breed?” He grinned his brown toothed grin.

“Have you been following me?”

"I was following both of you. You lost your friend as well as your way, eh? Very careless."

"Fuck off, Tosspot. I'm not in the mood."

"Don't weep, demon. I know the way out." He skipped on the spot. "Know the way t'the Shadow house. That's where you're after, ain't it? Need t' find the good father, eh?"

His appearance and offer of help was a little too timely. I tasted the air, just to make sure it really was him and not some sharp cove cloaked by a spell. It was Tosspot all right. No mere demon could replicate the frowsty stink of self-abuse that clung to the dirty old cull.

That he was here did not sit well with me, and neither did his claim to have followed me and Cyrus without either of us spotting him. Unfortunately, time was prancing on like a homebound urux and I needed to find the priest.

"Show me, and be warned, I'm in a killing mood, so you cross me at your peril."

He laughed and skipped along the tunnel. Again, I got the distinct impression that I wasn't being taken seriously. We doubled back to the last branching passage. It turned out that Cyrus hadn't led us far wrong. Perhaps he'd intended to do for me then find the priest himself. Tosspot turned off the main path and through a side tunnel to where a fissure had cracked the roof in a much earlier collapse.

"So how did you know this was here?" I asked, nosy as a lurcher. Tosspot smiled, got out his pel pipe and licked the sticky residue from the bowl.

"I bin exploring, having a look-see while you were playing with fairies."

"Eh? You mean the Annurashi? I'd love to hear you call her that to her face."

Tosspot capered like a drunken puppeteer was yanking his dangle. "You're moving up in the world, Breed. Up, up you go." He flapped his spindly arms. "I'm going to find Clary, get her to cadge me some pel from her mousy dimber damber."

"Aye, you do that. Oh, and Rubin." He stopped, spun on his heel and eyed me suspiciously. "Don't tell anyone you've seen me, eh?"

He just laughed and skipped out of the tunnel. I chimneyed up the fissure and along a narrow crawl space that had been hacked out of the rock. The old lunatic hadn't played me false, the tunnel came out on the other side of the grilled storm drain. From there on it was only a matter of wading through relatively clean runoff water that flowed ankle-deep along the outlet. I say relatively clean, I still had to dodge the occasional floating island of fatty and decaying agglomeration, but I felt more at home here than I did wandering around Nightside or Dayside Valen.

It was dark when I crawled out of the drain. As Cyrus promised, it came out beside the monastery which was surrounded by a culvert overflowing with trailing vines of red viper's tongue. I could hear singing coming from the building. It was the usual loud, pompous dirge favored by religious culls although the singing was nowhere near as pompous as the temple itself which was a gilt-edged nightmare.

The whole edifice had been painted a lurid shade of red. It was so screamingly bright that even at night it hurt my eyes to look at it. But that wasn't the worst thing about it. Oh, my no. Some demented genius had decided to imbed spells into the walls, which wasn't unheard of except these spells weren't wards. The monumental waste of money had been spent on a purely decorative effect and I use the term 'decorative' loosely. I watched as every few seconds, deep red shadows rippled around the building. It was horribly, tastelessly literal.

Like a competent glazier, I quickly spotted an open casement. Satisfied that I was unobserved, I scaled the wall and took a look-see inside. As befitted an order dedicated to a shadow, the prayer room was dark and joy of joys, it was also empty. I hopped inside as another ripple of shadow crossed the building.

Getting inside was always going to be the easiest part of this venture. Finding the hammer was the tricksy bit.

It might take all night to search the place room by room, so I resolved to lay hands upon one of the sanctimonious little arseweevils and persuade them to tell me where it was being kept. I was about to go hunting when I heard footsteps coming towards the door. I dived behind the altar as the door opened and a couple of gospellers bumbled in.

“That went really well, didn’t it?” His voice was strained like he was carrying something.

“You think so? I thought the choir was off tonight and Prenam’s sermon was the same one he gave last week.”

“Was it?”

“Aye. Don’t you remember? He quoted Chankuk the Venerable’s speech to the masses at the slaughter of Riven Eye Gorge.”

“I don’t think he did.”

“He did, I’m telling you, he just swapped a few paragraphs around.”

“Well, I liked it. Yay, I say unto thee that rivers shall choke on the corpses of our enemies and we shall know glory.”

“You missed a line.”

“No, I didn’t.”

"You did. After the rivers shall choke on the corpses, there's a bit about flowing with blood."

"Not in Prenam's version." I'd heard enough.

They'd brought a lamp with them but it was small and cast more shadows than light and so I risked a peek from behind the altar to check where they were before I made my move. There were two of them stacking books on a shelf. I leaped from my hiding place, grabbed one by the neck and bashed his head against a wall. The other I punched in the mouth before he had a chance to shout. The one I was holding went limp, but the other was staggering about, moaning and clutching his face. I let go of the unconscious one, drew a knife, and slapped the moaner on the pate.

"Shut your yap or I'll vent you," I said. That got his attention and very wisely he did just that. I slid the door bolt and gestured for him to sit. "Right, you, where's Augustra stashed my fucking hammer?"

"I, I don't know."

I slapped him on the head again, a little harder this time. "Don't tell me you don't know, or I'll clip those shells from either side of your head as they are apparently a waste of skin and I hate waste. Course, I'll have to cut out your tongue first, just to keep the noise down."

"Shekeepsthehammerinherstudy," he blurted. Tears smeared his red eye make-up and ran down either side of his snot-bubbling nose.

"Slow down." I slapped him again.

"Her study. Third floor, big door at the end of the hallway, you can't miss it."

"Good lad. Best close your eyes, eh?"

Blubbering, he closed his eyes and fell to his knees. "Please, don't k—"

I laid him out with a punch and stripped his robe before divesting the other cull of his garb. I put on the one that looked to be the closest fit and tore the other into strips which I used to bind the pair of them. As usual, my feet stuck out of the bottom of the robe, but it was blessedly dark in the hallway, and I managed to reach the stairwell without bumping into anyone else. All the noise seemed to be coming from the lower levels. The air in here was thick with the smell of incense laced with pel and the underlying odor of unwashed human.

I crept up the stairs, beneath the painted arrogance of gilt-framed hierarchs who stared down disapprovingly from the walls. My feet sank into a carpet, so luxurious it felt like I was walking on clouds, the walls were likewise draped in a fortune of red silk.

If the intention had been to make the place look imposing it had failed. It looked more like a high-class brothel than a temple. Of course, I didn't know much about the order of the Sanguine Shadow. It might very well have been one of those sects where to fuck is to pray, in which case it had struck a reasonable balance. The Pantheon had hundreds of cults, all competing for patronage and membership. Each had their own unique twist, but the sex and drug cults were always popular.

A splinter of light squeezed from under an imposing door at the end of the hallway. I drew my blades and hoped Augustra wasn't in. Alas, I was out of luck. A woman's throaty laughter rang out.

I listened at the door. There was no way I was going to rush her. Like Tobias, she was a sorcerer, and like him, she could burn me down to the nub before I got within a yard of her. I sheathed my blades and had a look through the keyhole.

Standing against the glare of a roaring fire was Augustra. She was wearing a loose red robe and had a dildo strapped around her nethers. More importantly, above her on the mantelpiece was the Hammer's hammer.

"Just sign the confession and I'll stop. Unless you don't want me to?" She smiled at someone I couldn't quite see. I angled myself and managed to see that the unfortunate cull she was talking to was bent over a table. His brown, homespun robe was pulled up around his waist and his drawers were bunched around his ankles. I heard chains rattle and gagged shouting. My headache vanished in an instant. It was Tobias. I'd forgotten all about the poor cull.

Augustra adjusted her borrowed member. "Still won't? Then you leave me no choice."

There was more muffled shouting.

"Don't blame me. Your father said he'd kill me if you have so much as a bruise when I hand you over, but I must have that confession. You see my problem?"

He shouted almost intelligible curses. I could see he was shaking, straining against his bonds.

Augustra laughed. "And you a priest. What would Saint Bartholomew think? Now, where were we?" She walked over and squared her hips behind him.

It was an ornate door, heavy, highly decorated, inlaid with shell and polished bone. Funny, the things you notice in those rare moments of absolute clarity. As well as beautifully decorated, the door was also unlocked. It took me just three quiet strides to reach her. I didn't bother to announce my presence, swear any oaths, or make any promises, I just snapped her neck.

I stepped over the body and pulled the priest's robe down. He was chained to a table. A sheet of parchment was crumpled beneath his stump and a quill lay beside it. Ink was splattered all over his hand and sleeve and had soaked into the table top, clouding the bright inlay.

The chains might have been marked with a ward against sorcery, but they weren't proof against me smashing the lock off with a hammer that happened to be lying close at hand. I say a hammer because as soon as I picked it up I knew it wasn't *the* hammer.

Now I'd freed him the priest tore the gag from his mouth and steadied himself against the table. His gaze fell on the body of Augustra.

"Oh, Breed."

I girded myself for the inevitable admonishment, but it didn't come.

"Is she dead?" he asked.

"Yes."

He shook his head. "You're too late. The Synod voted. The Senate will follow…"

"Not now," I said. He was trembling and what little color he possessed had bled from his face leaving it a pallid mask. "We need to get out of here."

"They told me you were dead." He stared at the body.

"What, again? You really need to stop listening to them." I tossed the hammer, across the room.

Tobias looked horrified. "What are you doing?"

"It isn't the hammer."

"It's clearly the hammer," the priest insisted.

"It's clearly *a* hammer, but it's not *the* hammer."

"Of course, it's the fucking hammer. I've had to listen to Augustra telling me about how she opened the tomb and took it. It has to be the hammer."

He was shaking and furious, but not because of the hammer. He was bundling all his rage together because he was in shock. The thoasa in me had never felt what he was going through, the human half had a vague idea. Nether part had the desire or patience to deal with his pain right now. "My guess is that the Hammer and his hammer were never in that tomb," I said and took a shufty out the door.

His mouth twisted into an ugly sneer. "And you're an expert now, are you?" His fist was clenched, the air charged.

"You've been hurt, you're itching for a fight, I understand, but you're looking in the wrong place. The hurt will pass."

"You seem to know an awful lot all of a sudden. Has your demon been educating you?"

"A demon, aye, but not the one you think. Mother Blake trades in flesh as much as any other commodity. They come in all shapes, ages, and sizes, bound for the brothels, many are unwilling. I've met a lot of people like Augustra."

"I knew you were despicable."

"That's enough." I was trying to be understanding, but he was asking for a punch. "I stayed away from that part of the business. Mother says it's a weakness of character, says I wasn't well rounded, but then, she talks shit."

"You might not have participated, but you knew it was happening."

He seemed determined to pick a fight, to vent his rage. I didn't blame him, I just didn't want it to be with me. "So does anyone with eyes in their head. We all live in the same fucking world, just about. The difference is that some of you sail above the shit and some of us have no choice but to wade through it."

He ran his hand over his stubbly head. He was struggling to make eye contact as though he was embarrassed or ashamed. I didn't think it would do any good to tell him that there was no need. We both knew he hadn't done anything wrong, but that didn't matter right now, so I held my tongue.

"How do you know this isn't the real hammer?" he asked.

"I don't know. I just know it isn't."

"How? Where does this insight come from? How do you know?" Pain was fueling his anger, never a good thing for a sorcerer, or those around them.

"I don't have the answer, Tobias, I'm sorry."

“It isn’t fair.”

I shrugged. “No. It isn’t fair and there’s no justice, I know, and now so do you. Come on, let’s get out of here.”

Tobias said a prayer over Augustra. I opened the door a crack just in time to see a handful of red-robed figures coming up the stairs. Closing it quickly, I signaled to Tobias. He looked at me but didn’t seem to be taking anything in.

“We can’t go that way.” I braced a chair behind the door. “We’ll have to go out the window.”

“Allow me.” Tobias raised his hands, the air crackled.

“You sure the angles are right?” I asked.

“Fuck the angles.” Before I had a chance to try and calm him down, he blew the wall out.

I’ll give him this, he didn’t believe in half-measures. As he crumpled, I scooped him up and slung him over my shoulder. A light drizzle misted the air, damping down the clouds of dust rising from the rubble. I scrambled out of the gaping hole and climbed down what was left of the outside of the building. When my feet hit the cobbles, I ran like a dragon was chasing me.

***

“Sweet salvation, I didn’t expect that to happen,” the priest said when he came to.

I'd legged it as far from the Sanguines' temple as I could, avoiding busy thoroughfares until I found a derelict house tucked at the end of a quiet, residential street. I broke in and hid in the cellar with my unconscious charge. It would do for now, but we couldn't stay here. Given what we'd just done, the clanks would tear the city apart to find us.

"You killed Augustra." Happily, there was no hint of recrimination in his voice, he was just trying to recall what had happened. Being slightly fuddled wasn't a bad thing for him right now. Being raped was hard to bear so perhaps it was best that his memory was hazy.

"I did, and you blew a massive hole in their temple."

"Oh. Yes. I did, didn't I? They will not forgive either act. We're in trouble, Breed."

I laughed. "For a change. I think a trip abroad might be in order, somewhere like Shen, perhaps?"

"None of this would have happened if they hadn't been so damn greedy." He put his head in his hand.

I decided that I wasn't going to abandon him just yet. No matter what my next move would be, I was going to need coin and Tobias was my best chance of getting it without going on the rob. Given my somewhat strained relationship with Duke Leo, it was probably best to avoid robbery as all fences were bound to be affiliated. Though I hated to admit it, I was running out of room to maneuver and gaining enemies with every stride. The only useful ally I had was the demon, but I'd be damned if I asked him for help.

"You should get a message to your friends in the order."

He shook his head. "No, absolutely not."

"Unless you're planning on swimming to Shen, we're going to need coin."

"I haven't decided what I'm going to do yet, but I cannot go to the order. They're in enough trouble because of me. I won't endanger them further."

This wasn't what I wanted to hear. "They'll probably do much better now that Augustra isn't on their backs. You said it yourself, your brother's a halfwit. And Sister Kyra will be desperate to know what's happened to you." I thought that sounded rather good as persuasive arguments went. The priest shook his head again. There was just no pleasing some people.

"I don't know if I can trust her. Someone told Augustra our plans, it could have been her, and why do you care?"

"I won't dignify that with an answer." I couldn't, the truth was, I didn't care. I just needed money.

"I'm sorry, Breed. I'm sorry about everything. I'll get word to Kyra, somehow."

'Somehow' involved me swapping clothes with Tobias and sending him off to find a bakery.

I waited anxiously for him to return while wearing his scratchy, too-small robe. He was a thin-shouldered cull and no mistake. He came back with a loaf of fresh bread.

"Did you do what I said?" I asked.

"Yes, yes."

"Nobody saw you? Nobody asked any questions or saw what you did?"

"Gods, Breed. Paying a baker's boy to deliver a loaf of bread is not beyond me. Do you want your clothes back?"

"Yes, I bloody do. You put the note inside the loaf, right?"

"I'm not even going to answer that." We exchanged clothes. As before, he didn't know where to look while we dressed. I didn't give a shit, a body's a body, clothed or naked but humans, like arrachids, have some strange ideas when it comes to modesty.

We waited out the day in the temporary sanctuary of the cellar. It was raining outside and if a search was being mounted they hadn't made it this far yet. The street was quiet save for the usual sounds of children shouting and wailing and neighbors passing the time of day. While we shared the bread, I told him about what had happened after we were caught. I didn't tell him about the flies and the demon sigil, instead of that I told him I'd escaped into the sewers after overcoming one of the clanks. I did tell him about the Annurashi which was a mistake.

"How stupid can you be, Breed?"

The shock of his ordeal seemed to be wearing off as he sounded more like his whiny, judgmental self, although I could smell anger lurking just beneath the surface. He pored over the mark in my palm, turning my hand this way and that while muttering to himself.

"Hold my hand much longer and we'll be betrothed," I said at last.

He let go. "This could be very bad. The Annurashi don't do anything by chance."

I held up my hands. "Nothing to do with me, your priestship. I was helpless, lying on a couch. Blame Clary, in fact, blame yourself. Clary had her boyfriend save me because she wanted me to save you, not that I wouldn't have anyway." I smiled.

"Oh, I believe you. After all, it's not like you have a choice." His gaze drifted to the bonding cuff.

I was an unlucky cove, I'll grant you, but right then I was thankful that I was me and not him.

Chapter Nineteen

On the way to the singular dump where Tobias had arranged to meet Kyra, I broke some rules of the Court and dipped a few pockets. I also lifted a couple of cloaks.

With a basic disguise and a handful of coin, the priest and I settled into a corner of the designated backstreet cellar-dive with a couple of mugs of the vilest ale I'd ever drunk. Tobias paid a yawning link boy a copper penny to keep an eye out while we got down to the serious business of cradling our flat beer and waiting.

The cellar was a real dump and in marked contrast to the sumptuous palaces and guild houses that I had lately frequented. I had no idea if we were still in Duke Leo's domain or if we'd crossed into the turf of another lordling. Wherever we were this was a wretched hole of the lowest order.

This place felt like one of those places that no one ever claims, somewhere that's fallen through the cracks. It was holes like this where poor culls with nowhere left to go fetched up; flotsam's end, which was appropriate given our situation, or rather my situation. Tobias would be all right, he had friends who'd look after him, but I had no idea where to start looking for that damned hammer.

I supped my ale. It tasted like the dregs of a pool of stagnant piss that someone with a bag of hops had once walked past. "This is more like it," I said to the priest. He grunted and curled his stump around his mug but didn't touch a drop.

"My father knew where I was, but he left me there. Nicus Lutius, Mattarax Vulsones, Hero of the Battle of Gutomer, soldier, senator, advisor to the Empirifex, and bastard." He raised his mug.

"I'll drink to that." I took a drink of my terrible ale. Tobias had changed since I'd first met him. He looked a little sadder, a little wiser perhaps, but that was no bad thing, despite the route he'd taken to get there. "Look on the bright side. At least your father didn't put a bounty on your head. He just wants you out of the way until this is sorted in Senate and Synod, and he becomes even wealthier than he already is. It's going to make for a fine inheritance. Think how many brown robes you'll be able to buy."

"I foreswore wealth when I joined the order. This is the only robe I own."

I almost choked on my ale. "You're a very strange human."

He held his stump close to his body as though protecting it. "What do you mean by that?"

And then it hit me like a kick in the cods, which was what I deserved for being so dense. All the time, it had been right in front of me, tickling my senses, and I hadn't noticed. Tobias was touched. That's what happened to his hand, or whatever it had been before it got lopped off.

I drew a sly breath, tasted the air to confirm what I'd known all along. Soft as a feather, there it was, that subtle, peachy taint edging the smell of human sweat. I glanced at his stump. His cheeks flushed.

"I said, what did you mean by that?"

"Nothing. It was just a joke," I said. He looked away.

After a couple of hours of not speaking to each other and listening to the old sots fighting over slops from the penny barrel, a robed figure heaved his bulk down the stairs. Wrapped in a heavy cloak that was glittering with raindrops, the newcomer slowly made his way over to our table. There was no sign of Kyra, but Tobias obviously knew this panting cull and beckoned him over.

The corpulent fellow didn't look like a stranger to overindulgence. The whites of his eyes were bloodshot. His wine-soaked face had collapsed in on itself like a soggy pudding. Before sitting down beside Tobias, he tipped me a nod of acknowledgment.

"I'm so sorry, Toby," he whispered. "The guard at the hall betrayed us. Kyra is devastated."

Tobias clasped the old man's hand. "Never mind that now. What's going on, Jared?"

The fellow shuddered like a speared brachuri. "The Synod's in uproar. Soon after your escape, Marius convened an emergency session where he called for the order to be excommunicated." His rheumy eyes glittered, his lip quivered. "He's understandably furious about Augustra's death and is trying to blame the order. Dear gods, Toby, you didn't kill her, did you?" Tobias looked like the arse had just fallen out of his world. He stared at the table.

"No."

"Of course you didn't. Forgive me. And Marius won't get his way. None of the Synod would want that precedent to be set and then, well." He leaned in. "Your father has been in talks."

"What do you mean 'talks'?" Tobias narrowed his eyes. "What's happened?"

"Your father was summoned to the Senate. I, that is, we, have agreed that you will be spared, and the order will be given a substantial donation." Jared put his hand on Tobias's arm. "Substantial, Toby, but only if we support the Sanguine Shadow in the Synod and agree to put this whole episode down to interference from *undesirable elements*." His gaze flicked in my direction.

"What? You mean Breed?" Tobias sounded shocked. I wasn't. "No, that isn't right. And this is more important than a new statue."

"More like an entirely new monastery to put the statue in, Toby." Jared licked his lips. "Would you have us cast out just to prove a point?"

Tobias slammed his stump on the table. "The demons are returning. The fate of the fucking world is at stake."

Jared looked around to see if anyone had heard Tobias's outburst. They hadn't or if they had, they didn't care. "There's nothing we can do. Kyra thinks it's best that we stick together. A united front against the chaos. It's too complex, Toby. We don't know.' He glanced at me again. 'We don't know who's with who, but we know who we are. Sweet Salvation, the fate of the order is in your hands. I'm begging you, Toby."

Tobias looked at me as if I had the answer. I felt colder than when the dragon had breathed on me. Numbed to the core, I shook my head as the stitch-up was laid out right in front of me. Jared gave a sly smile and pressed his point.

"You need to leave Valen, my boy. The Empire in fact." He cast another wary glance over his shoulder and oozed a bit closer to Tobias. "I've taken the liberty of booking passage for you on a ship leaving for Shen. For your own safety, I urge you to take it."

Tobias gestured to me. "What about Breed?"

I knew where this was going. I could tell by the way the cull had been giving me the shark eyes. I leaned in close. "Aye, what about me?" I asked, more out of sport than a desire to learn their plans. I knew I was being offered up as the lamb for this job.

"I, we, that is…" He couldn't look me in the eye. "Kyra and the order thought it best that you find your own way."

I waggled my wrist. The silver cuff gleamed. "I can't be separated from Brother Tobias. I'm bound to him."

The old pissbag fumbled under his cloak, wafting the vinegary stench of his unwashed flesh into the air as he flapped the sodden wool aside and produced a bulging pouch. He slid it across the table to me. I flicked the lacing open. The unmistakable sound of gold hitting the table got the attention of the locals. I bared my fangs and they went back to their own business.

"That should be enough to pay a sellspell to break the enchantment before you suffer any ill effects due to separation." Jared smiled. "And there are coins to spare."

I nodded. “But what about finding the hammer? The one Augustra had is a fake.”

“Is it?” Jared looked to Tobias for confirmation. Tobias looked at me. I folded my arms. He had to decide for himself.

“Aye, it is,” he said, conceding the truth. “I’m not convinced we shouldn’t try to find the real one, as we initially planned.”

Jared blanched, licked his lips. “Kyra doesn’t think that’s the best course, and I have to say, I agree. We have a chance to smooth things over with the Senate and save the order. This matter can be looked at in the future. For now, everyone has agreed it should be put aside.”

Gloom doused the conversation. The barkeep sluiced the floor. I watched old rushes sail furiously on the sudden tide while I contemplated the coin-induced change of heart of the order of Saint Bart and, more importantly, how it would affect me. The straws foundered against table legs as the beery tide drained away. This was what I’d wanted, wasn’t it?

I snagged the pouch, tucked it into my shirt. “That it then?” I expected nothing from Tobias, he looked beaten, spent. I, however, had to find the damned hammer. Tobias didn’t look at me. An ocean of awkward silence washed away the sandy knot of commitment we’d briefly shared.

"We'd better get going, Toby," cooed Jared. "I've arranged a place for you to stay until we can get you out of the city. It should only be for a few days."

"Wait, no. I can't. I won't abandon Breed."

The older man frowned. "You're not abandoning Breed, Tobias. Think, man. The two of you are known. A one-handed human and his warspawn companion are hard to miss."

"He's right." I patted Tobias's arm, like we were friends. "Together we stand out like cocks in a henhouse." That I'd had every intention of leaving him and had even been charged with killing him was not the point. At this moment it looked like I was doing the decent thing and I liked that picture. It wasn't one that I often saw.

"You didn't abandon me."

"You better go," I said. I was enjoying the brief and utterly false sensation that I'd made a noble sacrifice. "I'll be off now. You should wait a while before heading out." I grinned. "Take care, priest."

Jared sagged like an overcooked soufflé, visibly relieved that I wasn't going to be difficult. Tobias always looked like a whey-faced pup, so it was hard to tell what he was thinking.

The Order of Saint Bartholomew had sold me out in the politest way I've ever been sold out in my life. It made me smile. I pulled up the hood of my stolen cloak and left. I didn't look back.

The inn was on the lower level of the city. Overhead, rain-washed walkways wrapped around stairwell towers and grey daylight filtered through the filigree ironwork to pool in the rutted mud. All the storehouses that framed this lonely ginnel were shuttered against the bucketing rain. The central drain ran thick and swift. I had no allies in this city that I could go to. I was hunted by the law, the Sanguine Shadow, and probably Duke Leo and his courtiers.

And then there was Shallunsard.

I didn't know the demon well, but from our few encounters, I guessed that he wasn't going to be pleased when he found out that I hadn't killed the priest or found the bloody hammer. I was about to work myself up into a righteous lather of self-pity when I caught the familiar scent of calthracite and blood wefting through the warp of the rain.

"How forgetful of me." I drew my blades.

Sebastian Schiller stepped into the lane about thirty feet away. About the same distance downwind, an ogren stomped into the middle of the road. I took a step back so that I could keep an eye on both of them.

"Ah. There you are, Breed. That is what they call you, isn't it? Most amusing." Schiller whipped a rapier from its scabbard. Against the rain, it was nothing more than a fish-scale flash of silver, a thing made of light and menace. “I would say you’re hard to find, but you’re not.” He smiled revealing his fangs. “Mistake the first was not killing me. Very sloppy for a Guild Blade if you don’t mind me saying. Mistake the second was leaving Marius and Cassia alive.”

“Only two? I’m just not trying hard enough.”

“You struck me as an underachiever.” He frowned shook his head. “I see you’ve lost my firelance. This is a pity, for both of us. For my part, I think I shall carve my displeasure in your hide.” He gave the rapier a casual flick to loosen his wrist. “Was that too much? I’m never sure with threats. It’s so tricky trying to find the balance between menacing and ridiculous.”

“I don’t suppose you’d take a promissory note in lieu of the lance?”

He rested the rapier on his shoulder, put his hand on his hip and smiled like we were old friends talking about the weather. “Oh, I would, but given that there’s a tidy bounty on your head, I don’t reckon you’re a good investment.”

“Oh? I thought the bounty had been paid.”

“Last I knew the bounty offered by one Pork Chop Jing was very much alive.” He whipped the rapier through the air. “You’ve managed to upset a lot of people. I’m genuinely impressed by what a troublesome cove you are.” He smiled and tossed a coil of dark ringlets over his shoulder. The ogren chuckled, spat on her hand, and hefted a double-headed ax.

“It was pure luck that I had business in Appleton.” Schiller made a practice lunge. “Lots of contracts up for grabs there right now, some sort of turf war. I do love a good turf war, don’t you? But yes, had I not been there I might never have found out who the sneaky bastard was who’d stolen my lance.”

“Would that be the same firelance you shot me with? Only, I think you’re way ahead of me in the sneaky bastard stakes.”

“Let’s not quibble over details.” He paused, tilted his head, and sniffed. “Ah. You brought a friend too. The priest didn’t mention you had a crew.”

I had no idea what he was talking about, though I was keen to find out if it was Tobias who had betrayed me. “And which priest would this be?”

Schiller shrugged. “I don’t suppose it matters. Brother Jared is such an odd creature, the man has the heart of a viper wrapped in the body of a pig. He sold you cheaply, Breed.”

“I think you’ll find that—” I didn’t get chance to finish as, with a roar, the ogren rushed me.

I say rushed, but, sweet salvation, she was a slow cove.

While keeping an eye on Schiller, I waited for her to come on. I let her swing and swayed away from the ponderous blow. Using the lumbering bravo's arm as a step, I hopped over her shoulder and drew my blade around her neck. Hot blood sheeted the ground. Her ax spun from her grip and smashed into the wall as she dropped to her knees clutching her throat. It was a deep cut and the weight of her massive noggin ripped the bud from the stem, as it were. Stunned and blinking, the ogren's head rolled away from its twitching body.

Schiller sighed. "Well, that was a waste of five crowns."

I flicked the blood from my blades. "That's the least of your worries."

"I'm not the worrying kind," he said, and then darted towards me.

Not only was he tougher than he looked, but he was extremely fast. I fended off his first flurry of resounding blows purely by reflex.

He paused, stepped back and cracked the bones in his scrawny neck with a side-to-side head toss. "You have some skill. It's almost a shame that I have to take you in."

I set my guard. "Less talk, more fight."

You know those times when you regret saying something, but can't take it back? It was like fighting air. The muddy spray flew as we danced, every attack I made was met with a blindingly fast riposte and so it went, along the length of the street and back again. He only slipped up once and lunged clumsily, leaving the slightest opening. I pressed my attack, realizing too late that it was a superb feint. His blade slid into my right bicep. I swung with my left to keep him at bay as the blade in my right hand slipped from my fingers.

Schiller smiled, sniffed the blood on his blade. "Sweeter than I'd imagined, with floral undertones and a subtle hint of halfwit if I'm not mistaken."

"Do you ever get bored of the sound of your own voice?"

He laughed musically. "Not so far, and I'm older than I look. Urgh, these stockings are ruined. Pure arrachid silk, cost a fortune." He rushed me again. His wings were a droning blur, his blade a flicker of light.

I just about managed to hold my own against him. My arm hurt but it wasn't as badly injured as I first thought. Truth be told, I was enjoying myself until I caught another familiar scent on the breeze which quite soured my mood. It was akin to old leather boots that had been soaked in lemon juice and earthworms. I dared a glance over my shoulder, just to confirm it was who I thought it was.

"Mistake the third," Schiller said. I looked down just in time to see his blade slide under my guard and skewer me between the ribs.

The wicked splinter burned a breath-stealing path right through me. I fumbled my remaining blade and would have cursed had I been able to draw breath, instead, I settled for gasping.

Schiller withdrew his rapier and flicked my blood from the blade. The desire to sit in the mud quite overcame me and I folded like a freshly laundered sheet.

“Easier than I thought.” He took a silk kerchief from his sleeve and dabbed his lips. “Jing wants you alive. Apparently, he’s going to make an example of you, more’s the pity.” With a glittering flourish, the tip of his blade tickled my chin. “I find heads so much easier to transport than whole persons.”

Before I had a chance to tell him what I thought of his plan the scent of arrachid bloomed in the air, drawing both our attention. I looked up to see a familiar outline crest a rooftop.

It was the arrachid that I’d tussled with in Appleton. “This scum is mine,” she said. Her foreclaws twitched beneath her green haori.

“I don’t suppose that you’d believe me if I told you that I wasn’t trying to kill your father?” I gasped.

She glared at me. “What you say is irrelevant, vomit-sack. You broke into our home and shamed our house.” She then turned to Schiller and gave him a hard, four-eyed stare. “You will leave now.”

The Mosquito tucked his bloody kerchief up his sleeve. "Now, just a minute, milady, the contract is open, any cove can collect."

She reared. "I am the daughter of Shu Lo Jing. You will yield to me or my father will put a bounty on your head."

"And just how will he know to do that?" I asked, keen to foment discord between them.

"Breed does have a point, milady."

The arrachid smiled and dropped to the ground. "Is this where I'm supposed to say, 'because I'll tell him' so that you can say, 'not if I kill you first,'?" She unholstered a pearl-inlaid handcannon.

Schiller pouted. "I wouldn't dream of saying that. Oh, all right, perhaps I was. What can I say? I'm inclined to the dramatic. Now get thee gone, fustilugs afore I'm forced to school you like I did young Breed here."

The arrachid leveled the cannon at Schiller and fired. He was already moving, up. The shot missed as he leaped into the air. She cursed and drew a Shen blade that was sheathed across her back and advanced. Schiller grinned and came back down to earth. I lay quite still and tried to stay conscious, just in case I got the chance to scarper while they were giving each other a basting.

While I gathered my energies, Jared and Tobias emerged from the cellar. It was at least satisfying to see the look of horror on Tobias's face when he saw what was happening. Jared ushered him away sharpish, half dragging him down the street. I watched him go. He kept glancing back as he let himself be led away. The hard, heavy rain stung my face.

The arrachid and the Mosquito circled each other. They were evenly matched if very different fighters. She had a blade and a cannon, Schiller was quick and precise. By the time I had the strength to make my move both had drawn blood.

While they were busy making confetti out of each other, I seized my chance and attempted a slow and rather painful escape. I didn't have a hope in hell of outrunning either of them, but I did catch wind of something that might help me hide from them should they notice I was gone and give chase.

A few streets away I came upon my destination and stumbled gratefully into the fish market. The cobbles were slick with blood and speckled with scales. The air was wonderfully pungent. Schiller and the arrachid wouldn't be able to track my scent through here with a pack of hounds. If I could just make it out the other side I might be able to lose whichever one survived to pursue me. Unfortunately, my strength was fading quicker than that slight hope. You'd think a body would get used to this kind of thing, become inured to discomfort.

It doesn't.

I was leaking like the proverbial when, halfway across the market square, my legs buckled beneath me. I flailed as I fell and managed to tip a whole bucket of brachuri fry all over myself. This spectacular, possibly final act of self-sabotage elicited gales of laughter from the crowd and curses from the stallholder. To gild the lily of my misery, a couple of clanks strolled around the corner just as I was being berated by the brachuri dealer. I tried to get up, but my strength had fled so I sat there like an unstrung puppet all too aware of my fate.

"Well, what do we have here?" one of the clanks enquired.

I was by now resigned to an untimely and painful death. If they didn't kill me, someone else would. "What the fuck does it look like, you rusty-haired, tin-arsed self-abuser?" A baby brachuri squirmed out of my shirt, looked up at me with its bulbous eyes before wriggling away to join its brothers and sisters who were escaping down the drain. The clank turned as red as his hair, he and his sniggering companion drew their blades. The world began to darken at the edges.

"Breed!" Tobias shouted, just before someone snuffed out the candles.

Chapter Twenty

I drifted back to consciousness after the strangest and most exhausting dream involving pickle barrels, prostitutes, and fireworks. Wherever I was, I was comfortable. It was cool and dry and tasted of dust, wood smoke, and familiarity. A breeze stirred but didn't trouble the languid air to blow harder than a gentle caress.

I opened my eyes. I knew this place. Above me, the uninspiring, but seemingly happy life of Amari Geran stretched in fading, painted panels across the ceiling of his tomb. I remembered the fleshy, ample-breasted wife, the tow-haired children, and the favorite hound from my last visit. Their idealized images were slowly fading from the stucco while the man himself lay scattered like a broken puppet in the robbed-out tomb beneath me.

With consciousness came awareness and, as was usual these days, almost everything ached. I sat up. My side burned but had been neatly bandaged, as had my arm. I was naked save for a cloak thrown over me and I smelled of vinegar.

"Why do I smell of vinegar?" I said to no one in particular.

Tobias was sitting by a fire. He had a black eye and instead of his customary brown robe, he was wearing a pair of voluminous Guldistani slops, black bucket boots, and a turquoise kurta. He smiled. Tosspot and Clary wandered in from an adjoining chamber, Clary had a brace of rock rats in her hand and was wearing an oversized and dented knight's helm, which would have been worthy of comment had Tosspot not been dressed in a rather fetching floral gown. They looked a little crisp around the edges, soot-streaked and singed.

"It's from when you was in the barrel," Clary said.

"Did she just say, 'when I was in the barrel'?" I looked to Tobias for clarification.

"Yes, the barrel," he reiterated. "Don't worry, you weren't in it for long." If I wasn't mistaken, he had a twinkle in his eye, which was most unlike him and more than a little disconcerting. "And at least it helped clean off the bear grease." He looked at Clary and Tosspot who both nodded. "The fire got quite close to where the lovely ladies and gentlemen of the Blossom House had hidden us, and I didn't want you going up in flames. How are you feeling?"

"Confused. How long have I been out? And where did those two come from? What happened to Schiller and the arrachid and Brother bastard?"

Tobias blushed. "Ah, yes, Jared. I can only apologize. His holy abilities run towards calculating the very best way to put across his point."

"Eh?"

"He's incredibly persuasive. It took me a while to throw off his influence, but if it's any consolation he did help us to get out of the city."

"No, it isn't. How long have I been out?" I swung my legs off the tomb. "And where are my clothes?"

"The spider and the fly scarpered when all the clanks showed up." Clary beamed from under the helm. "You've been out for two nights and today. Lady Greenstone said you'd be out for that long and she was right. Your clothes got a bit burned. But we got you some more."

"Burned? Who the fuck is Lady Greenstone?" I managed to stand up but felt as weak as a newborn. "What have you three been up to?"

The three of them exchanged guilty looks. They were behaving like a novice crew who'd just pulled off their first rum job and were as proud as kings of the manor. I gave up. "Just give me the damn clothes."

Tosspot produced a fan and gave himself an angry wafting. "Well, there's gratitude."

* * *

They spent the next few hours giggling and talking in the code of a shared experience, one to which I wasn't privy. I did not like that they'd been up to things and I'd been there, but only in the flesh.

What I did manage to glean, other than they'd rescued me from the clanks, was that they had negotiated with a Nightsider to fix me up and then, while that was happening, Tobias had found and beaten the damnation out of his brother. Though I'd rather rip my tongue out than tell them, I was quietly proud of their achievements.

Evening settled over the cemetery, and we sat down for a meal of roasted rock rat and stale bread. My side was sore but had healed surprisingly well due, I was told, to the ministration of the mysterious Lady Greenstone. From what I gathered from their chatter she was a brachuri. How one of those fearsome crustaceans had become the madame of a landlocked brothel was beyond me. I'd always thought they were strictly monogamous and somewhat prudish when it came to sex.

I kneaded my right arm, it felt heavy, but at least it was working. Being a thoughtful crew, they'd remembered to filch me a couple of hunting knives along with a pair of black breeches, a linen shirt, and a rather fetching, if slightly too small, brocade waistcoat. I gave myself a dust bath before dressing which dampened the higher notes of the vinegar smell but didn't get rid of it entirely.

"So how did you get us out of the city?" I asked the priest, who was looking very unlike himself, sitting there, all prinked up in his rum-duds, gnawing on a rat leg like it was peacock.

"Jared lacks confidence in his skills and so it didn't take long for me to come to my senses. I ran back to where I last saw you and followed the arrachid and Schiller. While they had words with the knights over ownership of your good self, Jared and I dragged you out of there." He grinned. "And after we'd rescued you, I had words with Jared. He confessed that he'd sold you out to Schiller and begged me to forgive him."

"Which you did?"

"Naturally. He was eager to atone so I made him hand over his purse. As I was in a conversational mood I left you in the safe house with Jared and went to find Marius."

"Not sure that was wise. I'd have preferred it if you'd vented the snakish cull."

"I'm sure you would but he and Kyra thought they were doing the only thing they could do. There's no excuse for Marius, he's a prick of the highest order and so I gave him as you would say, a basting that he won't forget in a hurry."

"That's when we found him," said Clary. "You should have seen him take those Sanguines to task, Breed. He done ever so good."

Tobias blushed. "Really it was nothing, the Sanguines are not Scienticians."

"So why did you bring me back here?"

"Safe innit, demon?" Tosspot was still fanning himself and remained garbed like a gutter-run slamkin.

"I still don't know what you lot have been up to." The world tilted, my stomach lurched like a ship in a gale. "And I'd really like to know because I'm getting bored with being stabbed, beaten, and shot."

"'S'none of your bizzy, demon," Tosspot said indignantly.

"None of your bizzy," Clary echoed.

I eyeballed Clary. "You're learning too many bad habits from him. And as for dear Duke Leo, that little sly-boots paid Cyrus to scratch me from the ledger." I stretched, it hurt. Everything hurt. Everything always hurt.

"It wasn't Leo." Clary stood up and planted her fists on her hips, which was quite the most ridiculous sight, as she was still wearing the helmet. "It was his brother. Leopold was very angry with him."

"His brother? I never even met his bloody brother, have I?"

She frowned. "Of course, you have. It was his brother who was with me when we found you in the sewers. Took a dislike to you, he did."

"You were alone, save for that great ugly dog rat. Ah. The dog rat is Leopold's brother?"

Clary nodded.

"That's strange. I can't think for the life of me what I did to upset him. Anyway, never mind. I'm still not happy about being in this pot of arsepickle. Not happy at all."

Tobias sighed. "I know, I'm sorry, Breed, and I intend to make it up to you. Leopold has arranged safe passage for us on a ship bound for Shen. We'll go there for a few months, work out our next move. This isn't over."

"What, you mean the prophecy? What about the Synod and the Senate?"

"Fuck them." He laughed. "I never thought I'd hear myself say that."

"Me neither. I didn't think you had the stones."

"I mean it. The Empirifex is half mad and lives in the clouds and the Senate and the Synod will never learn. They're all too caught up furthering their own petty ambitions to see the danger that awaits them, to see further than their next banquet. Nothing changes, nothing ever changes." He got up, paced to the door. "That's why this place is a cemetery."

I leaned against Amari's tomb. "I did not know that." Or where this speech was leading. It occurred to me that he might have lost his wits to the Paradox of Power, either that or he was being poetical.

"This valley and the surrounding area was where the original city of Valen stood until the demons leveled it. After the war, the citizens buried their dead here near the ruins and rebuilt Valen where it is now. Even then, when the demons came the first time, the Synod and the Senate were too busy vying with each other for power that they didn't see the danger until it was too late. That's where the warspawn came in." He leaned on the broken door and gazed into the gloom of evening. "I've had enough of them and their games." He backed away from the door and kicked dirt over the fire.

"What is it?" I went to see what was wrong.

"I was sure we weren't followed," Tobias insisted.

"Uh-uh," I said as the clanks crested the far edge of the valley, their menacing silhouettes hard against the milky light of the dying day. With them were a dozen or so greenshanks. The more lightly armored guards were clambering amongst the tombs.

I looked at Tobias.

"Well, I didn't think we'd been followed." He rubbed his head with his stump. That was the old Tobias. I could see his confidence shrinking. "I'm not sure I can deal with, sweet salvation, there must be fifty of them."

"If not more." My side was healing, but the bright spot of blood on the bandage told me that, just for a change, I wasn't fighting fit.

"If I must make another calculation, if the angles are wrong and I lose control…"

I laughed. "We'll take a lot of arseholes with us to hell. C'mon, it'll be fun, briefly."

I turned to Clary and Tosspot. "You two keep quiet and stay away from the door. Tobias and I are going to draw them away." I looked at Tobias. He nodded.

"Why don't you just go down?" Clary asked.

We both looked at her. "Down where?" I asked.

"Down into the depths, down, down, and out to the city that was, stupid demon," Tosspot rasped. He looked terrible. "Down to where the rock rats live among the roots and bones."

Tobias and I looked at each other. The greenshanks were getting closer and the knights weren't far behind. It wouldn't be long before they found us. "If you know a way out, lead on," I said.

Clary straightened her helmet and ran off to the back of the tomb with Tosspot in tow. Tobias and I followed.

She led us into a second chamber that held three more ransacked sarcophagi. One of them had tipped into a hole in the floor. By the looks of it, grave robbers had tossed the lid off the coffin and the weighty object had smashed through into another chamber buried below.

Like good thieves, they hadn't wasted the opportunity and several more tunnels led off from the lower chamber that was scattered with bones and rock rat nests. Giggling, Clary slid down the lid, followed by the rest of us although Tobias and I didn't giggle. Rats squealed and ran for cover as we tumbled into their domain.

Chapter Twenty-One

We followed the main passage for about a mile as it gradually angled upwards. When we emerged, I could see the walls of Valen looming darkly against the bleeding edge of the horizon.

At first, I thought we'd come out near the ruins of a farm as stones lay scattered across a hummock of ground that was too rough to till. On closer inspection, I saw that the stones were dressed and carved and that the ghostly outlines of buildings stretched across neighboring fields, punctuated here and there by fangs of broken columns and remnants of walls too stubborn to yield entirely to decay. The ground sloped down into a shallow valley in the middle of which was a small mound that was stripped to the bare earth save for scabs of crusty rubble and half a dozen standing stones each about six feet tall. A large flat slab lay blackened and cracked near the mound.

"This is where the demon hordes were finally vanquished," Tosspot said with uncharacteristic clarity as he kicked an urux turd. "Right here."

"I can't say I've ever been here before," Tobias said.

"And you call yourself a scholar." I went down to the mound in the valley. Other than the standing stones it looked a natural rise. "Any idea what this was for?" I asked Tobias who was already heading away from the city.

"That? No. Anyway, come on, we need to get going, they can't be far behind."

I started to follow, pleased that the priest's confidence was returning but there was something nagging at me that made me slow my pace. I stopped. Clary skipped after Tobias. Tosspot was hopping along behind them, trying to take off the dress. I went back to the mound.

The slender stones were unmarked and unremarkable save that they were standing and mostly intact. I touched one and immediately withdrew my hand. It was vibrating.

"Breed? Breed!" Tobias pointed at the tunnel. "We have to go."

"Get going, I'll catch up." I'd heard the din of armor long before he had, but it now echoed loudly as the knights pounded through the tunnel. I knew that I should go, but something held me, something about the stones.

"You seen something you like, Breed?"

I glanced round to see Tosspot was standing behind me, watching with interest. I touched the stone again, put both hands on it, and twisted. It turned. I wasn't surprised. I'd expected it to move.

"What the hell?" Tobias made to come back, but Clary grabbed him and tried to drag him away.

When I felt I'd turned the stone enough, I moved on to the next. Nothing happened. I touched a third. Again, nothing. Formless panic prickled my gut. I moved on to a fourth and was again rewarded by a skin-tingling vibration that was running through the stone. I glanced at Tobias.

"Do you know what you're doing, Breed?" he asked.

"No fucking idea." I turned the fourth stone. This time I knew I'd turned it enough because a space that shouldn't be there, an impossible angle began to open before me like a tear in the world. I stepped back as the dark gash widened.

Behind me, knights came charging out of the tunnel. Clary squealed but didn't run. She took the helmet off and stood her ground beside Tobias.

"In the name of the Empirifex, I order you to surrender," the lead clank shouted. His troops spread out, a dozen firelances were leveled at Tobias. "Do not fucking move."

"All right, Captain that's enough." I recognized Marius's voice.

"You should have let me shoot him," I called to Tobias as his brother limped out of the tunnel. He was dressed in the scarlet robes of his order and, like his brother, he had a black eye.

"Next time, ignore me," said Tobias.

"I can hear you, you know," Marius shouted from over by the tunnel.

"How are the angles?" I asked the priest. He shushed me with a frown.

"I see your friends are all here too. That'll make things easier."

Tobias gave his brother a wry smile. "Make what easier? Is this it? Do you think you can just shoot us down?"

"If only. You, dear brother, are coming back to Valen where you will damn well stand trial for murder, theft, and arson. Father was less than amused by your actions, unlike the Senate. You've done the one thing he will not forgive, Toby. You've made him look stupid."

"I exposed his and your greed," Tobias retorted. "I think that matters more."

"You killed Augustra." Spittle flew from Marius's lips. "Did you really think you could get away with that? You killed her, Toby."

"You don't know what she did to me." Tobias matched his brother's fury.

"Oh, for gods' sake what? What did she do that made you take her life? What could be so terrible..." He paused as realization of what had happened dawned on him. "What did she do?"

Tobias looked down at his feet. The air turned hot and heavy. A storm was brewing.

Marius looked shocked. "I, I didn't know."

A couple of the greenshanks sniggered. Tobias shrank, the confident cove who'd recently begun to blossom wilted. "I wasn't exactly going to shout it from the rooftops, was I? And the last time we met you were more intent on killing my friends than talking."

Marius swallowed and locked eyes with his brother. For a second, I thought that Tobias had got through to him and that I was about to see some of the vaunted brotherly love humans were always boasting about. "You should have told me, Tobias." Marius turned away. "Get on with it, Captain."

The captain saluted and raised his visor before pulling an official-looking document from his boot. He cleared his throat before reading the scroll. "I am charged by the Imperial Senate to arrest and detain Tobias Lucius Vulsones who is hereby charged with the crimes of murder, treason and arson."

Clary let out a low, keening wail and began to sob.

"Shut that fucking monster up, Toby, or I will," said Marius, sounding more like his old, detestable self.

Tobias put his arm around Clary and pulled her close to him. "She's just a child."

Tosspot backed towards me.

A look of disgust spread across Marius's face. "That thing is an abomination. Step away from it, Toby, and give yourself up. I promise you'll get a fair trial."

"What are you going to do with my friends?"

I looked at the smirking clanks, lovingly hugging their firelances. "I'm no seer," I said to Tobias. "But it seems pretty fucking obvious what they intend to do to us."

"Over my dead body," the priest replied.

Marius thrust his hands into the sleeves of his robe, whistled out a deep, sighing breath. "Toby, Toby, Toby."

It was a signal. Behind Tobias, a pale shade with skin the color of sand and eyes as white as bleached bone rose out of the dusty ground. Dirt dripped like water from her wispy hair and cobweb gown.

She spread her hands and the earth beneath her rippled and flowed towards Tobias in an undulating wave. A dozen small dust devils sprang up around him and seemed to bind his arms by his sides, trapping Clary with him. I saw him gasp as the swirling winds stole the breath from his lungs. Clary's wailing cry turned to choked coughing as they were both driven to their knees by the fury of the imprisoning, sorcerous winds.

"You didn't think I'd come unprepared, did you, Tobias?" Marius's voice carried over the howling gale. "I know what you're capable of." Before he had chance to pat himself on the back, a big rat sprang from the rocks and sank its fangs into the face of one of the clanks who had her visor up.

Taken by surprise, the guard fell backwards and discharged her lance into the air as the rat chewed on her face. The shout went up as dozens of rats poured from the tunnel and began attacking the Imperials.

"See, what did I tell you? Monsters. Shoot them," Marius yelled in panic. "Shoot them all."

I drew my blades, intent on throwing myself at the sorcerer who was attacking Tobias and Clary. Rats aside, we were grossly outnumbered and without Tobias's power we were as good as dead.

As I launched myself towards the sorcerer, Tosspot caught me off balance and shoved me into the space between the stones.

The narrow-angle opened on a vast, grey plain gouged with black blasted pits and mounded with the frozen corpses of every stripe of creature that had ever walked, crawled, slithered, or flown.

We were on a battlefield, standing by a mound that was almost the twin of the one we'd just left. The difference was that on this one a slab of granite was supported by half a dozen, unblemished standing stones. I took a step towards the oddly familiar monument. Beneath my feet, ice-rimed bones shattered like glass. It was so cold I could see my breath. I took a step back and bumped into Tosspot who must have followed me through.

I grabbed him by his filthy shirt. "What the fuck is this place?"

He patted my hand. It was such an unexpected gesture that I let him go. He grinned. "It's the last battle. The Mage Lords locked it in here. Too much Schism magic, too much poison, so they froze it and locked it away forever, or not." The cackling mania had vanished. He looked at the sky. Unlike the one we had just been under, this one was black and cloudless and as still as death.

"How do you know?" I had to ask, but I really didn't want him to say what I thought he was going to say.

"Because I was there."

"I knew you were going to say that." I drew my sword and held it to his scrawny neck. He didn't flinch, he smiled. "Start talking."

Heedless of the blade at his throat, he chinned towards the mound. "Best go look over there and then you'll understand better than I can explain."

I thought about it before doing as he suggested. "You so much as scratch your nut-sack and I'll gut you."

"No doubt." He grinned.

I sheathed my blade and climbed the mound. The stone pillars were the twins of those I'd turned to open this space. I didn't want to touch them, but something more than Tosspot was driving me, and so I hauled myself up onto the slab.

And then I understood.

Lying there, untouched by the vicissitudes of time, was the Hammer of the North. The real Hammer of the North. The reason I knew it was him was because he was holding a dirty great hammer, other than that, he looked nothing like the paintings and statues in the Hall of Heroes.

He was a good foot taller than me and wrapped in a ragged, fur-trimmed cloak. A bloodless gash ran diagonally across his face, marring the pattern of orange scales. His claws, like his cloak and his long, pierced hair spines, glittered with frost. Aside of a set of nondescript and battered leather armor, his clothes were patched and worn. His clawed feet were bare.

"You couldn't find any boots either, eh?" I spoke to break the spell of silence.

I don't know how long I stood there, looking at the truth while remembering the lies. It could have been minutes or hours. Eventually, I did what I knew I was meant to do and took the Hammer's hammer. The moment I touched it, I felt its power flow through me. This is what had drawn me to the mound, what had called to me across time.

It slipped surprisingly easily from his frost coated fingers as though he was ready to give it up. I hefted the weapon, it had weight, but it wasn't heavy. The metal was dull grey but sparkled when turned in the light, I guessed it was made of star steel. The twin heads of the hammer tapered to the middle of the sigil-intagliated shaft. It was a hammer, there was no getting away from that, but it was as graceful as a bludgeoning weapon could be.

I didn't examine the weapon because my attention was on the Hammer himself. I half expected him to crumble to dust or vanish, for Time and Fate to finally set him free, but nothing about the hero changed.

Despite the gash across his face, he looked at peace, serene almost. Something gleaming at his throat caught my eye. I took a closer look. It wasn't a diamond or sapphire, it wasn't a gem at all. It was a glazed blue bead threaded on a simple, silver chain.

Old habits die hard, and I unclasped the chain. It wasn't just because I was a thieving bastard, but also because it felt like the right thing to do. Truth be told, I didn't know what I was doing. I was adrift, lost in waters I would never have dreamed of navigating mere weeks ago. The only thing I could do was let the current take me where it wanted. I fastened the chain around my neck.

"He looks different in the paintings," I said to Tosspot, anger and sadness spiking my gut.

Tosspot, unlike the Hammer, looked like hell. "I know. That disservice wasn't the least of the indignities he had to suffer."

"No?"

He shook his head. "That popinjay in the paintings, the ones in the Hall of Heroes?"

I nodded.

"He was the worst of the lot if you ask me. He was supposed to be his friend, but instead, he helped them erase the real hero from the pages of history."

"What a cunt."

"Aye, a complete and utter tosspot." He bowed.

And now I knew why the golden-haired god looked so familiar. It was such a shock I laughed. "No. You?"

"Don't sound so surprised, I've been alive for over seven hundred years, followed him into more than a dozen Schism War battles." His shoulders sagged. "All that magic takes its toll on a body. Never mind the curse."

"That talking thing we were discussing earlier? You'd better get to it, sharpish."

"My name is Rubin, squire of the Hammer of the North." His eyes shone with tears. "I would have died for him, we all would, many did." He drew a shuddering breath. "But after the war, it was decided, that it was best to, well, to lie. The warspawn were deemed too dangerous to have such a legendary hero to look up to, someone they could aspire to, someone they might try to emulate. The Mage Lords were afraid that their creations would become their masters, as the Annurashi were afraid that the Mage Lords might become theirs. So much fear, so much jealousy." He laughed hard, blood flecked his lips. "I'm sorry, Breed."

I shrugged. "It's all right, it happened a long time ago and means nothing to me. But why did you go along with it?"

"The war took its toll. It was deemed best to pretend that the fabled hero was a human. The Mage Lords swore those of his companions who'd survived to secrecy." He coughed. "Civilization teetered on the brink of destruction. We thought it was for the best. We were wrong."

I had a practice swing with the hammer. It was far more elegant than the monstrosity painted on the walls of the Hall of Heroes. “Why didn’t you tell me when we met, save all this dancing around?”

“I couldn’t. By sworn to secrecy, I mean bound by a geas so powerful that I couldn’t tell you or anyone.”

“But you found me and led me here.”

“No, I just followed the road that was laid out for you. The Annurashi knew, Fate knew, I just tried to be there when it happened.”

“I don’t understand. I mean if he was as popular as you say he was, surely someone would have said no to the stitch up?”

He scratched his matted beard, chuckled softly. “Sweet salvation, she was angry. I got off lightly compared to some, but she damn near started another war when she found out.”

“The Red Witch?”

He nodded. “Her curse has kept me alive all this time, but only just. Nobody can curse like Halda.”

With all this lost legend waffle I’d forgotten about Tobias and Clary. “Oh, shit. Tell me about it later. We need to go back, now.”

Tosspot, *Rubin* shook his head. “You do, but this is the end for me. I’ve felt it coming for a while now. That’s why I knew you were the one.”

“You sure about that?”

"Aye, demon, I am. I've felt death's grip tightening ever since I met you. I knew it was a sign." He gripped my arm. "Promise me, when you're back on the other side you'll close the gate. There are things in here that no mortal should lay their hands upon."

"Oh, aye? Things like what? I mean, are they valuable things?"

He raised an eyebrow. "Breed, really."

"All right, all right."

I took one last look at the battlefield, at the thoasa, arrachids, ogren, amphibanes, and humans lying side by side amid the demon horde. The sacrifice was immense. I'm not given to sentimentality but right then I did something that I'd never felt another living body had ever deserved of me. I raised the hammer in salute to the dead, or so I thought. But all the lies, all the beatings, every injustice that me and the Hammer, and all those like us had ever suffered, boiled out of me and into the hammer. I held it aloft, felt an enormous pressure build within me until a gout of fire leaped from the weapon and burned the cold, black vault of heaven to molten gold.

"Looks like I can do more than just boil water. Mother will be surprised." I lowered the hammer. Tosspot didn't answer. I looked around, but he was gone. Above me, the fire spread across the sky like a sunset. On the battlefield, the gold light gilded the dead.

I gave a nod to the Hammer's bier before stepping back into my own world and absolute, fucking chaos.

Chapter Twenty-Two

On seeing the carnage, my first impulse was to go back inside and wait until they'd finished killing each other, but as I was in possession of the real Hammer's hammer, I felt I should probably do something to help my friends.

But first things first.

I took a two-handed grip on the weapon and swung it into the nearest of the standing stones. A neat crack raced across it and it broke in half, instantly sealing the rift between worlds forever.

I might have taken a moment to congratulate myself on a job well done, but a shot winged past my head and buried itself in the mound with a soft thump. At least two companies of knights and greenshanks were fighting swarms of rats of every size.

Clary and Tobias were taking cover behind the stones on the mound, which was surrounded by dead Imperials that had been charred to piles of ash and molten metal. The pale sorceress was standing protectively in front of Marius, who was cowering in the tunnel entrance.

"Breed!" Tobias shouted, just before he sent a blast of crackling energy at the sellspell. A wall of dirt rose before her and absorbed the lightning. "If you have any intention of using that bloody thing, would you please get on with it?"

I rested the hammer on my shoulder. "You missed me then?"

He sagged against one of the stones.

I called over to Clary. "Call your friends off." She didn't look convinced but gave a keening wail. The rats disengaged and scattered. The knight captain raised his hand and the clanks stopped firing and reformed their ranks.

Silence fell over the valley until the captain raised his visor and pointed at me. "In the name of his Imperial Majesty, Durstan the Seventh, I order you to lay down your er, weapon and surrender."

"Nah, I don't think so."

His eyes widened in disbelief, his cheeks flushed. "What did you say?"

"You heard me, clank. I will not lay down the Hammer of the North's hammer," I said it loud enough so that everyone could hear me, so that every jaw would drop, which they pretty much did. The smell of fear and excitement bloomed on the iron air.

"Listen to me, you fucking animal," said the knight captain, oblivious to the gasps from those around him. "You will lay down your arms and surrender, or by the All-Seeing Eye, I will put you down, and I don't give a donkey's fuck-piece whose hammer you've got."

The knight pointed his sword at me to emphasize his point. I pointed the hammer at him. The blast must have boiled every drop of liquid in his body so quickly that he exploded, splattering everyone within twenty feet with hot gobbets of Imperial fuckwit. One of his more dull-witted comrades roared a battle cry and charged me. I pointed the hammer at her and she pulled up so sharply that she fell on her arse.

"Breed, enough. I order you to desist." Tobias looked pale and scared, and well he might.

I tugged the cuff off my wrist and tossed it. "Sorry, priest, I'm done playing servant. Anyone else want to try their luck?" A couple of the knights weighed their swords but wisely stayed where they were.

Marius shoved the sellspell in the back.

"What?" she asked, indignant.

He chinned in my direction.

"Are you deranged? That's the Hammer of the North's hammer. You aren't paying me enough to take that on. The Empirifex couldn't pay me enough." She looked at me and pointed towards Valen. "Do you mind if I…?"

"Not at all," I said.

"Most kind." She tipped me the nod and then melted into the ground.

I turned to Marius. "Right, you. Get your arse out here."

He hesitated. I raised the hammer which prompted him to shuffle forwards.

"What do you think of the prophecy now, eh?"

"This proves nothing," he shouted at me, but his words lacked conviction.

I pointed the hammer at him.

He shrieked and raised his hands defensively. "Please don't kill me!"

"Say it then."

"Tobias was right."

I cupped my ear. "Sorry, what was that?"

"TOBIAS WAS RIGHT!" he bellowed. "Happy now?"

I scanned the faces of the knights. "You all heard that, right?" Nobody answered. I raised the Hammer and without looking, although I'd clocked it a moment before, fried a gull that was passing overhead. Its cindered corpse fell from the sky. "I said, you all heard that, right?" A chorus of affirmation followed. Satisfied, I turned to Tobias. "Well, that's that sorted." I was rather pleased with myself. "Fancy a drink?"

I should have known better.

No sooner had the words left my mouth than a shadow passed across the suns. The air turned cold, the sky roiled, and black clouds billowed overhead. Lightning flashed, followed by an earsplitting peal of thunder. The acrid stench of sulfur filled the air. The Imperials took cover where they could find it.

"You didn't forget about me, did you?" The demon Shallunsard had apported onto the scorched patch of ground where the knight captain had given his final, fatal speech. The last time I'd seen him in his own flesh he'd been naked. Now he was clad in burnished bronze armor, his horns were bound in rings of silver, and his wings were tipped with steel.

"No, of course not. I just had a few other issues to deal with first."

"So I see." His laughter rumbled through the ground. "You finally worked it out?"

"I did. No thanks to you. Why didn't you tell me?"

"I couldn't. That is the irksome nature of one of the many geas by which I am bound. You don't think they just locked me in my stronghold, do you? Actually, knowing you, you probably did, if you even thought that far."

"I have my own troubles to think about, why should I give a donkey's dangle about yours?"

The demon tutted. "So ungrateful, and after everything I've done for you." He held out his hand. My palm itched. "Now hand it over, there's blood-letting to be done."

Part of me wanted to give it to him and be done with this, but a more stubborn part didn't. I have a knack for making bad decisions, a gift for choosing the wrong path, or not choosing a path at all and just running blindly from one disaster to the next. I'm not going to lie, most of the time it's bloody good fun. But, as a friend once told me, there comes a time in everyone's life when they have to make a decision, take a stand. I looked at Tobias. He looked at me like the soft, soapy cull that he was.

"What about him?" I asked the demon.

"Why do you care?"

I looked at Clary, saw myself reflected in her dark eyes. In truth, I wasn't sure that I did care, given that I'd never been in the position where I'd thought anyone was worth caring about. I had, until now, treated the world with the same indifference with which it had treated me. I swung the hammer off my shoulder.

The demon's fingers twitched impatiently. Tobias said something to Clary and tried to get up, but she held onto him. I didn't hear what they were talking about, I was too busy concentrating on a spell.

One thing I did see was the shocked expression on Shallunsard's face when I belted him with the hammer at the same time as unleashing all of the pent-up sorcerous might I could summon. It was a good blow and caught him square in the chest, although it felt like I'd hit a mountain. I planted my feet and roared and poured my heart and what passed for a soul into reducing the demon to ashes. To hell with the Paradox of Power.

I didn't care.

I didn't care about anything and that was the truth and the key to my Paradox.

When I opened my eyes and peered through the smoke there was a crater around the demon, but the bastard was still standing. I have to say, I was a little disappointed. I'd hurt him, as the ichorous black blood oozing from the rent in his breastplate proved, but I hadn't dropped him. Nevertheless, I stood my ground even though my every instinct was telling me now was the time to run.

"We made a deal, Breed," he said.

"You tricked me."

"I did not. Well, not much, and not about the deal we struck about the hammer or killing him." He pointed to Tobias, who gave me a look.

"I didn't do it, did I?" I said to the priest.

"Give me the hammer," the demon demanded. The ground shook, lightning lashed the clouds. It was all very dramatic, but I knew it was bluster. He was unsteady on his feet and bleeding.

"No," I said.

"You dare say no to me. Don't you know who I am?"

"Of course I do, I just don't *care* who you are. Your time is over. It was over centuries ago. Now fuck off while I'm feeling generous." By generous I actually meant 'about ready to pass out'. I was exhausted. Those spells, half-formed and ill-conceived though they were, had drained me. I now understood why Tobias fell over quite so much. Casting spells was harder than it looked.

Shallunsard bared his fangs, in what could have been a grimace or a smile. "I'll make sure you live long enough to regret that decision, halfling. I will destroy everyone you have ever loved, everything you have ever cared for, and then, in the depth of your despair, I will destroy you, slowly." The demon threw his head back spread his arms and roared. Coruscating lightning lit along the ridge of his outstretched wings momentarily blinding me. I blinked, and he was gone.

"Everyone I've ever loved, eh? That won't take long, *prick.*"

The demon's explosive departure knocked everyone who wasn't wielding an ancient artifact off their feet. The leaden sky growled and rumbled like it had eaten something that didn't agree with it. Tobias was gawping at me, his expression a mixture of anger, hurt, and surprise. I rested the hammer on my shoulder and turned my attention to Marius and the knights who were staggering out of the tunnel.

"Right, you pox-mongers. Attend me closely if you want to live beyond your next breath." They all very wisely became instantly attentive. "Here's what you're going to do. You're going to go back to Valen, and if any of you so much as think about glancing over your shoulder, don't, or I will turn you into a cinder. When you're back in your pig pen of a city, you will tell the Senate and the Synod that Brother Tobias Vulsones of the Order of the Scienticians of Saint Bartholomew was right. I'm looking at you, Marius, you miserable, back-stabbing fuck-knuckle, and if your father has a problem with that, tell him to talk to me."

It took some longer than others to digest my words but with a little encouragement from their brighter friends, they all eventually seemed to get the message. Marius allowed himself to be ushered away by the Imperials, who all seemed very eager to get away from the angry thoasa with the hammer, demonstrating excellent survival instincts. As I'd expected, Tobias and Clary stayed where they were.

"Nice thing with the rats, Clary," I said when the last of them were out of earshot.

"Thanks. Where's Rubin?"

I didn't know how to tell her what had happened. They'd grown quite close and she was just a kid. "He decided to stay with his friend."

"He's dead then?"

A kid who knew more than most.

"Yeah."

She nodded. That seemed to satisfy her. She made a funny little squeaking noise and a fat white rat squirmed its head out of her pocket. She sat down and started grooming it.

"So I was right. You were the one," Tobias climbed unsteadily to his feet, a look of triumph on his face.

"And, so? What do you want? Only, I'm all out of thanking humans for their amazing insight."

"What is it?" He cottoned on quicker than me that something else was bothering me.

"You know those paintings in the Hall of Heroes, they're lies. Did you know that?" I was angrier than I'd realized. "The Hammer, the real Hammer, was a thoasa, a fucking warspawn. Tell that to the Synod when you see them next, if you dare."

Tobias rubbed his head with his stump. "I had no idea, Breed. Although, I suppose it makes sense. Humans have treated you and your kind poorly."

"Damn right they have." He folded his arms to hide his stump and blushed to his roots. "It's all right, priest. Your secret's safe with me."

He sighed. "It shouldn't be a secret, but my father insisted upon it."

"If you want my advice, see how this anti-warspawn thing turns out before you tell anyone you're touched, eh?"

"Aye, perhaps. Though I doubt that is the worst of my problems. What are you going to do now? Have you chosen a side?"

"Yes. My own. As to what I'm going to do, that's easy. I'm gonna keep out of it and let humans and the demons tear each other to pieces if they want. I'm done. If you're wise you'll do the same."

Tobias smiled and shook his head. "You don't mean that."

I laughed and fingered the bead I'd lifted from the Hammer. "Yes, I do, because I know how this story ends."

"What? Ah, yes. The Hammer." He looked away, embarrassed by that injustice, but unable to admit it.

"Yes, the Hammer. I'm not like that stupid bastard. I'm not going to sacrifice my life for anyone, especially not humans."

"No. I don't blame you. I'm not keen on them myself at the moment."

At the moment. "Suit yourself. Are you going back to Valen?"

"Yes. I have to try and reason with the Synod and the Senate. After seeing the demon with his own eyes, Marius won't be able to deny what's happening, and how much we need the warspawn, how much we all need each other if we're going to survive. Of course actually having proof would help. I don't suppose you'd…?"

I laughed. "Not a chance."

"I didn't think so. Still, it was worth a try."

We both laughed and when the laughter died we stood there in awkward silence, neither one sure how to say goodbye, for real this time. I broke first. "You'd best get going, see if you can catch up with the others and vent your brother before he gets back."

"What?"

"I'm joking." I wasn't. The arsehole should be turned into fertilizer rather than left to run around, flapping his lips, and sowing the seeds of hate. "Good luck convincing your father and the Synod."

"Thank you. I think I'll need it." He half turned but then stopped. "Just out of interest, when did you break the geas?"

I winked. "Look after yourself, priest, try not to get hung."

"And you. Take care of yourself, Breed." The soapy cull sounded like he meant it.

"Always do. Tell your people not to come looking for me."

He nodded and set off after the others. I noticed there was a new confidence in the way he carried himself. His shoulders were back, his head was held high, and there was a touch of swagger in his walk that reminded me of me.

I turned to Clary who had sat quietly as she often did, taking it all in and keeping her own counsel. She popped the white rat back in her pocket.

"You can stick around if you want," I said, not really meaning it. "It's probably safer away from Valen for the likes of you and me."

"Safe?" She squinted up at me, dark eyes bright with mischief. "What's the fun in that?" she said, and then did something nobody had ever done. She hugged me.

"All right, all right, that's enough of that." I gently pried her off. "Now get lost, and stay away from rat boy, he's a bad influence."

She grinned and scampered after Tobias.

I watched the procession of knights march towards the city followed by Clary and Tobias. As I had no pressing engagements, I watched them until they were swallowed by the shadows of Valen's mighty walls. I didn't have the first clue what I was going to do now. I briefly considered going back to Appleton and killing Mother and Jing, but after seeing the Hammer that seemed petty and pointless, a bit like me. I sat on the broken stone by the mound. I had a hero's weapon, but I was about as far from a hero as a body could be.

A cold wind scythed across the fields as darkness closed the wound at the world's edge with glittering, night-strung stitches. I picked the brightest of those low-slung stars to be my guide, hefted the hammer onto my shoulder, and started walking.

You have finished book one, but Breed's adventures continue.

Type the following link into your internet browser to get your copy of *Tooth and Claw* now.
http://kdavies.net/atac

Free Books

If you haven't already read them; I would love to offer you two free *Chronicles of Breed* prequel stories!

I love telling the stories of Breed's exploits; *The Best Laid Plans* and *A Fistful Of Rubies* are available for free if you type the link below into your web browser.

http://kdavies.net/nldtk

Author's Note

Hi. Thanks for reading *Dangerous To Know.* I am really pleased that you decided enter Breed's world. I hope you enjoyed it.

I also hope that you will join me to find out what happens next in *Tooth And Claw.*

It would be awesome if you would consider leaving a review. They are really important for authors like me, we rely on reviewers like you to tell other readers how much you liked (or not) our work. Typing this link into your internet browser will make it really easy for you:

http://kdavies.net/rdtk.

Thanks again.

K.T.

About the Author

When I'm not writing books, I work the day job, wrangle my kids, four dogs, and a grouchy, old cat. I play computer games, ride horses, practice medieval martial arts, grow vegetables, throw axes, and read, not at the same time, that could get messy.

I have a website here http://kdavies.net

And a Facebook page at https://www.facebook.com/KTScribbles where we can hang out, have a couple of brewskis, and talk about the good old days.

You can also find me on Twitter @KTScribbles.

Once again, thank you so much for going on a ride with me and Breed. I hope I see you again soon.

All the best,

K.T.

12631999R00229

Printed in Great Britain
by Amazon